SMITH AND WESTON
CRIME CASE TALES

BY
DORIS NICKLES

Smith and Weston
Copyright © 2022 by Doris Nickles

2nd Edition

All rights reserved. No part of this publication may be
reproduced, distributed, or transmitted in any form or
by any means, including photocopying, recording, or
other electronic or mechanical methods, without the prior
written permission of the author, except in the case of
brief quotations embodied in critical reviews and certain
other non-commercial uses permitted by copyright law.

Tellwell Talent
www.tellwell.ca

ISBN
978-0-2288-8684-6 (Hardcover)
978-0-2288-8683-9 (Paperback)
978-0-2288-8685-3 (eBook)

The stories you will read in this book are fictional, the characters are all fictional, no name is of a real person. My stories were inspired by real life crimes and criminals, but they are told in complete fiction. This is only my second attempt at fictional writing. I found that during the past two years of the pandemic, writing became my company while practicing social distancing. I have made some lovely friends all over the world on social media like Face Book and Twitter. We shared some fictional stories based on certain television series. I want to thank my new friend Caroline Gilpin, who gave me some important critiquing on English literature rules. Most of my writing experience has been of spiritual research, poetry, sonnets, and essays. I do hope all who read my book enjoy the adventure of Smith and Weston.

Thank you
Doris Nickles.

INTRODUCTION

Smith and Weston

Jordon Smith - Detective first class, with the Police Dept. for five years. Twenty-nine years old, five feet eleven, dark hair, blue eyes, warm hearted laugh in life, best friends with Steve Weston and very much like brothers. They have been working together for past few years, also trained together. Jordon is from the east coast, and his father was a police officer, killed in action. Jordon is ex-military, served in the Canadian forces for six years, was posted in Kandahar for two rotations, was released due to a leg injury from battle hit. He would have stayed in the military, but had trouble with anxiety and panic attacks from combat. Jordon Smith can make connections easy with people and has a good rapport with witnesses. Jordon is an excellent sharpshooter, has worked in hostage situations, with excellent outcomes. Smith can sense situations better than most seasoned officers and detectives; he is able to assume many characters in his undercover work. He has a great arrest record; he enjoys being an upbeat positive being. Jordon's mom is still in Fredericton, and he has a sister and brother still living at home with mom. Jordon likes to check in on how the family is doing with him being half-way across the country. He left Fredericton because of his detective post in River City, Manitoba. Jordon was picked by his Capt. Shepherd for the position. He worked in Toronto for a brief time and moved around to different departments for experience and promotions.

He went back to Fredericton when his dad was killed in the line of duty, to help his mom. He was told by his Captain about a new division being formed in River City, into which he would fit. He was picked and off he went.

Steve Weston - Detective first class, six foot two inches, works out, and is a no-nonsense guy, does not like games of drama, attention seeking, or emotional manipulation. He is divorced, a Med. School dropout, had a football scholarship, was studying Medicine, made it to his second-year residency, but found he was not happy, so went into criminal law. He is blond, blue green eyes with a killer smile and twenty-eight years old. He is into fitness training, healthy living, and sports. Steve is a motivator; he looks for where he can connect on a mental level with people. He does self-defense seminars on the side. He likes to make a difference in his community. He volunteers at community drop-in centers and drags his best friend Jordon Smith with him to volunteer. Steve has his mom and dad still around and moved from Toronto to River City for his job. His older sister is a lawyer in Toronto, his father is proud of her making a name for herself. His father is a chairman on a board of directors for various charities. He comes from old money. Steve's mom has always been a stay-at-home mom, who has devoted her spare time to her church charity work, and a hospital fund raising board. His mother also has a large family that did well in the 70's investing and making their modest riches grow. Steve really does not want much to do with any of it. His father and he do not agree completely on his choice of career, his mother worries about him being hurt. He has an uncle who is a farmer, his dad's brother Robert; he is proud of Steve and his choices. Uncle Rob is more of a dad then his father is. Steve was with the Toronto Police Dept. and was moving from post to post writing his exams for promotions and heard of a special division being formed in River City, and he applied for a post. He was chosen by the captain in charge who picked him for a position. So, Steve left for River City, and ended up running into his best friend Jordon.

They were paired up together as partners, after they finished their probation year.

Their Captain is Capt. Neil Shepherd. He was promoted and made Captain to his special division of investigations. It was developed to deal with Gangs, Drug smuggling, Human trafficking, and Kidnapping/extortion cases. They all work undercover for different divisions at times, and at times their own cases they find or volunteer for. Capt. Shepherd is married with three children, two boys and a daughter: 13, 11 and 5. He's been married 15 years. He is six foot five, and quite stocky like a brick wall. He is athletic and tries to keep fit. His department has eight teams of partners. Sixteen detectives in various levels of investigations. They are an elite group, handpicked by their Captain, from across Canada. Capt. Shepherd has a commanding voice, he will raise it if he needs to, but he is also able to be discrete when necessary. Shepherd is good looking with brown eyes and light brown hair, he has a beard, and he wears eyeglasses for reading he is thirty-eight years old. He's tough but fair, no goofing around. Stay focused and stay safe is his command watchword.

CHAPTER ONE

The first case:

Smith and Weston walked into the squad room, and their Captain was briefing everyone with the city's latest crimes, and what was getting attention.

"We have a few robberies in the downtown area: these were committed with the use of machetes. No one was hurt. The perpetrators were youths, a group of four ranging in ages thirteen to seventeen. It is thought it may be gang initiation. We are keeping an eye out for groups of youths up to no good on the street. I'd like to see them caught and off the street.

"We also have a missing woman, Trudy Wilson, sixty-three. She went missing yesterday at approximately 0730 hours. She was reported going for a walk and never returned home. The family is concerned as this is not her typical behavior. They have been searching for her since yesterday afternoon at 1530 hours. I would like Detectives Gains and Woods to investigate and gather information on this case. Report back to me, and we will decide what is needed.

"Anyone working the streets, if you hear anything on the missing woman, I would like that passed on to the detectives. We also have a report of a gang shooting out by the General Hospital. The member shot is twenty-one-year-old Raymond Profettie and he is a member of the Indian Posse. It seems they've had a grudge on the River East Creepers. Detectives Barnes, Wheeland, Smith and Weston, you will work with some uniforms canvassing the area of the shooting for witnesses, also check with Detective Cornwall and Brennon: they worked the nightshift and have a report for you to start follow ups on.

"We also have a few small fires during the evening and night that were deliberately set. The Fire Chief thinks it may be the work of a fire bug. No idea of age or sex but the chief would like to catch this one before someone gets hurt. Detectives Leroy, Baskon, Chartrand and Noland, I want you to check out the fires, speak to the Fire Chief, and then canvas the areas of the fires. Put together your reports and gather info on some of the firebugs known who are on the streets. Everyone else is on cruise today on their usual areas. Be careful, stay focused and safe. That's it for this morning's report."

Smith, Weston, Barnes, and Wheeland got together to talk about their assignment and review the reports. They decided to do door to door canvassing for information, and witnesses to the shooting. They asked their captain how many uniforms they had for the canvass.

Capt. Shepherd told them, "You have four uniforms, and if you get behind on the canvas, let me know I'll see if I can get any others in on it."

So, off the detectives went. They had a map of the area, and streets that needed canvassing.

Smith asked Weston, "How have you been doing these days?"

Weston said, "I'm doing great buddy, how about you? Anything new going on with you?"

"Neah, just the same old same old. I think I am done with Janet though. She got so wasted the other night at the bar, I had to practically carry her out to the car. Then of course there's the flirting she does, she gets guys worked up and then fights break out. I can't deal with that."

"Wow not too cool. I would say she likes the idea of being rescued. One of these days, it's going to get serious, and someone will be hurt seriously. Are you going to tell her you're done, Jordon? Or give her a chance to fly right?"

"Well, Weston, I don't think she will change, she really likes the booze. I think I am getting too old for this. Maybe I need a more mature girl. Grown up and responsible."

"So, you are done with Janet. So maybe you'll have time to come to the community club for some basketball training?"

"Aw, Weston, there you go again, filling my schedule with volunteer stuff." Jordon's face was crinkled up from the thought of more teens all over him.

"Well, buddy, you need me to keep you busy, don't you?"

"I swear I am going to match you up with a woman you'll have to marry and then you'll be so busy, you won't have time to volunteer."

"Nope, Smith, won't be happening anytime soon. Well, here we are. Let's meet up with everyone and split the canvas."

Weston parked the car and got out to speak with everyone.

"Okay, we have a radius of ten blocks to canvas. There are eight of us, so we each take a side of the street, and start knocking on doors. The last few streets will be done by those who finish first, and the rest will join them when they are done. Everyone has a radio, use channel three if there's any trouble. Keep your eyes and ears peeled for evidence of any kind. Sometimes, the simplest thing can give us the biggest lead. Take notes of names and addresses, we can check the computer later for details."

So, all the officers went out and started knocking on doors. Weston was halfway down the block when his radio called out: "Detective Weston."

"Yeah, Weston here, what's up, and who am I speaking with?"

"Officer O'Reilly here. I got a lady at my last house. She has two young adult sons and she thinks they came home acting guilty last night."

"Ok, make a note of the address, and did you get their names? Also did you let the lady know we may get in touch with her very soon about the information?"

"Yeah, I got all that done. She expressed concern because they went out on foot. She doesn't know what they are up to. They told her to mind her own business."

"Okay, I hope everyone got that message. Keep a sharp look around for possible gang trouble in the neighborhood."

Everyone responded with: "Roger that."

It was a long day of canvassing, and everyone was tired and thirsty. They all ended up meeting at the end of their canvas.

Weston stated, "Let's all grab a coffee and go back to the squad room, we can discuss freely what we've learned, then we can type up our reports. I need to figure out how much work the detectives' services office will have to do for us for tomorrow."

Weston and Smith walked back to their car.

Weston asked, "So what have you got planned for tonight, Smith?"

"Well, I think I will be going to bed I am pretty bushed from the canvass, and I am not sure we're going to get home all that early tonight. My gut says we may end up being late."

"Ok, Smith, so you think I will keep you late tonight, ha-ha, I am a work slave, I guess. Look, we'll keep it brief. You know my questions and my idea. I like to prioritize the gut feelings with the details, we both know it's our best info to go on."

"West, you know I am kidding you. Let's get our coffee and get back to the squad room."

Everyone regathered and shared their notes. No one picked a leader, but Steve Weston is just one of those guys that take the lead, and everyone feels comfortable. He is easy to work with and he seems to know the right questions to ask his coworkers. So, he started right in, and started asking his questions.

"So, Officer O'Reilly picked up a feeling about one of his canvasses. Tell us how that came about will you, O'Reilly?"

"Yeah, so I got to this one house on Dufferin Street. An older woman answered the door. She has two sons aged 22 and 21. They live in her basement. I told her about the incident last night with the shooting. I asked if she had heard anything or knew anything about it. She told me she heard her sons talking about it when they got home last night. They stopped talking when they saw she was still up and hurried into the basement. They were quiet while at home today, she said. I got the feeling she knew her sons were up to no good. She mentioned they had been hanging around some young men who were always getting arrested. I gave her my card and asked her to call us, if she finds anything out, or maybe needs our help."

"So, what is the name of these young men? And did you get the woman's name and phone number?"

"Well, her name is Naomi Chartrand, and her boys' names are Collin and David, with the same last name. And their number is 204-925-9865. She will be home tomorrow all day."

"Ok so we will need to get detectives services to pull any possible history for these two for us. Get on that request and let them know there may be more work coming. That's good work, O'Reilly. Any other gut feelings in your canvas?"

"No, Weston. That was one of my most interesting interviews."

"Officer Bill Kelly, what have you got for us?"

"Well, I can tell you, there were a lot of don't know, don't care slam the doors, and a number of would not answer their doors. But there was one lady, who preferred not to be identified. She spoke of two young men, didn't know their names, but that they were bad news. They tend to offer help to seniors then rob them. She said they scare her. I asked where she thought they lived. She told me a few blocks over towards Dufferin Street. Kind of fits with O'Reilly's information."

"Ok, that's great, did anyone else get information like that or similar?"

"Detective Dave Barnes had a few conversations that might have been interesting," Jimmy Wheeland stated.

"Ok, Dave," Weston said, "Give us what you got. Thanks, Wheeland."

"Well, you know I was one block over from you. I got this one old man, he said he was robbed by these two young punks. He said they offered him help bringing his groceries home. Once they were in the house, they ransacked the place, stole a bunch of valuables, as well as money. He was able to remember them calling each other Dave and Collin, no last name, but he distinctly remembered those two names. He couldn't remember if they lived nearby, but he thought they were very nice at first, but then they went mean. He did file a police report, so who knows we may be onto something."

"Ok, you got the old man's address and name, so request the history on the report. Now what about you, Wheeland, what do you have?"

"Well, I got a few homes that gave me a bit of different information on the gang member happenings. Up on Sinclair Street there was a father who answered the door, he works nights. His name was Mr. Desjarlains. He reported to me something happened to his fifteen-year-old daughter one evening. She was coming home from her part time job downtown. She got off the bus and started walking home. These two men pulled her into a dark corner. They scared her because she started to scream and kick. She said they did not hurt her, but they tried to assault her. The dad now meets her at the bus stop after her shift and walks her home. He said he will beat the crap out of those punks if he ever catches them. He did not know their names, but he is sure they are part of a gang. His daughter was not home to question. I suggested they come into the division and file a report. He says there is a report on file. I gave him my card and told him bring his daughter in. She can look over mug shots if she does not know their names. I can request any reports on sexual assaults for the past three months to see if I can match any of them. Another home down the street named those men right out as the robbers in their home. They also sexually assaulted the wife in that home invasion. I think if we get those two in here, we could sweat them for names, maybe they'll talk about the gang."

"I would say the canvas has given us some leads. Jordon and I have some stories that are much the same. We asked a few people to come up and look at mug shots. We should make sure those Chartrand boys are visible. And you're right, Wheeland, maybe we can squeeze them for a shooter. Well, let's get those reports typed up, get a hold of detective services and then we can make a report to Captain Shepherd."

The guys got all their required requests together and typed up their reports. They met with Capt. Shepherd. He was pleased with their canvas, and he encouraged getting people in to identify these young men. He liked the idea of sweating these men for info - that they may be able to get these guys to turn snitch to avoid charges, and to get clean and fly straight.

Capt. Shepherd was happy. "Ok, you guys are almost at the end of your shifts. I'll see you tomorrow and keep on this case till it's solved."

Detective Services brought up stacks of files to the men, and Weston was caught off guard with the amount of case files that arrived. "What the heck is going on here? Is this a joke? That cannot be all of our requests can it?"

"These are the files on the Chartrand boys. We still have more files on assaults and robberies to bring up. Sorry but you detectives requested everything we have on these two men," the woman from Detective Services replied.

Steve Weston was shocked at all the files; his mouth fell open. "Well, thanks, Cheryl, for the heads up. We will read these carefully. Well, guys, we have a few files to go through. Shall we divide and conquer for tomorrow?"

Smith suggested, "Ok, how about we just grab a pile of files and start reading and make notes. We can do an hour of work then go home get some rest and pick up where we left off tomorrow."

"I agree with Smith. We can get through this if we each take on a bit of the reading. Set files aside that are important that could lead us to what we need to know, who the shooter is." Weston had a look of excitement about the case, he was sure they were on to something. Weston's eyes seemed to gleam like headlights when he became intent on solving a case.

Smith went and put on a pot of coffee for all of them. He was also hyped to find the evidence they needed. He turned and looked around at all the guys; they were all intense while reading the files. He thought, *"West sure knows how to motivate everyone involved, just with a look. He's a natural born leader. From the first time I met him though, no one would have known, he was so introverted, and quiet, always solemn in situations. But West has confidence now and is more extroverted than ever before."*

Smith admired him; he had come a long way from who he used to be. Smith sat down and dug into the files.

Everyone was quiet while reading as the other detectives came and went in the squad room. They were so absorbed in the files, none of them realized how much time they had spent reading. Barnes's phone rang at his desk and snapped him out of his trance-like search. "Oh damn, I forgot the time!" He picked up the phone and answered, "Detective Barnes." It was his wife. He answered, "I'll be home in half an hour; I am sorry I'm so late." He hung up and grabbed his coat. "Got to go guys, see you in the morning!"

Then the rest of them decided they had better get going too.

Smith and Weston got up, and Smith asked," Hey, you want to grab a pizza and some beer on the way home?"

West finished the coffee on his desk and said, "Sure. Why don't we take it to my place? You can stay over if you want to save time in the morning."

"Ok, let's do that. We can talk about how things are going for you. Ha- ha, I'll find out if you have been solitaire or if you have a secret girl hidden away."

"I am not seeing anyone; it's just I am trying to form a basketball competition for the community clubs in the city. It is keeping me plenty busy. We have a chance at a government grant for sports initiative in communities. If we can get a regulation competition going amongst all the community centers, we may win the grant, plus I've applied for funding and sponsorships to keep the basketball competition going year to year."

All Smith heard was 'we', "So who's this we you speak of?"

"Well, Diana and me. She is the sports coordinator for Sports Manitoba. We met at a community meeting; we were exchanging ideas on encouraging youth accessing the community clubs and staying off the street. I came up with basketball camps, she suggested team tryouts. I have been recruiting coaches from various city departments to volunteer. So far, I have most community clubs covered, I still have five of them to fulfil and then we can get teams forming. It's one of the few sports where we don't have to cut players. We want everyone involved."

West stopped the car to get the pizza they needed. Then they took off to pick up their beer.

"So, this Diana how old is she?" Smith had a huge grin on his face as he asked the question.

"She's about twenty-five. She is very nice, polite, I don't know much about her other than that."

"So why don't you ask her if she is spoken for or if she might be interested in dating?"

"Smith, why don't you give up? Your match making isn't going to work. She's nice, she's smart, I don't want to scare her off, as I have invested so much time into organizing all of what we have done."

They arrived at Weston's and went up the stairs to his apartment. They put the pizza in the kitchen and the beer in the fridge. They made themselves comfortable and of course Smith could not let go of his questioning.

"So, what kind of sponsors are you looking for, along with finances on these teams?"

"Well, if someone is interested in sponsoring a team, we find out what they are willing to donate. Such as enough for uniforms, shoes, or long-term financing in exchange for free advertising. I arranged for advertising signs at participating community clubs. I am looking at keeping the youth busy, so I am not looking for them, like these gang members. I even have the mayor sold on the idea, so more funds are moved towards the clubs."

"Sounds great! So, what does Diana look like? Tall, dark, or fair, do tell?"

"Well, she is about 5 feet 5 inches tall, dark hair, wears glasses, fit build, nice looking. She's a graduate from the university's athletic programs. Is that enough for your prying nose?" West had a huge smile, as he knew Smith was using his easy way of getting others to give up information in conversation. So, he decided to turn the tables. "So, Janet, what's up with that? You were telling me something about it this morning."

"Well, we went to the bar a couple of nights ago, she was drinking rather quickly, and then started dancing with the band. She was dancing provocatively and teasing guys at the bar. She would get them interested, then play them off one another. I asked her what she thought she was doing, and she called me a party pooper. Imagine me a party pooper. I am usually easy-going, love fun, but she looked horrid behaving the way she was. I suddenly didn't see her as the cute feisty girl I thought she was. I cut her off and said we were heading home. She was falling all over the place. I put her in the car, took her home and put her into bed."

"So, what's your plan with this situation?"

"I think I am going to meet her at my place and tell her we are done. I think once I paint a picture of our last past dates, she'll realize. If she doesn't, I'll tell her she needs to date someone younger, as I can't do this stuff anymore."

"Well, Smith, no....You got serious with Jennifer; she was a grounded solid girl. Then you lost her the worst way possible. This Janet sounds like a High School girl. Mind you I only met her once at bowling. And yeah, I thought she was too young for you. I let it slide, as I didn't get to know her too well with just one night."

"So maybe we need to have a get together party in our coming time off. Meet some new ladies or get out to the bar more often. You seem ready to start getting into a steady relationship, West. You think you want to start dating?"

"Aw, I don't know, I think so but, I don't want to just go out and get someone. I would like to just meet a few interesting ladies. Get to know them, really know them. You get too excited each time I show an interest and you force it. I appreciate your excitement, but I need you to ease off the gas pedal then I won't feel pressured."

"Ok, well, now you're talking. I can work with that. Our next few nights off we will start to circulate a little. So, what's on T.V. tonight? Any good movies?"

The guys were still eating pizza and West got up and got two fresh beers, then came back to sit down in the armchair, Jordon was on the couch. They found a western movie to watch. They enjoyed the movie and then called it a night. They decided to go to bed as they had work in the morning.

CHAPTER TWO

The following morning West was up and making breakfast, and he woke Smith up, Smith went and showered, and came out and grabbed a coffee. "So did you sleep well?"

"Yes, I did, I was very relaxed after chilling with the movie. How did you sleep?"

"Yes, slept very well, getting used to your couch. So, let's have breakfast and get going, got a bunch of files to go through."

The guys ate and cleaned up then took off to work. As they drove, they discussed the case. West suggested they see if they have enough information to get warrants to bring them in and question these two guys.

They arrived at their precinct, and it was noisy as they approached the squad room. There were people there from the neighborhood they canvassed. They walked to their desks, looking around the room. All the detectives were busy, handing out papers and pens.

Det. Barnes came over to Smith and Weston, and said, "Hey Smith, I guess our canvas stirred up the neighborhood, a bunch came in to give us statements, hoping to help catch the shooter, and maybe get rid of the gang violence. They are fed up with being scared, pretty great, right?"

Smith looked at Weston with a surprised look and then back at Barnes. "What can we do to help?"

"Well, we have everyone here taken care of. Next new ones that come in you two can look after, ok."

Capt. Shepherd came in the squad room, and asked, "What the heck is happening here?"

Weston was still pulling himself together and said, "Captain, these are people from the neighborhood we canvassed. They have all come in to give statements and help us with our leads."

"Well, carry on then."

Then Cheryl came in carrying a bunch of files, which she was pushing in a cart. She said, "I have more files for you guys to read. I'll have one more cart of files to bring up for you. There was a lot of information relating to these two names. I think they have been very busy in their short lives."

Smith was shocked. He said, "We have more than a month of reading to go through."

West was just as surprised, "Well, let's dig in and get started, we will be better for it, when we get into it."

West was looking around and then he saw Wheeland trying to type some stuff up. He walked over to Wheeland, "Hey so what are you typing up? Is there something I can do to help?"

"Well, I am typing the statements out that people have made related to the case. Maybe you could start typing as well. You'll have to read a lot of different handwriting."

"I am used to that. Give me a few to type - I know none of us are proficient with our typing! Plus, I get to see what we have for evidence."

Smith went over to Wheeland, and requested some typing as well. The whole squad was pitching in to get the work done. "Just make sure they sign the typed statements, or they will be no good." Wheeland was worried there might be some missed signatures. As all the men worked the squad room got a bit quieter, and the chaos became an organized calm noise. Then a big surprise came, a polish baker came in the squad room with coffee carafes, and trays of baked goods and sandwiches.

"What is this?" asked Smith, "Someone knew I was hungry obviously."

A secret in the squad room was Jordon Smith's appetite.

"I am Mr. Polanski, and I could see you all working so hard to help our neighborhood. I thought the least I could do is bring you lunch. I am sorry I am a bit late."

"No, you are not late, right guys? Thank you Mr. Polanski, we appreciate this very much."

Jordon had a very large smile on his face, and the men all stopped what they were doing to shake Polanski's hand and thank him. Both Smith and Weston finished typing their reports and getting the signatures, prior to stopping for a much-deserved break.

The men were very surprised at the neighborhood response to their canvas. Capt. Shepherd came out of his office and looked around. Wheeland told him what happened. He went over to Mr. Polanski to thank him. Then he turned around and called, "Smith and Weston, I need you in my office!"

Both Smith and Weston got up and went to his office. They closed the door behind themselves.

"Yeah, Captain," was said simultaneously.

"What's up, what can I do for you?" Weston got quiet as he saw a man and a teen girl sitting in his office.

"What's going on here, Captain Shepherd? Can I do something for you?" Smith asked while looking around.

"This is Mr. Ron Desjarlains, and his daughter, Sicilia, her family calls her Sisi. They came in to look at mug shots and complete a complaint for an assault on Sisi. I have assured them we will keep their complaint anonymous, until or if it makes it to court, and they understand in court it must be revealed. We will give them ample notice if it is to be revealed, so they can stay safe. They have stated they do not feel safe with those brothers on the loose. I have another couple in an interrogation room. They are amending their complaint of assault and robbery. The same goes for their statement. Meantime, I have assured them I have two extra squad cars that will patrol and watch their homes."

"I have called up for arrest warrants for the two Chartrand boys. We should be getting them soon; I want you to pick them up and bring them in for questioning. You men understand what I am saying. We bring them in and get them talking."

"Ok Captain. As soon as the paperwork gets here, we will go and pick them up. We will need to take six men with us so we can take them in without trouble. Smith, you go let Barnes and Wheeland know what we are doing, then talk to O'Reilly and Kelly. Get them ready for the arrest."

The men went back into the squad room, and spoke discretely with their fellow colleagues. They formed a plan and hoped it would be an easy arrest, but they had gut instincts that said, with a shooting prior to this, it could be difficult. Most of the people were gone from the morning and the statements were done, it was just files that needed to be reviewed. So, with that said, they sat and started to read the case files, they still needed to build their case, so needed to check the history and the present of the Chartrand boys.

Capt. Shepherd called out to Smith and Weston, "Get in here. I've got your warrants."

Both Smith and Weston went into the captain's office and got the paperwork. Capt. Shepherd told them, "Make sure you have your vests on, and stay focused, and stay safe."

"Captain Shepherd, I will be careful and so will the men we take with us." Steve Weston took the warrants and went back into the squad room. "Ok men let's get our vests on, and remember we surround the house first. Have your radios working, and let's hope there wasn't too much chatter on the streets. We want to arrest them without a scene if possible."

Smith and Weston pulled up a few houses away from the address, then they radioed the others, "Everyone in position?" Steve waited till he heard from everyone. Then he said, "Ok, we are heading to the door."

Smith and Weston walked to the door and knocked on it. They waited till someone answered.

"Mrs. Chartrand, I am Detective Weston, and this is my partner, Detective Smith. Are your sons home today?"

"Yes, but they are in the garage in the back."

Smith and Weston, headed to the garage in the back, and radioed the officers about what they were doing. They carefully checked the big door. It was closed, and so was the passage door. Weston was on one side of the door, and Smith on the other side.

Knocking on the door with the barrel of their gun, Smith called, "Collin and David Chartrand, it's the police. Open up we have a warrant for your arrest."

A few moments went by. "Open up or we will need to bust the door in."

Suddenly there was a noise of a motor starting. Smith and Weston knew what that meant. They ran to the big door, guns drawn. Smith radioed: "They're going to try and run." Then the door was smashed open, and Smith fired off a round at the car. Smith jumped out of the way. He aimed his gun at the tires and shot them flat. They chased the car for a few moments. It wasn't going far on flats. The two men got out and opened fire at Smith and Weston.

O'Reilly came up from behind and told them to: "Freeze! Police!"

They turned and aimed their guns. Smith fired and one went down but fired with his gun aimed at Weston. O'Reilly fired and the second one went down. Weston was down; he was hit in the arm.

"We need paramedics, and everyone come into the alley. We've got them down," Smith radioed.

Smith went to check on his partner after cuffing the two men. O'Reilly read them their rights. They were upset that they were shot in the arm and leg.

"So, how's the arm? Let's see it?"

Steve Weston said, "It's just a graze. Nothing serious."

"Looks like you may need sutures for your arm, buddy."

Sirens were whining away in the air, and people were peeking over their fences and out of their yards. The detectives were flagging the ambulances and fire dept. toward the alley.

Barnes was announcing: "Nothing to see here, folks. You can go in your homes, go on with your usual business."

So, Smith said to Weston, "Well I guess you'll be ok to ride to the hospital on your own. I'll get Barnes and Wheeland to ride with the prisoners, and the officers to bring their cars to them."

"That's a good plan partner, I'll be good as new in seconds once I'm stitched up, then we will go do the paperwork and interrogate those two goof balls."

CHAPTER THREE

So, all involved either went to the hospital for care and to guard the two men or drove cars back to the precinct. Steve had sutures to his upper arm; he had only been grazed. Of the two boys, one needed surgery to his leg, as the bullet traveled up the leg as it ricocheted off the bone when it hit. The other had his wound cleaned and closed. Once the two men were released from the hospital, they were taken in to be processed and hopefully questioned. Smith and Weston typed up their statements and turned their guns in to IIA and awaited their reports and findings. Capt. Shepherd spoke with them briefly on how the arrest took place.

"It was a clean shooting; Barnes tells a similar take down on it. You men need not worry, but I insist you be more careful. I don't like hearing of my men getting shot."

"I was grazed Captain, I wasn't hit. I underestimated how far over I needed to move to avoid. I am hoping to start interrogating these guys asap."

As they left the captain's office, Jordon asked, "Should we order supper as we are going to be late getting out of here tonight?"

"Oh yeah, the stomach speaks, sure we could do that. I know it's been a long day, but we are close to making an arrest on the shooter. I believe it's one of the two we have that pulled the trigger. I figure once ballistics is done checking their guns, we will have our guy." West had the biggest grin; his eyes were even grinning.

"So, what do you feel like eating," Smith asked, "Pizza, Chinese, Thai, or sub sand? I could eat any one of these. What do you prefer?"

"Well, I wouldn't mind something simpler, a burger and fries from Zack's Pit, we know the owner he will deliver!" West was still grinning ear to ear about their case. "Smith, you order the food, I'm heading down to the Crime Lab for the preliminary reports."

So, West went down, and he was looking for his expert on the guns. "Anyone in here?"

Then a voice came out of a test room: "Yeah, I'm in here, West!"

Sherry came out with the file and walked over to the printer which was busy printing the reports on the tests. "You are going to be so happy, West; the results are the answer to your investigation."

"What do you have for me, Sherry? All good, I am hoping. I suspect I am right in my theory."

"Well, one of the guns matches the shooting of the gang member, Raymond Profettie, and the prints on the gun match Collin Chartrand. It was his gun in the shooting."

"Yes! I had a gut feeling this afternoon about this case. I knew it was going to go this way. Give me the file and I am going to take it to Captain Shepherd. Thanks Sherry; you sure work fast."

Weston raced up the steps with his file, he was taking giant steps clearing the floors to the third floor. He ran into the squad room shouting, "We got him, we got him." He went straight into the captain's office and laid the file down on his desk. He had the biggest grin looking at his captain.

"Careful Weston or you will injure yourself with that grin on your face." He read the file and slammed his hand on his desk. He was pleased with what the files had said.

Smith came in the room and could tell they had their man as the two others had the look of "Got Yaa."

Smith and Weston were the only guys left of their team at the office, so they couldn't tell anyone, and celebrate. So, they decided they would go straight into interrogation, and get these men to talk.

Their supper arrived so they sat and ate, no taking their time though, they were too hyped by what they knew. They talked good cop bad cop scenarios for their questioning. They had their script laid out, so they were hoping these two would not lawyer up on them. West called holding to bring the Chartrand Men up for interrogation. The captain was about to join them in the questioning. They went into the room Collin Chartrand was in.

"Ok, Collin, we are not going to waste our time with a dance of getting a name for the murder of Raymond Profettie. Your prints are on your gun, and your gun matches the one that killed Raymond, do you deny that?" The captain towered over Collin and had a menacing look about him.

Collin took a deep swallow and said, "No, that's impossible! It can't be my gun, I can't shoot anyone, never!"

"Well, you took a shot at my men on the street; that tells me you are desperate. You had something you were running from, if not the shooting what then?"

"I wasn't running, it was David who was running. He didn't want to be arrested. I didn't shoot anyone, I swear! I don't know why my gun matches, but it wasn't me."

"So where were you at 1115PM on the 17th of the month, you better have a good alibi, with good backups, 'cause your brother won't do!" The captain looked hard and unforgiving.

Then West was in Collin's face, "Make it good, because we already talked to your mother yesterday, she answered this question, and she didn't know you were involved. We will turn your alibi inside out."

Collin looked around and then said, "I want to talk to my lawyer; I'm not saying anything else till I get a lawyer. My brother wants a lawyer too." Collin had a huge evil grin on his face.

Smith asked him to stand up. He cuffed him and read him his rights and stated he was arrested for murder one. He added,

"Your brother must invoke, and he hasn't so you will sit until your lawyer talks to you."

Smith, Weston, and the captain went to the next interrogation room to talk to David. They told him his brother was charged with murder one. They told him the evidence they had and asked about alibis.

David was surprised, "I am not sure what you are talking about."

"Where were you at 1115PM on the 17th, what were you doing, and make sure someone other than your brother can back your alibi."

David cowered down in his seat as he was hovered over by Capt. Shepherd.

"I…I..I was hanging out with my brother at a friend's place, we were goofing around and drinking, h….h….honest, I'm not lying."

West slammed a pad and a pen on the table. "Start writing, all the names of those who can back up your story, and if even one deviates from what you said, you are going to be charged with aiding and abetting." He was looking tough and hard as well. Smith was nodding in approval with his arms crossed looking very stern.

"I…I…I W…W…Want a l…l…lawyer," David stammered as he pushed the pad away, refusing to write anything. They cuffed him, read him his rights and charged him. They let him have his phone call and took him to holding till arraignment.

The detectives walked back to the squad room with their captain. They decided to type up their reports, and go over files, and collect as much data on the two brothers as they could. They were hoping to close any possible holes in their case. They started going through files, the captain came out to say goodnight. He was going home. He said, "You two should go get some sleep as you will be busy when the arraignment comes up in two days."

So, Smith and Weston decided their captain was right. They got up and grabbed their jackets and headed home. West dropped Smith off and then went home as well. West was more tired than he cared to admit. So, he took a shower and went to bed, not even noticing someone had been in his apartment.

The following morning, West got up, he proceeded to put coffee on to brew, and then there was a knock at the door, he shouted, "It's open! Come on in!"

"Hey, hey, am I on time for breakfast?"

"Come on in, Jordon, I was just getting it started."

"I'll get the eggs if you would like and the butter, scrambled would….," Smith opened the fridge and stopped mid-sentence.

"What's up, buddy?"

Smith had a look of disgust on his face. "You check your fridge lately or is this a new diet plan?"

"What do you mean partner?" West looked and on a plate in the fridge was a gutted rat. "Someone was in my place I guess; I was so tired last night I didn't notice."

They started looking around to see if there was anything else to notice. West threw out the rat. West was a bit unsettled by the discovery and thought it might be a gang thing, as they arrested two of its members.

"Hey Smith, how about we get breakfast uptown? I kind of lost my appetite. I would like to disinfect my fridge before I cook anything."

"Yeah, if you insist, we can go get breakfast at the 'I hop', if you want. I'm starving so let's get going." Smith, of course, was always the hungry one. Even he was a bit turned off by the finding of the rat. The guys turned everything off and left. West found his car with flat tires; he was unhappy about that.

"I guess we are taking your car, Smith. Mine is out of Commission! I really hate today; seems I've been tagged for harassment. I will have to request extra patrol around my place." West was not happy.

They got into Smith's car, and off to the office they went. They picked up breakfast to go and headed to the precinct for their shift. When they arrived, their captain noticed, they brought breakfast with them.

"You guys get up too late for breakfast?"

"No, Captain. My fridge needs some work, so we picked up breakfast."

"Well, I guess those things happen."

"We are going to eat quick and then get right to work."

"West, you and Smith don't have to rush, you are hard workers I know, so just relax."

The guys sat and ate. They were reading the case files while they ate. They made their notes, compared their notes, and came to realize these two men arrested were high up the ladder in the gang. They went to Capt. Shepherd with their findings. The captain encouraged them to type up their findings, and hand them in.

CHAPTER FOUR

By mid-day, West called Zack to come get his car keys and to get the car's tires changed. He ended up getting four new tires. He filed a report on the vandalism at his place and he did request extra patrolling for his own safety. Zack came by with Weston's keys, and he handed them to Weston.

Zack had a weird look on his face and commented, "I got the tires done, but I think the paint job will have to go into the shop to get done."

"What are you talking about Zack, I don't need a paint job."

Zack took out his phone and showed West a picture of his car, it was spray painted with the word 'pigs' across the car, in different directions.

"Aw…. these guys are just nasty, they ruined my car."

"West, you know your car wasn't the greatest to begin with."

It so happened that Capt. Shepherd came into the squad room. He saw the guys looking at something and that West did not look happy.

"What's up men, what are you looking at?"

"West's car ended up being revamped by vandals."

Capt. Shepherd looked surprised. "What are you talking about?" The captain was looking at the picture.

"So, the gang knows where you live and that you got their men in jail. Why wasn't I told of this right away?"

"Well, West's apartment had been visited yesterday, but we didn't notice till this morning. We opened the fridge and there was a gutted rat on a plate in the fridge."

"And that's why you had to pick up breakfast." The captain picked up the phone, saying, "Get me CSI department. Hello to whom am I speaking? Ok, listen up Lieutenant Sappiatto, I want you to get your crew and go over to Detective Steve Weston's and go over the place for trace evidence and fingerprints. Come upstairs and get his keys. I want any evidence found reported to this division. Thank you."

"So, Steve you are not going home for the next little while. We will have some uniforms watch your place. Smith, was your place fine last night?"

"I didn't notice anything, I went home I went to bed, and left for West's this morning. I didn't pay much attention just like Weston."

"Well, that's just great, my top detectives, and they don't notice things!"

"Captain, with all due respect, we stayed late and left late. We were tired. We did not think a gang was going to tail us or find our homes."

"If we can't go home, where are we supposed to stay? When there are gangs involved, I'm pretty sure we will not get to go back for a long time."

"Smith, we will worry about all of that later. For now, you're picking a hotel, and you are sitting quiet, till after the court arraignment."

"CSI is here. Could you please give them your keys to your place and car? You too, Jordon. Hand them over."

"My spare key is just over the door; it lies flat on the frame. Just drag your finger over the frame you'll feel it."

"Weston, why would you leave your spare key so accessible? You men make it too easy for someone to get at you! I cannot believe it. I want the CSI to change your locks, and no easy access to the spare key either! That is an order! How about you, Smith, do you have an easy access place as well?"

"My spare key is under a fake rock on the deck. It is for emergency access as well, so if something happens to me Captain, honest."

"Boy, you men sure make it easy for the crazy ones to get at you. CSI, you know what to do when you get to their place. Where is your car, Jordon?"

"It's out on the street, why?"

"So, no one has been able to access it, or is it easy to access by anyone?"

"Well, it is out in the open, but if you are bold enough to access it, it could have been played with."

"Give Barnes your car keys, he can bring it round to the garage, and we will let the techs check it over."

So, the CSI techs went to check the detectives' home, they did the whole nine yards for fingerprints and evidence collection. They even took food samples to test. Turns out they found something in Weston's car. It was serious. They came back and ran all their tests, and Smith's car was checked over as well. While all this was being done the guys were checked into a hotel, and were relaxing watching a movie, and eating popcorn. They were joking around and talking like nothing was wrong. Except there was, their lives were being threatened. West was worried about missing a basketball meeting for the Thursday evening. He had hoped, once all things were checked out and given a pass, he would resume his schedule. The guys called it a night and went to bed.

That following morning there was a heavy knock on the door. Smith got up to answer it.

Then from the other side of the door he could hear: "Smith, Weston, it's me, Captain Shepherd."

Smith opened the door and let the captain in. Weston came out scratching his head. "So, what's up Captain, come to tell us to get to work?"

Capt. Shepherd was looking very serious. He said, "Men, sit down. CSI finished the preliminary tests, and investigation. You men are lucky to be alive. You must have a guardian angel or something watching over you both."

"What are you talking about Captain, what did they find out?"

"Steve, your fridge was full of cyanide powder in everything they could put it in. As well, it's a good thing you ordered all new tires. They removed a bomb from your trunk. It could have injured you seriously or killed you. You fellas have a few angry enemies. Jordon, your place wasn't much safer, again cyanide in your foods, and nitro tucked into your couch. You guys had the CSI's and the bomb squads very busy."

"So, they found it all. Is there anything else we need to worry about, Captain? We would like to get back to work. We can't hide out for too long. West's got commitments and I wanted to finish the files that are sitting on our desks."

"Smith, you can forget about work for the foreseeable future. The gang has it out for you two. You are out of commission till we figure out what we are doing."

"So, we can't go back to work, what are we supposed to do? We can't stay in a hotel room for ever. Can't we round up all the gangs lock them up and stick charges on them?"

"Well, we are reading the files you started, we are trying to connect the crimes to gang members, and hopefully find evidence to charge them. Once we get the heavy hitters, then we can look at letting you two out. I'm not going to lose two good men, all because you need to move about."

"So, we are stuck here, Captain, maybe you can bring some files here for us to read and research. Also, do you think Wheeland or Barnes could bring us some changes of clothes, and our hygiene products? Otherwise, we need to go shopping."

"Weston, we can't bring you files, and yes you are stuck here but alive. You two don't seem to appreciate the fact that you are not maimed or dead. I will see if I can find some sort of work for you two to do while you're stuck here. You can watch all the movies you want while you're here, if that's any consolation for you."

"Well, Captain Shepherd, we can't stay here forever. It's insane, we need to be out there working, and I really wish we could go home. I don't like someone packing for me. And my car needs to be driven it can't just sit there."

"Smith, your car has been moved to the police garage to be inspected. I am sure they will run it from time to time. And yes, you will stay hidden until I say otherwise. Wheeland and Barnes are going to interrogate the two men we have tomorrow, we are going to squeeze them for info. Or we add Federal charges, for the attempts on a Police Officer. They will squeal, I am sure."

The captain left and wished them well, as the two men settled in for the evening. Popcorn and movies, and some cards, they did not like it, but they knew it had to be this way for now.

CHAPTER FIVE

So, after all was said and done, the guys waited it out for over a week. Smith and Weston were chomping at the bit to get out and work their jobs. They contacted Capt. Shepherd, and he asked them to come in, via a patrol car. They did so.

They arrived at the precinct and were told that the Chartrand boys finally started talking. They gave up their boss for ordering the shooting of the young Raymond Profettie. There were warrants for their gang captain and many of the higher-ranking gang members of the Indian Pose. So, the task force of officers set out to do all the arrests at the same time. They had many officers to assist in the take down of this gang. All together they arrested fourteen gang members, two extra for assaulting the officers, to try and protect their President of the gang.

Capt. Shepherd was excited to see the arrests and see Smith and Weston out on the street working. He ordered patrols to monitor their safety the first week they were back on duty. As there were no further attempts, Capt. Shepherd was relaxing the patrols.

Smith and Weston were again out on the streets making busts. They were back in the saddle and happier for it. They were reconnecting with their snitches, and those on the street that were their friends or peers that had businesses to run. The streets became quiet and calm, after so many in the gangs were taken in and charged, then found guilty. Smith and Weston were known as tough but fair cops, they had a reputation of being clean cops, untainted. They were respected throughout their city. Sometimes if there was a problem for someone, they would seek out Smith and Weston. They could usually help resolve problems. Smith and Weston were back out on their regular patrol, with updates of complaints, and crime in their travels of their section to patrol, they would make stops along the way to drop in on some of their snitches, just to get updates of what is going on in the streets. At some point they got a tip about a runaway, making themselves at home in homes where people were away for vacation. The runaway wasn't stealing, but was just utilizing the homes, for a safe night sleep.

A New Case

Rumors didn't have an address, but the homes were upscale, and easy to access. No one seemed to know if the runaway was male or female, so age was thought to be twelve to fourteen years of age. So, Smith and Weston thought they would follow up on this report and inform their chief. They felt a kid on their own needed to be home with their family or foster family if they were without. They were not sure how they were going to catch the suspect, so figured talking it out with the team would give them ideas on how to seek and catch. They already knew they would look at reports of break-ins and complaints made for the same. Then find out if there is a neighborhood, that is favored by this little break and enter expert. So, their next chance in the office they were going to work on the files. They put their requests in from the Detective Services' office.

The next day they sat and read files, they mapped out the addresses of the complaints. They studied the dates of occurrences to see if any habits were forming as to picking the home to stay in. Weston had a theory he was working on; he thought the kid might be making friends in the neighborhood into which they were breaking. Friends tell everyone their plans, even new friends. This kid would study the homes and know when it was empty to enter. He could stay clean and kept, and nice appearance, so no one would be suspicious. Weston didn't have a theory as to why this kid was on the streets though. After studying the map, he decided the kid was hitting the homes in a new subdivision of the city. So, Capt. Shepherd assigned them to evening shifts for a few weeks so that they could patrol and observe the neighborhood.

So, Smith and Weston made their way to the neighborhood called Woodridge, all new homes with big layouts. There were work crew sheds at the edge of the development. Steve thought a kid could hide there until he figured out how to enter the homes.

Smith said, "West, you scare me how you think like a perp! Were you a troubled kid growing up?"

"No, I just read a lot of the "Hardy Boy's" mystery books, and other books when I was young. I guess it gave me ideas in my subconscious."

"Well, when you share your theories, it is so easy to believe as you have it all figured out how it would work."

"I just process the thought and think of the scenarios that could crop up, and answers to those problems. I guess I have a mind that thinks like a deviant or even a perp at times. Do I still scare you, Smith?"

"No, you don't scare me. Your theories can scare me, as they often turn up correct."

The two men kept their patrol up and monitored the area for the normal activity and anything that might look strange, or out of character.

"If we see anything unusual, we can go to the door, and have whoever is home answer it. If a kid answers we give a fake story why we're there, an adult we can just show our badges, and discuss the neighborhood. A kid will likely believe anything we say. But the kid will either look like he fits in or is not from the neighborhood. Got that, Smith?"

"Sure West, I got it! Like I say, scary thoughts."

So, they staked out the neighborhood, and watched the activity for a few evening shifts until, finally, out came this kid, tall and skinny, with hair that was medium length, with an old crumply jacket, from this nice house. They watched where this kid was going and what this kid was up to. They could not tell if the kid was a girl or a boy. The kid walked to the nearest convenience store to pick up some groceries and walked back to the same home. Once Steve saw the kid go in and settle, that's when they made their move. They walked to the door and knocked on it.

"Hi, is your mom or dad home this evening?" Steve asked the youth that answered the door.

"No, my parents are at some school meeting. They'll be home soon. Can I help you with something?"

"Well, we were hoping to catch one parent to talk to them about their cable service. We have a special offer for those who want to save. We will try back tomorrow evening about our special offer."

"Sure, that would be great, try tomorrow."

Smith and Weston walked away. They got in their car and discussed what was observed during their encounter.

"No way he belongs to that house, West! He was wearing his muddy shoes in the house. My mother would have killed me if I did that!"

"Well, he sure kept his cool and calm self, he just acted like he lived there. He made a slip with that at 'some school meeting' comment. Kids know exactly what the meetings are. He was also unwashed, and his clothes needed laundering. That's a kid that's not had parents around for some time."

"We going to arrest him tomorrow?"

"Maybe or maybe not. We are going to stake out the place all night, see what this kid does overnight. Then maybe we arrest tomorrow evening. We want to be sure, and collect our observations. If the parents don't come home tonight, then we know he is on his own. I have an idea, why don't we do a door-to-door canvas, see what the neighbors might know."

So, Smith and Weston went door to door asking questions about their neighbor at 122 Sycamore Crescent. They finally hit a neighbor four doors down who knew the owners who were gone on a business trip/holiday. They obtained the names of the owners, and they were ready to cheer, but kept their cool. They began walking back to number 122. West was pumped, and forming his take down plan. Smith was very eager to make the arrest.

Steve knocked on the door and waited for the kid to answer. "Hi, we're back. My partner reminded me, I forgot to get the name of your parents for our canvas list."

"Well, why don't you come back tomorrow, my parents can give you their names."

"Well, I need the name of the household to give my supervisor when I am done; that's how I get paid."

"What can I say Mister. I am shutting the door now."

Smith stuck his foot in the door, and said, "We just need the last name to confirm we knocked on the door, kid."

Weston pushed the door open with his hand; the kid froze in place. "You don't live here do you kid?"

The kid was just staring at Weston. Then he started backing up, Weston reached forward and grabbed the kid and snapped the handcuffs on him so quick, the kid was in shock. "You are under arrest for break and entry, and illegal squatting. There may be more charges added as we investigate further. You have a right to legal representation," as Weston continued with his rights, the kid was starting to shake. They got to the car and Weston put him in the back seat. Smith and Weston locked up the house, and took the kid in.

The boy sat down at Weston's desk, he did not look up or around, and his leg kept shaking as he was so nervous. Weston sat down next to the kid, and began with, "So can you tell me your name? I need it for my report, and I would appreciate knowing to whom I'm talking." Weston had that big infectious smile, as he bent down to meet the kid's eyes. The kid barely looked at Weston, but he did. Weston kept his eyes connected to the kid's, and slowly got the kid to raise his head. "It's ok, you're not going to be in a lot of trouble, if you are honest. I just like to have a name of whom I am speaking with." There was quiet from the kid. The kid stayed quiet. "Ok, so it's John Doe, so John, can you tell me why you were in those people's house? I know they were gone away on business and a holiday."

"Smith, can you call Child Protective Services so that John Doe has representation?"

"Sure, Steve will do."

Capt. Shepherd came into the squad room, and asked, "So how are my men this evening?"

"Captain Shepherd, this is John Doe, I picked him up on a break and entry."

"John Doe, it's nice to meet you. I hope you were advised of your rights?"

The kid just nodded yes. He was a bit perplexed about the whole John Doe thing.

"Carry on, men. I am off to home and a nice hot meal. Winnie makes a mighty fine pot roast if I do say so myself." Suddenly the kid spoke up.

"He sure is a happy captain! Is he always that happy?"

"Every time we get a runaway youth, he gets a little more thankful of a stable home and a hot meal with family," was Weston's response. "I guess you have not been away from home long enough not to miss the hot meals and a warm bed, right John Doe?"

"Stop referring to me as John Doe! I don't like how it sounds!"

"Well, that's what we are using as you refuse to tell us your name, so we call you that, until we find out your real name."

"Fine, then call me Eric."

"Eric, ok, and do you Eric have a last name we can refer to?"

"Sanderson, my name is Eric Sanderson."

"Ok Eric Sanderson, do you have an address you used to live at or an Identification card on your person that I may see?"

"No, I don't have anything, and I don't want to go back there so what happens if I don't tell you that? I want to know what happens," He demanded to know.

"Well, Eric, I will tell you that Child and Family Services picks you up and places you in a Youth Detention Centre, until they find out who you are, then if appropriate, they place you in to foster care. My next question is: have you been arrested for any other crime aside from this one? I advise you to tell the truth. Yes or no?"

"You just want a yes or no to that question?"

"Yes Eric, that's all I need. I don't need details. Bookings will do a search with your picture and your name to find the details that we need for you. It just takes a bit of time. When you are more forthcoming, we move a lot faster."

"I was picked up and charged for something, yes."

"You were arrested, ok thank you Eric, that's good." Steve was typing in a bunch more stuff on his report. Then he decided to ask a gnawing question to see if he could get an answer. "So, Eric, why do you not want to go home or say where home is? How bad was it at home?"

Eric was warming up to Steve and finding it hard not to answer his questions, he tried to resist but started to open-up. "Well, my dad is never happy with me, no matter what I do. He smacks me around, and fights with my mom all the time."

"How is that Eric, how does he slap you around?"

Eric's eyes got big, and they were beginning to tear up as he thought about his dad. He was looking down at the floor, his breathing was getting heavy and his leg was bouncing again.

"Eric, this is you talking to me, not an interrogation. You don't have to tell me, but I am interested in how you ended up on the street."

Eric looked up and around the room and started to talk, but no sound was coming out. He was struggling. He was not crying, but tears were falling from his face.

Steve got up and then said, "Eric follow me!" He walked him to an interrogation room and shut the door. "Now why don't you speak to me, Eric. No one else can hear us. What's happening at home?"

CHAPTER SIX

"Well, my dad started to punch me, last time I yelled at him to leave mom alone. He yelled at me. He said that he is the one paying the bills and doesn't need a little bastard like me telling him what he should do. He then grabbed me by the neck, punched me, I flew across the kitchen, then he kicked my ass so hard, I could hardly stand up and walk. I went to hit him, and he grabbed my fist and twisted my wrist till it cracked. I never got it checked out. I just pulled it straight, and taped it for a few weeks, till I ran out of tape. My dad did not care. I left with a black eye and bleeding nose, and I don't know about other injuries. I can't go back home. I can't watch him push my mom around. I don't want foster care either. I'm almost eighteen, two more months then I'm of age."

Eric was sobbing heavily, and Steve just hugged him and let him cry. Steve felt bad and angry, as the kid was right. When Eric was near calm, Steve asked what he said was his last question.

"So, were you in school, and how were your grades until you left?"

"I was doing ok, I was having trouble in math, but everything else was good, my marks were up in the eighties towards the nineties."

"Ok. Let me talk with CFS and see if we can get you back in school on an emancipated case. Where are you from can I ask?"

"I am from Brandon, Manitoba, sir."

"Cool, let me see if I can pull off some magic. I'll see what we can pull together for you, Eric."

Steve had his infectious grin going and Eric had half a grin returning. They walked back to Steve's desk. Jordon came back to the desk.

"Hey Steve, CFS is on their way, so we shouldn't be much longer on this case."

"Jordon, I need to talk to you about something. Hey Bryant, can you watch over my friend, Eric, here?"

Steve and Jordon went to a closed room and Steve filled Jordon in on what was discovered. Then they came back into the squad room and sat at their desk.

"Thanks Bryant, that was great. We got it from here."

Steve began typing the rest of his report, and then put a file together. Then he called Detective Services to ask for anything on Eric Sanderson.

"Hey Jordon, are you hungry?"

"Yeah, I am, should I call Zack's Pit?"

"Yeah, get me my usual, and get Eric the big boy plate. Get whatever you want, ok."

"Will do."

The social worker walked in about a half hour later. "Hi, I am Eileen Sangster. I am from CFS. I'm here for a youth you called for."

Steve stood up, "Hi, I am Detective Steve Weston. Can we talk in another room privately for a moment?"

"Sure where?"

Steve led her to the interrogation room and proceeded to inform her about their case. They were well into the discussion when Jordon knocked on the door and opened it.

"The food is here; you want me to pay?"

Steve stood up and gave Jordon fifty bucks to pay. Without skipping a beat, he asked, "So do you think he can get emancipation, no matter the charges?"

"I don't know. There are certain things we need, like evidence of child abuse, interviews with teachers and parents. I can get the ball rolling on the interviews, but he will have to go for a physical assessment for proof of physical abuse, by a physician."

"I can take him in on an urgent exam and see what the E.R. physician can do for us. In the meantime, where will he stay?"

"Well, it's been busy with the nice weather, there is no room in the center at the moment. We may have to place him in a hotel, with a youth worker."

"What if he stayed with me until a spot opens up? He is used to me, and I got him to open up."

"It's highly frowned upon, you know that. We are not supposed to get emotionally involved."

"Too late for that. You know I am involved with youth and getting them off the street. You know my background, could you vouch for me?" Steve gave one of his grins and waited.

"Ok, for one night then we can reevaluate tomorrow, here at noon in the squad room."

"Oh, thank you, you won't be sorry, I promise you. As soon as we finish eating, I will take Eric to the hospital for X-rays."

Everyone returned to the squad room, and Steve sat down with his grin and his eyes filled with a bright blue green twinkle, "You are staying with me, Eric, eat up because we have an E.R. to visit."

For the first time Eric had a grin on his face and seemed very relaxed with that news.

"Thanks Eileen, we'll talk tomorrow," Steve said.

She called back as she was leaving, "We sure will, Steve."

"Do you always get what you want with that smile of yours?" Eric asked.

With a big grin on his face, Weston said, "Yeah for the most part, people can't help but give in to what I want, when I ask nice, smile and bat my eyes at them."

"Thanks for the burger and fries, I was quite hungry. You guys picked me up before I could make my meal. By the way, I never stole anything from any of the houses I stayed at. I paid from money I made on the street. Usually doing someone's homework, or I hustle a game of pool where I can."

"You hustle in pool? Didn't you say you had trouble in math?"

"Yeah, just when I am tired. Like when my dad never let me sleep, the numbers get all jumbled in my head." Eric was beginning to look at the floor again, like there was a certain amount of shame felt in him.

"Well, nothing wrong with that, you recognize that you need your rest to be on your toes. Do you know if you are dyslexic, or you just figured out yourself what your issue was?"

"No, I am dyslexic, my mom caught it when I was in grade one, she recognized the problem, and she got me a tutor, we cracked it, and I overcame it. My dad called me an idiot, and useless of course. I think because he had to pay for the help. He doesn't even look at my report cards."

"Well, from what I know, dyslexics are usually geniuses. Ok, you ready to get going. We have to get you checked out at the E.R..."

"Yeah, I guess so. If it's necessary - sure I am ready. Then what after this?"

"Ready Jordon, we need to get going so we can go home and get some shut eye."

"Yeah, I am ready, and we are off and running then."

So, the two cops and the kid took off to the hospital to get Eric checked out, and a report from the doctor to turn into the CFS worker. Steve was excited to help Eric solve his problem. He wasn't happy the kid had to go through all the trouble he has had, but he was excited to help and set the road right for this kid. They took Eric in, and he went for x rays and scans, and he was poked and prodded. They were all three sitting in a treatment area waiting for the doctor to return with his findings.

"Well, young man," was heard before the doctor entered the area. "I have a clerk typing up my report for you. You have a lot of trauma signs. When was your wrist broken and who treated it?"

"My dad broke it a few weeks back, I taped it up with Duct tape. No one treated it. I left home after that."

"It was not what I'd recommend. I believe it needs resetting, we will need to re-break and reset it for it to not give you trouble in the future. I'll finish giving my report, and then you think about coming in to have that done under a local anesthesia. Your tailbone is cracked and not in place, you will need that fixed by a spinal surgeon, I will put a referral through, and then they will call CFS, who will contact you for the consult date. You have a few cracked ribs, they have healed. Also, I see an old fracture in your skull, how did that happen, or can you remember?"

"I don't know how that happened, but it might have been when I was knocked out from my dad hitting me, and I flew across the room, I hit the wall and the plaster was busted to the wood."

"I am surprised no one took you for treatment. Your nose has been broken, you have a deviated septum, we can fix that during your wrist surgery, if you would like. I see a lot of evidence of abuse, son, unless you can prove to me you are into extreme fighting."

"No, I'm not into extreme fighting. It's all my dad. If you were to X-ray my mom, the way you did to me today, you might find she's in the same shape. My dad never took us for treatment at the hospital, as it would be apparent, he abused us. So, you want to fix my wrist and nose tomorrow?"

"Yes, if it's possible to bring you back in tomorrow, I will set it up through Admissions."

"I can have him back here. What time tomorrow?" Weston had a concerned look on his face.

"Bring him back for 7:30 AM tomorrow, and don't eat anything more overnight. Just water."

"Ok, we will see you tomorrow morning at 7:30 AM, nothing to eat, just water. Eric is staying with me, so easy peasy."

"Oh, here is the clerk with my report, thank you," the doctor took it and handed it to Weston.

So, the guys all left, Weston drove Smith home, "So do you want me to pick you up in the morning or will you take your car to the office for the evening shift?"

"I'll meet you at the office tomorrow in the afternoon, as I am sure you will want to wait for Eric while he is being fixed up."

"Yeah, I will hang out to make sure Eric does ok, and then I'll meet you at the office. Night Smith, see you later."

CHAPTER SEVEN

Weston and Eric went back to his place and they got ready for bed. Steve took the pull-out couch and gave Eric the bed. They said goodnight and then fell off to sleep, till the clock rang at 630 a.m. It was a short sleep. Steve figured they would catch up on their ZZ's during surgery. They got up and Steve threw Eric some clean clothes. He figured they were likely a bit big, but they would do for the day. Jogging pants and a sweatshirt.

"You are going to wait at the hospital, right?"

"Of course, I am going to wait. I would never let a friend of mine go it alone."

Steve gave Eric one of his infectious smiles, and then squeezed his shoulder, while he was driving. They arrived at the hospital admissions and went through processing. The orderly came with a wheelchair for Eric to sit in it, and then off they went to the surgical floor.

Steve followed them, "I'll wait here for you, Eric, when you're done."

Eric looked a little worried. "Thanks Steve, I appreciate it."

Steve was told the surgery should take 4 hours to recovery and back. So, he got a magazine and sat and read. He paced a bit and then he read some more. Steve could think of better things he could be doing, but he was worried for his friend. Steve nodded off and slept a bit. Then he awoke as he heard something rattle and clamor down the hall. It was Eric on his way back from surgery.

He had a cast on his arm, and his nose was taped up. The Doctor was with him and had paperwork for Steve to take to CFS when they left.

"If I could tell someone off, I would. This kid's nose was a mess. Surgery went well, his wrist wasn't too bad. He is going to be sore when he wakes, but he will heal. I will need to see him in a week. He needs to come back tomorrow to take the packing out of his nose, and to place a brace on it. He'll wake up again in a bit."

Steve said, "Ok, thanks Doctor. I'll bring him back in tomorrow, and a week from now, here or do you have an office?"

"My clerk will give you the information before we discharge Eric. No blowing his nose or sneezing for the next little while though."

Steve sat quietly waiting for Eric to come out of his groggy state. Much to his surprise there was a visitor who showed up at the bedside. "Hi there Eileen, what brings you here?"

"I needed to get to you two first before anyone else did. Eric's father is on the warpath. He is driving in from Brandon to claim his son and take him home. I read the file report from the E.R. doctor, and I see how Eric suffered at the hands of his father. I called an emergency hearing with a family court judge, so that Eric can be kept in protective custody. I'm going to need him to show up at court this afternoon, and he needs an elected guardian with him for the hearing."

"They can't possibly give him back to his dad, can they? He'll just runaway again if that happens."

"I am asking the court to grant him Emancipation, with a guardian to oversee him. I am hoping you meant it when you said you would stand by him."

"I did mean it. I can handle it if the judge grants it no problem." Steve had his big smile going on again. He was excited, and wanted to see this so-called man, that is physical with his family. Just as they were finishing their conversation, Eric started waking up.

"Hey Eric, you're awake. You did good, the doctor said. I'm supposed to bring you back tomorrow to take the packing out of your nose. How do you feel?"

"I feel fine, my face and arm hurt, but I feel fine."

"Yeah, getting things reset isn't a lot of fun. I'll let the nurse know you are awake. I'll let Eileen tell you what's happening."

Steve left to find a nurse. He came back a minute later, to find Eric trying to get dressed and leave. "Woah, woah, hold on there, buddy, what do you think you're doing?"

Eric looked like a deer in the headlights, terrified. "I have to get out of here, I can't go back to that place. No one can make me." Eric had tears in his eyes.

"First of all, I won't let that happen, my friend. Second, Eileen has arranged a hearing so I can oversee you and keep you away from your dad. You run off and the court will order you home. Just sit tight, you're not discharged from the hospital yet, and you are with me. I will protect you!"

Eric settled down and relaxed. The nurse checked him over and told him, "You have to wait a while longer before we can release you. You must have your lunch and go to the washroom before we let you go. Also, your I.V. is not done yet, it has post op antibiotics. When I come back, I will check on you again, I am going to get you something for your pain."

"See let's listen to the cute nurse," Steve said. "I won't leave you high and dry. I am going to stick to you like rice. We will go to court; I will keep your dad away from you. In fact, I will go tell the staff, your dad cannot come near you, if it will make you feel better."

"No, it's ok, I am good, I'll just rest here a bit, kind of tired anyway." Eric lay back down and was trying to find a comfortable way to sleep.

The nurse came back with some pills for Eric. "Here you go, Eric, these are analgesics to ease the pain. Lunch is on the way, so make sure you eat well, then I can write a positive note in your chart. By the way, your father called up to see how you were. I hope you don't mind, but I told him, I could not give out that information. I also said you were not to receive visitors. I read your chart, and I hope you don't mind I took the lead on this."

"No, not at all, thanks a lot, I am glad you did that. And yeah, I am in pain, like I got a two by four in the face sore." Eric had a small smile on his face.

"See, what did I tell you, Eric? Cute and smart all in one package!" Steve had a grin from ear to ear, as the nurse walked away smiling at the compliment. Steve said, "When they discharge you, we will get you some clothes for court this afternoon. You can make a good impression with the judge."

Eric's lunch showed up. He ate a bit of what was on his tray, and then was just picking at it.

"Hey, what's up, you're not hungry or do you have an aversion to hospital food too?"

"I feel kind of sick, not sure it's the food, I think it's the surgery, I feel nauseated. The food is ok, not great but ok."

"We should tell the nurse when she comes in to get your tray. But maybe you are stressing out over your dad and court. Just remember you are not facing him on your own, and we will be there to support you. You have a bunch of us on your side rooting for you!"

The nurse came in and checked to see how well Eric ate. "Was everything ok, or did you have trouble eating?"

"I am feeling a bit nauseated, so I really couldn't eat."

"I can get you some Gravel for that. Would you like me to do that, and I will also bring you some soup and Jell-O, maybe some ginger ale as well."

"That would be great if you can do that. I would like to try that, thank you."

"Ok, I will be back in a minute and get you what you need." The nurse returned in a few minutes and gave Eric a pill, which he took. She also brought him a tray with a lighter lunch. She disconnected his IV and then she said, "You're looking good, might be able to kick you out of here soon!" She smiled at Eric. Eric thanked her for everything.

"I think she likes you, Eric, my man," Steve was teasing Eric, and Eric had a grin and he seemed happy.

"I think I am too young for her, but thanks for thinking it, Steve. Besides, I think I need to build up my scrawny body."

"Well, we can work on that. I go to the gym often; I'll take you with me. I'll show you how to get fit safely. Do you like basketball?"

"I like shooting hoops; I don't know about playing the game. My dad never let me join teams outside of school hours."

"I am involved in organizing a community club basketball competition. I'm looking at a regulation competition of the sport so that it could reach professional sport scouts. I might get you in to it, as we kick off the start. It could lead to scholarships I am hoping."

"Wow, that would be cool, how did you land into that pot of soup?

"I volunteer for youth programs in the community. I also teach self-defense to women, and others who are vulnerable. I lecture and speak at conferences all over the place on crime prevention, and youth at risk."

"You sure are busy, Steve. You have a lot of ambition. I bet you con a lot of your cop buddies into volunteering too."

"I do get my share of volunteers for youth programs. It's an important project for me. Nothing worse than busting youth for crimes committed due to circumstances in their life."

"Ok, Mr. Eric Sanderson, you are ready for discharge. I have some pamphlets for you answering those nagging questions of cast care for your wrist. I also have some information referring to your nose surgery; I suggest you read that carefully, it will be helpful for issues as they come up. Also, I have a card with your appointment tomorrow at the E.R. to remove the packing in your nose. And this card has your appointment with the surgeon a week from today. This is the prescription for oral antibiotics and pain management pills. I hope you heal well, and good luck with your challenges, I hope they work out for you. Take good care of Eric for us, ok Steve."

"I will, I always take care of my friends." Steve waited for Eric to finish getting ready, and then they left.

Steve checked in at the squad room and filled Capt. Shepherd in on what was happening with Eric's case. Capt. Shepherd was concerned about the amount of time that Steve was building up for overtime. Steve reassured the captain that he wasn't going to expect time off when it was far too busy in his squad. Steve was honest and said that he hoped he would get a chance to go camping in the woods with Jordon, who has never had a good camping experience. Capt. Shepherd wished Steve well with the hearing, as well as Eric.

Steve was gathering paperwork for the court hearing and was almost ready to get going. He looked at Eric, and then took a deep breath, "We have to go get you some dress pants a shirt and a jacket, then we'll head back to my place to change, then to court."

CHAPTER EIGHT

They got back to Steve's place and quickly changed and got fixed up. Then Steve said, "We have to boot it to make it to the courthouse by two pm." So, they took off and Steve used his sirens and dome light to get downtown in record time. "I don't know if this was fun for you, but it was for me."

Eric said, "If I were a kid, I might have found that exciting, but I am glad I wasn't in the back seat." Eric had a huge grin on his face.

They entered the courthouse and went straight to the court room they needed to be in. They sat at the table with CFS and their legal aid and Steve handed his file to the lawyer to review. Eric began to breathe heavier and shake, as he noticed his dad sitting across just glaring at him. Steve leaned over, and he spoke to Eric, "Just take deep slow breaths, buddy. I'm here, you are ok, nothing bad is going to happen to you, ok, just relax." Steve put his hand on his shoulder and squeezed it reassuringly.

Eric slowed his breathing and looked straight ahead. He worked on staying calm, then he was looking around the courtroom, and towards the back, avoiding looking at his dad, then his jaw dropped, he saw his mom walk in the court room. He turned and stared at his mom, and said softly, "Mom."

Steve turned to look in surprise as Eileen said quietly, "I invited her to come if she could. I guess she made it. Please come sit down over here behind Eric."

Eric hugged his mom, and she hugged him back and said, I love you Eric, and I've missed you so much."

Then a door opened, and the bailiff said, "All Rise." The judge came in and sat down, the bailiff sounded off, "The honorable Judge Horton presiding in the case of Sanderson vs. Sanderson, everyone may be seated."

Judge Horton began, "This hearing, I understand, is to decide on the emancipation of young Eric Sanderson from his parents, Mr. John Sanderson and Mrs. Harriet Sanderson. Young man, would you stand up please?"

Eric stood up and remained quiet. He waited for any question the judge could ask.

Judge Horton looked over the youth, "Do you wish to live on your own without parental supervision?"

"Yes, sir I would like to, your honor."

"Ok, you may sit. I am glad you seem to be polite and respectful of the court. You dressed accordingly and addressed me with respect, that's impressive, thank you son." The judge looked across the court room. "I understand the parents are also in court today, could they please rise?"

Eric's dad stood up and his mom stood up.

Judge Horton observed they were not together. "Mrs. Sanderson, I see you prefer to stand with your son?"

"I am in agreement of my son not coming home for his safety and wellbeing." It was a very soft, shaky voice that she spoke with.

"You agree that your son should be granted emancipation from your parental rights. Is this what I heard?"

"Yes, your honor."

"Thank you for your honesty. Mr. Sanderson, how do you feel about this?"

"Your honor, Eric has been a troubled young man, and difficult to handle. He can't follow rules and is disrespectful of his father. His own mother has difficulty with him. She'd like nothing better than to cut him loose. I believe he is better off at home with a stable routine and rules to follow. If he is on his own, there is no telling what kind of trouble he will get into."

"Well, I have his arrest report here. Young man, please stand again."

"Yes, sir, your honor."

"Is it true you broke into a home where the people were on vacation, and you knew this by befriending their son? And would you make this a regular activity if you were to live on your own?"

"Your honor, I did that so I did not have to sleep out on the streets, I would like to state I did not steal anything, I cleaned the home up before I left. I was making money out on my own to pay for my food. I had no intention of making 'break and enter' a part of my way of living, respectfully, sir. If I were to be on my own, my wish would be to finish school and possibly go to college to study in the social sciences field. I met an awesome detective, who has treated me fairly and inspired me to fly straight, your honor, sir."

"Well, that is commendable, but are you prepared to face the charges and take your punishment, should you be found guilty?"

"Your honor, sir, if I were to be found guilty, I would serve my punishment with acceptable behavior and remorse for what I have done. I am also planning, I might add, to volunteer at a community club for youth and basketball. I would also be willing to tutor younger youth to repay society for my wrongdoing, your honor, sir."

"Well, that is admirable of you. Who is this detective, is he here could he stand up, please?"

Steve stood up and waited for the judge to address him.

"Young man, I might have known it was you, Steve. Did you coach this young delinquent?"

"No, sir, I did not. I spoke with him, I listened to his problems and have taken care of him while he was medically treated for injuries, but I did not coach him."

"Ok, you may sit, I would believe you, and if you had, I was going to state you need to coach pleading guilty with an explanation. I am impressed with this young man; you will go far with your attitude. Mr. Sanderson, in reading Eric's file I have a troubling medical report from an ER physician, which persuades me to believe this young man has been abused severely, without the doctor spelling it out to me. Can you explain this?"

"Sir, I have had from time-to-time trouble with disciplining my son, he is defiant of my rules and punishment, and he gets physical with me."

"Mr. Sanderson, you appear to be approximately six foot five, you are broad in stance and likely weigh approximately three hundred and ten pounds. Your son is at the most five feet ten inches, and maybe one hundred and sixty-five pounds. He gets physical with you. I have here a report that he needed his wrist reset from an improper healing of a break, his nose was badly broken it had to be surgically fixed. He needs back surgery for a displaced broken coccyx, he must wait to see a spinal surgeon, there is proof of healed broken ribs, a skull fracture recently, old bruises of various stages of healing. Explain to me just how he could get so physical as to cause you to hurt him this badly, and never take him for medical care."

"Your honor, I am telling you the truth, he is defiant and will get physical."

"I find that hard to believe, and it's a good thing I am not swearing you in to tell the truth, or I would find you in contempt of court and have you arrested for child endangerment."

"Mrs. Sanderson, please stand again. Tell me clearly and with a bit of a louder voice what you have to say about Eric's father. Does he get physical with you and, if you took a medical, would we find similar injuries?"

"Your honor, I find it hard to stand here and tell you what my husband does to me, but I do not deny the notion that I am abused, yes I believe you would find similar injuries." She turned and looked at her husband. "I am sick of you bullying our son, you've gone too far this time, I am not returning home either, as

I know I would suffer a beating. I say all of this respectfully, your honor."

"Young man, I am ordering the court to grant you emancipation. I am also ordering Detective Steve Weston to be your overseer and to supervise you. CFS case worker, Eileen Sangster, will visit you. You will be assisted through the CFS and Juvenile detention systems. And Mrs. Sanderson, I am directing you to be placed in protective custody, and assisted through legal aid to obtain legal separation. As well I am ordering a no contact order against Mr. Sanderson. You understand, Mr. Sanderson, you are not to go within five hundred feet of your son or wife. You are not to contact or make threats against them. I also expect you to respect any orders directed at you by the courts, or you will find yourself under arrest for the abuses you have caused. This case is closed, good luck young man. Case dismissed."

Everyone quietly cheered, hugged, and celebrated. Eric was subdued, he wasn't sure what to do, he was happy, but heart broken. He was worried about his mother, but he also was feeling weird from his surgery. He noticed more pain when he fought off crying.

Steve noticed Eric's pain and facial expressions; he knew Eric was feeling confused. "Eric, are you ok, buddy?"

"I am feeling strange, I think it's from my surgery, but I'm in pain. If I start to cry and fight it, it hurts. I know crying is putting pressure on my sinuses. I think I need a week's sleep. But I am happy with the ruling."

"Well, we haven't given you a pain killer since the hospital. I maybe should take you home and get you in bed for a rest." Steve turned to Eric's mother. "Mrs. Sanderson, we haven't formerly met, I am Detective Steve Weston. I have been looking after your son. He's tired today as he had surgery this morning. I'd like to take him home for a rest. Would you like to go with him? I would be happy to have you as a guest. I just think this has been a lot for him to experience."

"Oh, I don't want to impose on you, but I have missed Eric so much, maybe I could go for a while, and find a hotel for the night to stay at."

"I insist you can stay with us, a hotel is costly, and we can work something out tomorrow morning. It's not an imposition. I will insist so no sense arguing with me." Steve gave her his famous smile.

"I can't seem to say no to you, thank you for your generous hospitality."

"Ok, Eileen we are going to get going. Eric is tired; he needs his rest. I will catch you later, let me know if I have to sign anything. Thanks for all your help I appreciate it."

CHAPTER NINE

So off they went, they had the courts officers escort them to Steve's car, to make sure they left without any trouble. "We'll be home soon, 20 minutes there, Eric, and then you can rest. And you don't have to go anywhere for some time. Mrs. Sanderson, I hope you won't mind, my place is small, but homey. I didn't have time to grocery shop, so I may be ordering our supper tonight, I hope you don't mind. It'll be like a celebration for both of you, both being free."

"I am just happy to have Eric close by, and know he is taken care of. I am so thankful you happened to find him. You are an angel that God sent to us. Eric's running away, made me decide to leave his father. I promised God, I would leave him to take care of Eric. Whatever you have to offer is most appreciated."

They drove for a while. Steve parked and they all went upstairs. Steve found the door wasn't locked, so he went in ready for trouble. Then he got in and was very surprised it was Jordon that was there. "What are you doing here Jordon?"

"The Captain gave us the night off, and the next two days off, since we solved our case, and he heard you were going to be looking after Eric. I thought I'd surprise you by cooking dinner for you both." Jordon saw that there was a woman present.

"This is Eric's mother; Mrs. Sanderson She is my guest tonight. Mrs. Sanderson, this is my partner, Jordon Smith."

"Isn't that interesting, your names are Smith and Weston. Do you get teased a lot by that?"

"Actually, everyone expects us to live up to our names in the field. We like to call each other Smith and Weston." Then the smile came out, and Steve's eyes lit up the room.

"Do you know when you smile your eyes glean like a light?"

"I have been told that. Jordon, what are you cooking that smells so good?"

"I thought a roast chicken would be good, I made mashed potatoes and glazed carrots. It's almost done. I hope you don't mind I did some grocery shopping; I knew you wouldn't have time today."

"Man, you are a truly good friend, I don't mind. Eric, why don't you lie down on the couch for a while?" Steve turned and saw that Eric was on the couch asleep.

Steve went out to his green space and rolled a cot into the corner of the living room, for later that night. "Mrs. Sanderson, you can have the bedroom to sleep in tonight. Just let me know if you need anything."

Jordon and Mrs. Sanderson set the table. "Dinner is ready everybody!"

"Mrs. Sanderson, you may sit here." Steve pulled the end chair out for his guest.

"Just call me Mom. We don't need to be so formal, Steve."

"Ok, Mom, I will just go wake Eric up for supper."

They all sat around the table and began their meal, "May I make a toast, to new beginnings." Steve had his big bright smile on his face and was very happy with his victory.

Eric, however, was feeling less celebratory, as reality was sinking in. He was going to have to grow up fast and do everything right to survive now that he was on his own, so he had no smile, and he was in a lot of pain as he had fallen asleep before getting any pain med from Steve.

"What's up, buddy? You don't seem too relaxed there?"

"It's nothing," Eric answered, "I am just having a lot of pain in my face. And I am realizing I now have a lot of responsibility on me."

"We forgot to give you your pain med, let me get that for you, buddy. I'm sorry we forgot. We have to stay ahead of the pain." Steve got up and got Eric his pills, as well as his antibiotic, and brought an icepack for his nose.

"Thanks, Steve, that's great, and you had an ice pack handy. It feels great on the nose, thanks." Eric held the ice pack on the bridge of his nose, he felt some relief.

"Eric, buddy, you're not going it alone on the next road of your journey. Jordon and I will be around for advice and help. Your Mom is going to be close by, so you will always have her wisdom with you. No one is going to abandon you, I promise."

Eric then had a smile on his face and seemed very relieved to hear what Steve said. They all ate happily and had a great conversation. At the end of the meal, everyone pitched in to clean up. Jordon saw the time; it was quite late, and it had been a long day.

"Well, I had better get home, it's getting late. I need to put a load of laundry on as well. I am happy to know all worked out for everyone. Have a good night." Jordon put his jacket on and headed to the front door.

Everyone was saying, "Goodnight."

"Hey Smith, thanks for everything you did for me today, I owe you big time. I will see you tomorrow, right?"

"Yeah West, you know it. I'll bring the paper by so you can apartment hunt for your two borders."

"Great and thanks again." Weston slipped a few bills into Smith's hand. "That's for the groceries you paid for, if it was more just tell me."

"No, that's more than enough, thanks West. See you tomorrow."

Weston went back into the living room, and both Eric and his mom looked done. They were tired and Steve knew it. "So how are you two feeling this evening?"

"Well, I haven't slept for over a day. The bus ride into the city was exhausting and finding my way around very tiring. I would like to go to bed."

"Ok, Mom, you can use the bedroom. Did you want to have a shower first or just hit the hay?"

"If you don't mind I would like to Shower to unwind. It's been a long day."

"So, Eric, you can have the sofa bed to sleep on. I'll help you pull it out. You can't shower with the cast and your nose or arm for tonight, so you'll be able to nod off to sleep."

Then Weston went to work on pulling the cot open and fixing it to sleep on. He was quite exhausted to say the least. It had been an exhausting week, but it was ending on a good note. Weston was pleased with the results.

"Goodnight Eric, see you in the morning."

"Night Steve, and again thank you for all your help!"

CHAPTER TEN

Eric slept, but he had a restless sleep, Weston heard him thrashing and moaning. Weston figured that the meds, being overtired, and everything he went through was the cause of his restless sleep.

Weston awoke the next morning. He intended to get up and fix breakfast for his guests, but quietly to let Eric sleep. Eric's mom had beat Weston to it. She was getting the coffee going, and was whipping up pancakes.

"I hope you don't mind, I thought I would make breakfast for everyone. I found everything I needed. I think Eric needs his sleep; he was quite restless last night."

"Yeah, Mom he does, he's been through a lot. I got up quietly to do the same thing. You beat me to it, thanks. I hope you slept well!"

"Oh, I slept great. Your bed is very comfortable, thank you again."

"You are welcome! My mom would never forgive me if I didn't offer help to you! I was thinking later this morning when Smith gets here, we could look for apartments for you and Eric. No rush or pressure, but we may as well find what you need, right Mom?" Weston had a huge smile again.

"Oh, Steve you are a good boy, your mom did well with you." She brushed her hand up against his cheek then hugged him.

"So how about we cook some bacon with those pancakes, Mom?" Steve pulled the bacon from the fridge and smiled at the thought.

"Steve, that's going to be a big breakfast."

"Well, I need the energy if we are home hunting, right Mom?" Came erics voice from the doorway. "What's going on in here?"

"Hey buddy, you woke up! How do you feel this morning? I'll get your pills."

"I feel ok, but my face hurts. I thought I would try the ice pack again instead of pain pills, that's why I got up."

"Sure, it's in the freezer. How about you go lay down for about a half hour, get some more rest, and then breakfast will be ready."

"Ok, sure, then I will help with clean up, ok." Eric went back to lie down with the ice pack on his face.

There was a knock on the door, and then Jordon poked his head in the door to check if everyone was up. "Hey, is it safe to come in? I brought the paper, and I brought some Danishes."

"Hey Jordon, we don't need the Danishes this morning, we are having pancakes and bacon for breakfast. Mom's cooking up a storm, come in and have a coffee."

"Wow sounds great. I'll put the Danishes in the fridge for another day. Thanks Mom!" Jordon gave her a kiss on the cheek. He was of course happy as he was going to eat well. He poured himself a coffee, and sat at the table. He was looking over the newspaper.

As they all enjoyed their breakfast, they discussed what kind of apartment they would need to find, and how much they could afford, and the schools that were close by. Eric did not want to live too far from school, as well as Weston, and he was hoping his mom could find a place close by. Weston said they would find places close by then he would feel good about Eric being on his own.

Smith spoke up and said, "There is a new building opening up close by, they have single bedroom and bachelor suites available, we should go look at that one. It's only a couple of blocks from here. They are taking applications today and tomorrow."

"Well, what do you two think? Should we hoof it on over and see about the apartment?" Steve asked.

"I would like to check it out. It might just be what Mom and I need."

"Ok, let's tidy up and grab our jackets and walk over there. It's a start, isn't it?"

They all got up and put the dishes in the sink and put everything away. Weston told Eric, "We can do the dishes when we get back."

"Smith can keep looking at apartments available as we look around."

They all walked a few blocks over and saw the new building that had been finished in construction. They walked inside. The main floor looked like a courtyard, it was very nice, and it had elevators. They were greeted by a representative for the management of the new building. He gave them his card and pamphlets explaining the suites and rent. He asked who was looking, and Eric and his mom spoke up.

Steve added, "Sam, Eric and his mother are relocating from Brandon. Would we be able to see the suites, for options they might have?"

"Of course, let me take you through a few of our models. Let me explain how each floor is set up. You see the main floor has a courtyard. Each apartment entry is right off the courtyard. The second floor through the seventh floor have center halls and apartment entries right off the halls as well. Our plan is to have a social area for tenants with card tables, and possibly pool tables, and shuffle boards. We don't have those big game tables yet; we are hoping to hear about them soon. We want the tenants to feel this is their home, a small community so to speak. We will also have exercise equipment and social evenings. Some suites have balconies. The rent is a few dollars higher. There is central air, and electric heat. Electric is to be paid by the tenant; water and phone are included in the rent. This suite is a bachelor apartment all one room, and a bathroom. You can see it's a decent size, and the bed area is sectioned off by a three-quarter wall. There is a kitchen and dining area. It's quite spacious. The rent is five hundred and ninety-eight a month. Would the young man be interested in applying for this apartment?"

"I think it's a cute apartment, I would be happy in it, what do you think Eric?"

"Well Mom, I like it. The fact it's new means it's clean. How do you like it, Steve?"

"It doesn't matter to me. It's you two who need to be happy. The rent is right."

Sam said, "Well, let's move on and see the one bedroom, it is a great suite. This one has a large living room a kitchen, and dining area, and a bathroom. There is lots of storage. In fact, the big storage room here, if you'll look in, it is large enough with the door open you can make it a study room. Put a desk and shelving and you can study. The rent is six hundred and ninety-eight. This apartment has a balcony, it's not huge, but it is sufficient. Get a nice bistro table and chairs set and you can enjoy your private fresh air. Are you two on limited income, may I ask?"

"I know I will be," Eric answered. "I am not sure about my mom, but I think she will be too, is that good or bad?"

"Oh, it will be good, as the government would supplement your rent if you were limited. I will give you all the forms you need to fill in and submit. Can you get them done by tomorrow and back to me?"

"I will make sure you get them back tomorrow, thank you for showing us the building it's fantastic." Weston shook Sam's hand, as they began to exit the building. "So, let's head back to my place. You can fill out the forms. I need to make some calls while we are there and I need to get some information for you two."

Back at the house, Steve noticed his partner and buddy was very quiet indeed.

"Smith, you are awfully quiet, what are you thinking?"

"I was thinking those apartments are so nice we should apply to move in there ourselves. The appliances are nice, and dishwashers in each suite. I really liked the building; I can't get over the rent and the size of the suites."

"Ok, so we all like the first ones we saw. I like that they would be close by. Nice neighborhood too. I need to call social services to see what it is they will cover; I am sure Eileen Sangster can give me those answers." Weston got on the phone once they got home and started making his calls.

Weston was getting frustrated because he was having to wait for call backs, and he was making calls everywhere to get his answers. Then Eileen called back. She was making many calls herself, she explained to Weston, on behalf of the mom and Eric. She was explaining how the housing worked. Then she asked for the number of Sam, so she could call. She told Weston she would call him back with the answers to all his questions. So, Weston got off the phone, and went to help with the forms, as Smith was already helping. Weston was a bit concerned on the finance end of things. He was not sure what the rental allowance would be. He wanted his new friends to be ok.

The phone rang again, and Steve picked it up and answered, "Weston residence."

It was Eileen on the other end, she was a bit hurried. "Steve, I have some answers for you. It seems if both Eric and his mom want the bachelor suites, their rent is covered. They could live there easily; I have had their names added to the tenants' list. They need to take their forms in, but you need to write on the finance line these case file numbers. For Eric, his case file number is ES one three eight two five, and for Harriet, her case file is HS nine two five three. Write those in the rental forms and turn the forms in and they will get possession at the beginning of the month. So just a couple of days from now."

"So, I only have my guests two more days. Well, thank you for the information. I will get that on their forms, I have to take Eric to the hospital, so I will talk to you later. Thanks so much Eileen for all your help."

"Ok Eric, are you ready to get the packing out of your nose? I also have the information for your forms."

"Yeah, Steve I am ready, and here's my form."

"Ok, let me put the case file numbers on the forms. Jordon, could I ask you and Mom to take these forms back to the apartment block? Eric and I will head to the hospital and get the packing removed from his nose."

Everyone went off to take care of their tasks. Steve and Eric went off to the hospital and made it in time for their appointment. Eric went into a treatment room with the doctor. He did not enjoy the removal of the packing. It was the worst feeling, and he felt like sneezing. The doctor put the brace on his nose, and told him no blowing or sneezing, and taught him a few tricks to avoid a sneeze, and to clean his nose. The doctor said he was pleased with the results of the surgery, and dismissed Eric with: "I'll see you at your next appointment young man!"

"Thank you, Doctor, I appreciate your care."

"Well, you take care, and do well!"

Eric left and joined Steve in the waiting area. "I'm ready to go."

"Ok, let's move along and meet up with your mom and Jordon."

They arrived back before Jordon and Mrs. Sanderson got back.

CHAPTER ELEVEN

So, Weston was excited to hear from Eric's mom when they got back. His phone rang and he answered it. "Weston here. Yes, can I help you? No, Jordon Smith is not here now, I expect him back in a few minutes. Can I take a message? Ok, I will give him that message. Is there a number he can call if he needs further information? Ok, two zero four, seven, seven, two, one, nine, one, nine. Ok, thank you very much." Weston hung up the phone and was a bit curious as to how Smith would handle that call.

Eric was curious as well. "Was that something serious? It's like it wiped the smile off your face."

"No, I don't know, it'll be up to Jordon if it is serious."

Just as Weston finished his statement Jordon and Eric's mom came in the door laughing and joking. They seemed incredibly happy.

"Hey, you two are back. How did it go?"

"Well, I guess these two will be busy moving in two days. Eric's mom was telling me about the things they will need to start off."

"Well, that's great then. I think a few phone calls around the precinct we should be able to collect what they need, right Smith?"

"Yeah, the men in blue are pretty good with this sort of thing. I could type up a list of the things they need and drop it off at headquarters."

"Yeah, um Jordon, maybe," Weston got his partner's attention. "but first I have a phone message for you. It was the hospital. They wanted to talk to you about someone who used you as their emergency contact. Here I wrote the number down for you."

"Ok, I should call and find out what's up then."

"Hey Mom, how about I get you to make that list at the kitchen table while Jordon makes that call."

"Hello, this is Jordon Smith calling you back. Can I ask who this call is related to? Oh, I see, and is she ok? Do you know what happened to her? I will need to come and get a statement from her. Is she up to have the police come and visit? Ok thank you so much I will be there shortly." Jordon hung up the phone and looked at Steve in a shocked way.

"Hey partner, is everything alright?"

"It's Janet. She was beaten up outside a bar. She is in recovery from surgery, they had to fix her up. We are going to have to make a report."

"Ok, well, Eric, can you and your mom stay here? Heat up the leftovers for supper, your pills are on the window seal. We won't be too long, but this is Jordon's girlfriend, we need to check this out."

"Ok we can look after ourselves here, Weston," Harriet assured him. "You boys look after yourselves. I hope she's not too bad off."

"I'll drive Jordon."

A New Case

The two men made their way to the hospital, and went to the desk to ask, "Excuse me but can you tell me what room Janet Taylor is in?"

"She is in room five twelve G."

"Thank you so much," Smith took very long strides to the elevator, leaving Weston behind, but he waited for him in the elevator. They went up to the floor, and were heading down the hall, looking very serious, and a nurse stopped them.

"Can I help you two men?"

"Detectives Jordon Smith and Steve Weston to see Janet Taylor."

"Oh, ok. Just try not to react to her injuries, she is sedated, but awake. She sustained an awful beating."

"Was she drinking by any chance?"

"No thank goodness! We checked before she went to surgery. She was sober when this happened."

"When did this happen anyway?"

"It was around one a.m. this morning."

"Ok I need to talk to her then."

Smith and Weston walked into her room, she was all taped up, and she did not look good.

"Janet." She turned to look at Smith and began crying.

"Smith, I'm so sorry, you warned me about this. I wasn't drinking though!" She controlled her crying as it was very painful to her face.

"Hey, you have nothing to be sorry about. Try not to cry, it's creating more pain for you. Can you tell me what happened from the beginning?"

"Well, I was walking home after having coffee with my sponsor. I was happy I had three weeks' sobriety. We had talked that when I had a month how I was going to tell you. I walked by a bar, there were guys coming out fighting. I didn't pay attention; I was just happy I wasn't falling down drunk." Janet was crying and trying to reach for her water.

Smith picked it up and held it up for her to drink. "Continue when you're ready Janet."

"Well, this guy was yelling, but I kept walking, and then I was knocked to the ground. He jumped me, and was yelling, you…" The words were incoherent as she was crying. "He said he was going to teach me a lesson about what happens when you tease a man."

"Ok, just breathe nice and slow, and calm down. It's ok, you are safe, and we have all night if you need it." Smith was trying to be compassionate, but the anger was building inside of him.

Weston said, "How about you both take some deep slow breaths, take a moment to compose yourselves. Don't rush. Could you identify this guy if you saw him again Janet?"

Janet looked at Weston and began to nod yes, and then said, "Yes I would."

"So, when you are ready, Janet, continue," Weston had his hand on Smith's shoulder and squeezed it, so he would remain calm.

"I didn't know what he meant. He was punching me and kicking me in the gut. Then he kicked me so hard in the groin, the pain was so bad I passed out." Janet was crying so hard that the pain was getting to be too much, and she couldn't breathe.

"Do you remember which bar this was at?" Smith enquired.

"It was the one we go to all the time, close to your place, not Zack's, the 'Black Ball."

"Ok, let me call a nurse and see if they can give you something for pain, would that be alright?" Smith pressed the call button, and a few minutes later a nurse came in.

"Can I help you Ms. Taylor?"

"She's in a lot of pain from crying is there anything you can do for her; I won't be asking any more questions tonight."

"Ok, I will get the doctor, as he wants to talk to you as well."

Jordon pulled a chair up next to the bed and sat down, softly brushing her hair and rubbing her shoulder to calm her. He told her he was there and not leaving her alone. Jordon was almost in tears himself, and he was angry as she had done a thing wrong that time.

"Hello there, I am Doctor Schilling, I saw Janet in the E.R. and after her surgery. Janet, we are going to give you something to relax you and take care of the pain. You may fall asleep, but that is ok, you need to heal."

Smith asked, "How long will she be in hospital, do you know?"

"Well, she suffered some deep trauma, her pelvic bones were shattered. I understand she was kicked in the groin. She also had a broken rib that punctured her lung. And her face has had a lot of plastic surgery to fix it. She is in for at least two weeks minimum."

"Wow, she sure got a beating," Weston couldn't help making the comment.

"Well, I am afraid that's not all, in running our tests, we had to be sure she had no drugs or alcohol in her, we discovered she was pregnant. We want to do an ultrasound later this evening to see how the baby is doing. She is about eight weeks along, maybe ten weeks."

Jordon hung his head down, he felt sick. "For Christ's sake, how can a man beat a woman who did nothing to him?" The anger was seething out, he didn't know what to do, he wanted to kill someone. Weston wanted to comfort him but knew to give him some space. The doctor said that Janet should make a full recovery, and then left.

Janet was settling down but kept apologizing to Smith. "I'm so sorry. I know you warned me, I am sorry. But I didn't drink or do anything wrong this time."

"Ssshhh…., ssshhh…., ssshhhush, shush calm down breathe easy, it'll be ok. You are right, you were right, you did nothing wrong." Smith stroked her hair and whispered to calm her. Jordon sat quiet while she fell asleep, he didn't want to leave her alone. He turned to Weston, and said to him, "You find out if the cops are investigating or even showed up at the scene, and if not why. I want this guy found and charged. No woman deserves to be treated like this. I know what I said, but I never wanted this to happen." Smith was crying, not horribly crying, but quietly crying.

Weston approached Smith and hugged him, "Keep calm, just be with her. I will take care of this. I got you and Janet, ok." Weston left the hospital to go to the precinct, so he could follow up and get the information he needed.

CHAPTER TWELVE

Weston got up to the squad room and found Detectives Al Woods and Dave Barnes working on paperwork. Dave turned and looked at Weston. "Weston, how are you? I thought you were off for a few days?"

"I was until we got a phone call from the hospital. Smith is with Janet."

"Oh, so the hospital got a hold of you two. How is she?"

"She's a mess, and she might lose her baby, she was pregnant. What do you two know about this? Tell me something good."

"Well, we answered the call, it was awful, so many drunks. We got her an ambulance and sent her on her way. We had to look for the guy responsible. He is in lockup sobering up. He put up a fight but had no idea what he did. When he sobers up, we will read him his rights and inform him with what he is charged. He did a number on Smith's girlfriend."

"Well, I am going to do a number on him. I'll read him his rights first, then give him a wakeup call, about what he has done. I hope he is charged and processed before Smith gets here. I will make sure he stays with Janet, but if she loses the baby, I wouldn't want to be that guy."

"Ok, Weston you better keep your cool with him, we don't need a police brutality charge to follow."

"I am just going to give him a piece of my mind, then I'll come back and fill you in on what Janet told us." Off Weston went, to speak to the assailant.

He went to the jail cell where he was being held and looked in to see the man sitting on the bunk with his head resting in his hands. "What the hell did you think you were doing attacking that poor woman? You did a lot of damage to her, and she may lose her baby. What kind of freak are you? Did you get off on that?"

The man looked up and had tears in his eyes, and said that he was sorry and he had drunk far too much the night before. Then, he asked, "She was pregnant? I didn't know, I am sorry! I didn't know."

"Why though? What did she ever do to deserve the intense beating she got? She was just walking home from having coffee with a friend. She did nothing to you to hurt you! You're a coward, you crazy bastard, a coward."

"Really, I am sorry, I am sober now, I plan to plead guilty, I know I did wrong. I am truly sorry; I hope she will be alright. I was angry cause she was always in the bar teasing and leading me and other guys on, causing us to fight. I saw her and wanted to teach her a lesson. I lost it; I was out of control."

Weston wanted to beat the hell out of this guy, and he was glad he did not have the key. He told the man just as much as well. Then he left and went back up to the squad room. He got in there and saw Capt. Shepherd there. "Captain Shepherd, sir, what are you doing here in the evening?"

"Well, when I hear my men are on the warpath, I come out to check and make sure they are not committing a crime."

"No, Captain. I kept my head; I told the man off. He is just beginning to figure out what he did. He is pathetic. I stayed on this side of the cell."

"How is Detective Smith taking it? Where is he?"

"He is at the hospital with Janet. He is very upset. I swear if thoughts could kill the guy would be dead. Janet looks awful, and she didn't do anything wrong for the beating she got. I am going to head back to the hospital. I just want to fill the guys in on what Janet told us. We can question her formally in a couple of days when she isn't full of drugs."

Weston went on to fill Detective Barnes and Detective Woods in with what they learned at the hospital and then he spoke with Capt. Shepherd about his visit, and that what was said was off the record. He then said that he was heading back to the hospital to be with his partner.

Weston entered the room with a floral arrangement to give to Smith to give to Janet. "How is she doing?"

"She is hanging in there for now. Did you find out anything?"

"Yeah, he is in a cell sobering up, and he is not feeling all too good about himself. I filled in the arresting detectives and told them give her a couple of days to be coherent and not full of drugs and anesthesia."

"Captain Shepherd knows about all this. He said to keep your cool. Did they do the ultrasound yet?"

"Yes, they did, she's three months along. It's my kid, I'm pretty sure. She's all worried because of her drinking. I told her not to worry about it right now, as she needs to stay calm for the baby." Jordon was grinning ear to ear; he was not too worried about being a dad at the moment.

"Well, congratulations Smith. I hope it all works out fine for you both."

They both shook hands and hugged it out, like partners do.

"So, are you going to stay overnight with her?"

"Yeah, she is pretty scared, so I figure I can keep her calm and feel safe if I am with her."

"Ok, partner, give her the flowers; they are from you. I will stay just a little while and then get home to my guests."

"Oh, yeah you have the new family to take care of. Ok, you get some rest. I will talk to you tomorrow."

Weston said his goodbye and left to go home. He was upset for his partner and girlfriend, and he was feeling bad for Eric and what he went through with his dad. Weston was beginning to question humanity. Violence and not a good enough reason for it. He wondered why, what creates so much anger and craziness. He arrived home and parked his car, then went into his place. It was late, so he peeked in and quietly entered. He wasn't sure anyone would be up as it was late.

"I am home and happy to be here," he said out loud. Eric and his mom were sitting up and waiting for him. "Hi Mom, hey Eric, so how was your evening?"

"Come sit down, have a cup of coffee, how is your partner and his friend?"

"Thank you, I didn't expect you to wait up for me. Well, Jordon's girlfriend is in bad shape, and he is upset and angry with the person who beat her up."

"Oh, that is a terrible thing to happen to a young woman!"

"Yeah, they caught the guy, and he is in a jail cell for now. His reasoning is stupid as to why he beat her so badly."

"How bad is she from the beating?"

"Well, she has a broken rib, shattered pelvic area. She had to have plastic surgery on her face, so lots of pain from it and from her crying."

"Was she drinking, and she got in this trouble? Poor girl, she does not deserve to be man-handled like that."

"Well, she was sober, and was walking home from having coffee with a friend. She quit drinking a few weeks ago. This was a guy who had predetermined she would pay for teasing him. He kicked her so hard he shattered her pelvic bones. She did not deserve this. Just like you and Eric. It's not right and it's senseless."

"Oh, you are upset, I am sorry you're so upset." Mom got up and hugged Weston like a mother would. "It'll be ok and work out."

"I am upset, as Jordon's girlfriend did not know she was pregnant, and it's possible she may lose the baby, so far she is doing ok. Should have seen Smith - he was grinning ear to ear like a proud papa."

"What a surprise that is, so something good is happening at the same time."

"Well, I am hungry. I am going to throw together a sandwich then I am off to bed for a long rest."

"You are in luck, I made you a few sandwiches and kept them in the fridge, you just sit there, and I'll get them for you."

"Thanks Mom. That is great, so sweet of you, thank you." Weston sat with his coffee and ate his sandwiches with delight. Eric's mom made him feel good.

"We made our lists of things we will need for immediate move in at our new place. I think Eric and I could do some shopping at thrift stores and secondhand stores. It won't cost too much that way."

"Well, hold off there. I will make a copy of the list and get it out to the Department, then we will have donations dropped off at the apartments on 'move in' day. You would be surprised how organized the P.D. is in rallying for those in need. Then what you don't get I will take you shopping for the rest."

"That sounds great. We will need to get Eric back in school soon. Maybe the day after the move we can take him to be registered."

"Sounds like a plan." Weston turned towards Eric. "What do you think Eric?" Weston saw that Eric fell asleep on the couch. "I guess he is tired. I am going to take a shower and then go to bed, ok Mom." Weston got up and gave her a kiss on the cheek and put his dishes in the sink. He went and got his pajamas and went to the bathroom for his shower. When he was done, Mom had turned off the lights and had gone to bed. Weston covered Eric with a blanket, then went to bed. Steve was relaxed and hoped his partner would also be ok.

The following morning, Weston was up early and grabbed a quick bite before he went to head out with his list and to make his rounds. He went to the department first and filled in everyone, and put the word out about the list needs. He made copies to hand out and said he hoped everyone would check out what they were donating, so they didn't get duplicates. Then he spoke with Det. Barnes about the arrest. He was told the guy would be arraigned the next day. He was happy to hear that. He then returned to the hospital to see his partner and find out how he was doing.

"Hey there, Smith, how are you doing? How is Janet doing?"

Jordon looked up at Weston. He looked drained, and about to cry. Janet just turned her head away as she was crying.

Weston put his hand on Jordon's shoulder and squeezed it, "What's up partner, what has happened?"

Jordon moved into Weston's arms and was crying, he quietly said, "We lost the baby, he didn't make it. "Janet hasn't aborted him yet, but we've been told there is no heartbeat. We didn't get a chance to know him or love him."

Weston just held him and hugged him as he felt his partner's pain. He was sad for their loss. Jordon pulled away and wiped his face and sat down next to Janet holding her hand.

Janet turned to look at Jordon and saw Weston standing there. Weston moved in to hug Janet. He felt terrible. "I am so sorry Janet," Weston hugged her and moved away after she released her hold on him.

"The guy gets arraigned tomorrow. He will pay for what he has done to you two, you know that, right? Take time to heal, I'll deal with everything. I can cover court and I'll let Captain Shepherd know what's happening. Is there anything I can do for you two? Get you something to eat, or drink?"

Smith got up and said, "I need to get out of here and get some air."

"Well, air is one thing, but where are your thoughts going with what has happened partner?"

"I want that bastard to pay and feel what it's like. I will make him wish he were dead."

"You can get some air, but they will not let you near him. Believe me, he was feeling bad last night, he was crying and stated he was sorry. He told me he will face his charges and take the punishment. He was so drunk that night he had no idea how far he went till I told him. You have to stay away from him, partner."

"He needs to hurt and hurt bad. I want him to pay for taking our son from us."

"Smith, you're not hearing me. You need to stay away from the precinct."

Janet spoke up, "Jordon, I need you here for me, please. You can get a coffee and quick breath, but I need you at the moment. I don't think I can get through this without you!"

"See Jordon, Janet needs you, you two need to grieve together. I will get you coffee and something to eat, then you can think about the legal system taking care of this bad guy."

"You going to be ok staying here, while I go get you something?"

"Yeah, I'll stay put with Janet, I don't want to leave her alone at the moment."

"Why don't you go with Weston," Janet suggested, "and you two can talk, and you can have something to eat, Jordon. You need to vent; I'll be ok for a little while. I know you have bottled up a lot. Weston can help you de-escalate a bit."

"Are you sure, Janet? I think that's a great idea, but I don't want to take him from you either."

"I am sure. Jordon needs to find a way to forgive what has happened. As you said, the guy feels terrible, and I believe you. Go, Jordon, get some fresh air with your partner."

"Ok Janet, thanks. Let's go Jordon, let's get some food in your belly and a coffee to wake your brain up." The guys went down to the cafeteria, so they would not be far from Janet. "Janet has changed, Jordon, she has matured. I can't believe how she is handling things today."

"Well, overnight we talked. She is taking this A.A. seriously, she told me her and her sponsor were talking about me that night. She knew she needed to make amends to me over her behavior. She didn't know she was pregnant, she just thought her being sick was part of the withdrawal. You know we talked about the baby, I said we should get married, she said no, as she was planning to break up with me. She was over her hero worship. I was surprised, but also felt it was a good thing as I thought I was over her. She was going to keep the baby, and we talked about raising him together."

"So, you two had a real serious talk. You keep saying 'he' as you knew the sex of the baby. How?"

"When they did the ultrasound, we could see it was a boy. We got excited, as he was a little human, we created. I was already deeply in love with our baby." Jordon started to cry.

Weston hugged him hard and said, "I am so sorry for your loss, Smith. Let it out, let go, you can't keep that bottled up."

Smith pulled away and said, "No, not here." He wiped his face of tears. "I know I need to let go, but not in such a public place."

They got themselves something to eat, and a couple of coffees. They talked for a bit while they ate. Jordon seemed to be preoccupied with his grief and not stuck on the guy who beat his girlfriend up.

They started to make their way back to Janet's room. On the floor there was a commotion, then Jordon could hear the page for him. He went to the nurse's station, and asked what was happening. The nurse stated, "It's Janet, she is aborting the baby, so you will have to wait here."

"I am not waiting here. I need to be with her. It's our baby, and I know he died, she needs me with her."

"Ok, but if you act up it is you out of there!"

Jordon was at Janet's side and the doctors were there helping her. She was in tremendous pain as she was in a painful position to deliver the baby. Janet was trying to breathe as the doctors were telling her and, for some reason, Jordon automatically went into coaching mode for Janet.

"Ok, Janet, deep breaths, deep in and deep out, then push when I say push," she was instructed by the doctor.

"Janet, blow out the pain," Jordon said, "Come on you can do it." She was doing it, then she heard "Push" and she did. Then she had the feeling of a pop, and then the pain subsided. Janet felt better, and the nurses and doctors were helping to clean her up and remove everything, the staff returned her to a comfortable position and gave her something to relax her and ease her pain. The Doctor examined the fetus, and said, "Yes it was a boy. He would not have been viable as it was way too early for delivery." Jordon was very sad. He knew it was final and real. Weston came in the room when everyone exited.

Weston held Jordon, and said, "Let it go buddy," and Jordon finally released what he was feeling. He was devastated, and so was Janet. She was hugging a pillow and crying into it. The more Jordon cried the more Janet cried. Weston was looking at Janet and she was looking at him, they both nodded yes, as though thinking the same thing.

Jordon was crying, "I would have been the best damn father ever, I know that!" Weston released his hold of Jordon as he pulled away from him. Jordon went and sat next to Janet, and held her, they both cried together. Weston was hurting for them both. Then a lady came into the room.

"Janet, is everything alright?" It was her sponsor who came to see her. She had heard about the assault.

Weston turned to her and said, "Hi, I'm Detective Steve Weston, I am Jordon's partner."

"Hi, I am Sharlene, I'm Janet's sponsor. So that is the infamous Jordon Smith. Is everything all right here?"

"They just lost their baby. It's very hard and sad."

"Their baby? How, when, I didn't know Janet was pregnant. That's why her withdrawal was so rough."

"Yeah, they only found out after her surgery and all her injuries."

"Well, thank you for telling me, Steve." She turned towards the distraught woman on the bed. "Janet, it's Sharlene, I came to see you. I can go get a coffee, while you two take your time in grieving. I'm so sorry."

Janet released Jordon and reached for Sharlene, while crying.

Jordon realized that Janet wanted some time with Sharlene so he said, "I will go with Weston to talk. I'll be back; I'll bring us all coffee, ok."

Janet nodded yes.

Smith and Weston went out of the room to go talk, and found there was Captain Shepherd in the hall. "Did I come at a bad time?" He was holding a basket of fruit for Janet.

"We just lost our baby," Jordon wiped tears from his eyes and went to shake the captain's hand, but he grabbed Jordon and hugged him just like a father would.

"I am so sorry, son; I had no idea."

"We didn't know till the night before. As it sunk in, we developed a relationship with him. It's like having a lottery win dangled in front of you, you start a new life, and then it's yanked from you, but deeper and harsher. I am so angry, hurt, heartbroken, I just want to shred that bastard apart."

"Well, I hope Weston is planning to keep an eye on you to keep you out of trouble." Captain Shepherd gave the basket of fruit to Jordon. "Take that to your girlfriend's room for now."

Shepherd looked at Weston as he did that.

"I am sticking to him like glue," Weston assured the Captain, "I have been talking him down from his thoughts. His girlfriend is incredible in handling things. She has changed a lot. It's just that she just finished having the baby. It was about three months along, maybe a bit more. So, it is a shock for them."

Capt. Shepherd stated, "Take the time needed to help him and her. When you boys get back to the office, I'll put you on desk duty for a few days. Just till I am sure he will be fine out on the street."

"Ok, Captain, sounds like a good plan."

"Oh and, by the way, your call out for furnishings is gaining a good response. Where do you want the stuff delivered?"

"I thought I put on the call out that it's to be delivered to their new address. I'll get that for you later. They move in tomorrow. I figured it's better if it goes straight there and we don't have to move all of it."

"That's fine, son. I'll take care of it. Just don't forget to get the address to me."

"Oh, here comes Jordon. I will get that to you, I am just going to see what Jordon needs. I will talk to you later, sir." Weston went to catch up with Jordon, and to see about going for the coffee run."

"Hey Jordon, are we going to make that coffee run? I figure get out of the hospital and get some good stuff for the ladies, and us."

"Yeah, we can go get it, then we can bring it back, but after we will leave. Janet is very upset, she said we have no connection now, so I can be off and get on with life. I don't get it; we both lost a child. I know we were not going to get married, but I care how she feels still. How can she just cut and release so cold?"

"Her sponsor's still with her right?"

"Yeah, why?"

"She'll talk to her and comfort her. Sometimes a woman needs another woman. She may want to talk with you later. Leave it open for now. Let's go get coffee."

The drive was quiet. Jordon was hurting, but there was nothing Steve could say to make it better. He could understand, because it's a child, but he did not know how he would be if it were him this happened to. "Smith, I don't know how I would feel, but I would imagine I would feel devastated. It didn't happen to me, but I am here for you, alright! You are not going to go through this alone."

"Thanks West, I appreciate that. It just feels numb at the moment, I guess I will be ok, but I am not sure. I have a lot of anger, and I'm pretty sure Janet has anger as well." The guys talked and picked up coffee, then talked some more on the way back to the hospital. They went up to Janet's room. They had also picked up a variety of baked goods for the ladies.

"We are here with fresh coffee and baked goods." Jordon handed the coffees out and then opened the box of baked treats and put it in front of the ladies. "Help yourself, girls."

Janet had a slight smile, "Thanks, Jordon, that is sweet of you." Janet was hungry and dived in, and her sponsor also helped herself.

"I'm sorry, Janet, for everything that's happened to you. You did not deserve this, but I do hope you will get well soon." Weston gave her a hug, and then stepped back.

"Thank you, Steve, that means a lot to me. I should have taken an Uber ride home, but it was nice out, so I chose to walk, and my thoughts were elsewhere. I didn't pay attention to my surroundings."

"Don't blame yourself Janet! You have a right to walk anywhere peacefully."

"Jordon, it's all right, I'm not blaming me or anyone else, it just happened. I am alive, that's what is important. I plan to stay sober and get through this disappointment. My sponsor is helping me with acceptance, and forgiveness. I need to move forward in my life. The anger will stifle me and leave me stuck in the past. I think you should do the same, forgive the guy, for your own sake, accept that this wasn't meant to be, and move forward in life."

"I hear what you're saying. I will work on that with Steve's help. I am just worried about you. Are you going to be ok? I know we both realized we can't be good together, but I just want you to be ok and happy. If you ever need my help, don't be afraid to call me. If I can help, I will."

"That goes double for me too, Janet," Weston said. "Call anytime you need help we will come running."

Smith and Weston said their goodbyes and left for Weston's place to check on his guests. "I have to call the captain back when we get home. I need to give the address to him for delivery of donations for Eric and his mom. I feel I've ignored them this whole time, but I know I couldn't help it. You ok, buddy, you are so quiet."

"Yeah, I'm ok, I am just reflecting on my time with Janet. Sometimes I think I should have said something as soon as her drinking became a problem. Maybe she would not have gone through this."

"Well, partner, she may have not stopped on that information, she had to want to stop and get sober. You don't know what made her reach her conclusion. When we have lessons to learn, it is on a timeline that we don't control. I'm just glad she's getting it together. She's a nice girl, but needs to grow up, and she is doing that now."

"I just hate she had to go through all of this emotional pain."

"But she has the help of friends to cope with it. She will be fine. Well, here we are - home at last."

The two men entered the apartment and greeted whoever was there before knowing if anyone was even present. Eric and his mom greeted them, and made their concern and prayers known to the men.

"So how have you two been doing while left on your own?"

"We have kept busy with preparing dinner and cleaning, as well as watering all your plants, Steve."

"Oh, I guess there is a lot to keep you busy in my place. I am sorry I have left you both on your own to take care of things. I feel like I have been rude to my guests.

Please excuse me for one minute, I have to phone my Captain; he needs some information."

"If it's to give our addresses, he already called for it, and I gave it to him, I hope you don't mind, Steve. He felt, he didn't have to wait for you to call knowing we were here."

"Thanks Mom, that's great. You will have all the donations delivered straight to you then tomorrow." Weston was very pleased all was falling into place the way he planned it. Steve was tired, but knew he had to be alert for his friend Jordon, as he was still feeling the loss and a bit quiet with his emotion. "Jordon, do you want to sit and visit, and do you want a beer?"

"I'll just sit on the couch to visit, but I'll pass on the beer for now, thanks."

"Jordon, I am sorry for the troubles you are going through, you don't deserve that. I am saying extra prayers for you and your friend."

"Thanks Mrs. Sanderson, that's very kind of you," Jordon sounded sad and in pain.

"Call me Mom. You men are young enough to be my sons, and I consider you both more than friends, you're family. You have done so much for my son and me. It's so appreciated, bless your hearts."

"Thanks Mom." Jordon got up and hugged her, then sat back down.

"What's for supper, Mom? It smells so good."

"I've made a pot roast, it'll warm your insides, and you'll sleep well tonight."

"Yum, I can hardly wait, I'll wash up and get ready for supper."

Just then the phone rang. Steve picked it up and answered, "Weston here, how can I help you?"

CHAPTER THIRTEEN

"Oh, hi Captain, how are you doing this evening? Oh yeah, sure, we can be at the office day after tomorrow." Steve looked at Jordon to check if he agreed and Jordon nodded yes. Steve continued to listen to his captain, agreed with a few things, and then "I'll fill Jordon in," he said. "See you day after tomorrow." He hung up, and asked Jordon to follow him to the sink in the bathroom to wash up. While there, he started to fill Jordon in on what was said.

"The captain wants us on a case involving bad drugs on the street. There are three druggies who are dead in the past three days. Apparently, heroin laced with arsenic. He wants us to get this guy or whoever off the streets. There's a witness in the hospital detoxing, she gave her heroin to a boyfriend and he died in front of her. She apparently is not handling it well, now she wants to kick it. He is sending a sketch artist tomorrow to see her, see if she remembers who sold it to her. Then we can hit the streets running to catch this dealer."

"Ok so we have tomorrow off as well?"

"Yeah, the captain said he'd give us more time, but he can't; they are swamped at the precinct."

"Well, that's nice of him. We can help our friends settle into their new homes."

"Yep, so let's go see if supper is ready, maybe set the table for our meal."

The two men set the table and pulled out some wine for the dinner. They were eager to sit down with their newly formed family and have a family dinner.

"We should make this a regular family night dinner thing. Have Mom cook and enjoy a real home cooked dinner, then we can clean up, and play games after."

"Oh Steve, you are a sneaky one, but I do love the idea! What do you think Eric?"

"Maybe we can make a deal, when I'm stuck with my homework, Steve could help me study." Eric had a big grin on his face looking at Steve.

"It's a deal! I can live with that arrangement. I guess we won't stay up so late tonight though as it's 'move in' day tomorrow. Do you two know when it is you can go get your keys?"

"I believe it's nine a.m. in the morning. So, we will be able to keep decent hours tomorrow. The caretaker told me, when Mom and I went back with their papers, he was holding everyone else back till afternoon so that the elevators will be free for the deliveries."

"Ok, so up at seven then and there just before nine a.m. I think we can all handle that. Eh! You know, did anyone think about getting a phone hookup?"

"It comes with the apartment rent. The phones are all installed; we get our phone numbers tomorrow, Steve."

"That's great, Mom. Remind me to get both your numbers for emergencies and to keep in touch. Are you excited Eric? Your own place, independence. You're awfully quiet this evening."

"Yeah, I guess so, but I have been thinking about the school I'll be going to, I checked it out while you two were busy. It's a good school, I will have some catching up to do. I am a bit worried about it. I want to do good."

"Eric, the teachers will be aware of that, they also have to catch up with you. They do not know you so give them a chance. They need to get to know you to know what style of teaching you respond to. Teachers want successful students; it reflects well on them."

"Dinner is ready, everyone come sit down. You all must be hungry."

"I sure am, Mom, been waiting and drooling over the smells," Jordon said. "Just make sure I get invited to family night dinner! I'll even help with it."

Everyone laughed, as they knew Jordon loved to eat. He wasn't out of shape either, he was just always hungry.

"Oh Jordon, family night dinner would not be the same without you!"

"Thanks Mom, good to hear."

They all sat down at the table and began their meal with grace and then dug in. It was delicious, of course, and the men said so. Compliments circled the table. Mom was indeed very good at cooking. Then she surprised her boys with an apple pie; they were excited for that dessert.

"Apple Pie! Wow, that's terrific, how did you do that? I don't remember having apples in the house. You are spoiling us! You'll be gone, and we will be left to our own devices."

"Oh, I went down to that old corner store this morning, they had bags of apples for very cheap. I picked some up and made the pie from scratch. No trouble at all. And if you miss it, you'll remember we need a family dinner!" She smiled big and happy.

After dinner, Steve and Jordon cleaned up, and made a fresh pot of coffee, and pulled out a board game to play; Trivial Pursuit, a game everyone can play.

"I guess I will have to shop for games for us. I'll check to see what's popular and then we can give it a whirl."

"This game is good, Steve," Eric said. "I like these games; it challenges our knowledge."

"I'm just worried you'll show us up, being in high school with fresh knowledge."

They had their coffee and played the game. They were all laughing and having a good time. Jordon took a strong lead in the questions. He seemed to be getting lucky with each of the questions and having the correct answers. They had fun and kept ribbing each other when answers were wrong. Then it was getting on in time so they decided to wrap up the game, so everyone could go to bed. Jordon stayed as well, then he could be there in the morning for the move day.

Everyone was up early, seemed they were all excited about the move. Mom made the breakfast, Weston made the coffee, and Eric and Jordon set the table. The phone was ringing quite often. It was guys with last minute questions about furniture delivery and if they already had certain things. Weston was happy to relay the messages to Eric and his mom. They cleaned up after breakfast and left to walk to the apartment block. They chatted all the way and were happy when they got there. The manager met them with their keys, and they went up to the suites. They did the 'move in' walk through and both were satisfied. Eric was very happy finding his place looking so cool. They were there for a very few minutes and there were knocks on the doors. People started showing up with items for the apartments. They also brought grocery items with their donation. Both Eric and his mom were overwhelmed by the donations. Brand new beds, couch, armchair, even a T.V. for viewing. As each thing was delivered, they were set up in the place where they wanted it.

By late afternoon, Weston was making a list of what they did not have, which was very little. He needed the lists to do some shopping really quick for what they really needed. It was mostly the fresh groceries and linens. So, he left for a brief time, and then came back with the things he picked up. Weston and Smith helped make the beds and do the finishing touches. He got the phone numbers for their places and went over safety notes with them. The building was a secured building so there was no expectation of trouble, but Steve felt like the big brother and needed to be sure they would be safe on their own. Just in case the husband and father decided to try and contact them.

When it was about suppertime, Weston said they should get going. It was time to let the new tenants settle into their new home. Mom wanted them to stay.

Weston said, "No, Mom, you are on your own with Eric to keep you company. Don't forget that tomorrow Eric has to register at the school. I expect a call tomorrow on how the new school is for you, Eric, and I expect the latest gossip from you Mom. I put my number and Jordon's next to your phones. Let me know if you need help or anything else once you are settled in, and don't forget family dinners."

Steve and Jordon gave Mom a kiss and a hug, and said goodbye, then hugged Eric and said goodbye. Then they set out to walk back to Weston's place for the evening. "So, you want pizza and bear tonight, Jordon?"

"Sure, Steve, that would be great. I hope you don't mind that I have been quiet, still thinking of the baby. Half a year from now, I could have been a father! It hurts just thinking of all the things I am not going to be doing with my child."

"I can't say I know how you feel, but I can say you will get the chance to be a father, but maybe with the right woman. I know it would have been amazing, I know you would make an amazing father too. When we do settle down, it will be with the right person. Let's order our pizza, and we can watch a movie and talk more if you want."

The pizza came and Weston got them each a beer, then plates and napkins. He was standing in the living room when he noticed, outside his window, there were people moving into the building next door. "Looks like I am getting a new neighbor. Someone is moving in next door to me."

Jordon stood up and looked. "I wonder if they are female and single. I guess we will wait till they are settled in before we say our hellos, eh." He sat down and started eating.

"My neighborhood is beginning to grow again. It was getting empty, but now it is filling in. I am hoping I meet some young people along here in the neighborhood." Steve sat down and started to eat. He turned the TV on and found a movie to watch. Both seemed to be enjoying the movie and each other's company.

"Well, to be honest, I was looking at moving over this way too. There is a seven-floor apartment block just up the road, it's a bit older, but has been fully renovated. It has bachelor suites, as well as one and two-bedroom apartments. I saw the rent and it's very reasonable. I could walk home from here and as well it has underground parking. It is fully secured. You should think about it as well, Steve."

"Maybe I will think of it, I would have to see them first, but it sounds pretty good, and the captain would be happy we were in a secured building."

"Ok then I will make a viewing appointment for us. I know I am serious about moving. Oh, and one more thing the block has, is a fitness room. Work out whenever you want."

"Well, now you have sold me on it. I think I could enjoy that place."

"The only downer is it is not private laundry. They have a laundry room on every floor. That's according to the ad."

The two of them finished watching the movie then went to bed as they had work in the morning. They were up early and getting ready for the day. They had breakfast and cleaned up, then headed off to work in Jordon's ca. He liked his car better than Steve's clunker. It was sporty and looked good; a nice golden firebird, with pinstripes on the sides ending in flames on the back fenders. They got to the precinct and went to the squad room where the Captain filled them in on their assignment.

"We know there is a new seller on the streets. He is selling cheap, but it's cut with arsenic. We have a sketch from our one witness. She is in protective custody at the Detox Centre. She worked with the sketch artist yesterday. I want you to hit the streets today, and all your informants. Get the word out and hopefully we can catch this scum bag."

CHAPTER FOURTEEN

A New Case

"So, Captain, is there a chance we could interview this woman about her purchase of heroin? She may give us a starting place to find this guy."

"Yes, if you can get anything new out of an interview that is fine. Just type up what you find out, so to share it with other shifts coming through, ok Steve."

"Ok Captain."

"Do you want us to type up a summarized report from our street canvas from our snitches?" Jordon asked the Captain.

"Yes, Jordon, I would appreciate any info gathered to be shared via typed reports and put in the file. So, the two of you get out there, I know you can find out more than we have been able to."

The guys got up and left the captain's office and discussed the plan for their shift. First, they would visit Zack's and get the scoop from the street. Zack was very good at listening to the street and figuring out the 'what's what'. Then they would pay a visit to their witness. They were pumped to find information and get close to if not actually make an arrest. Smith and Weston entered Zack's bar and grill, and approached Zack to ask questions.

"So, Zack what's the word on the street when looking to hook up on heroin? We know there is bad stuff out there. Is there any talk about whom or where we can find the one selling it?"

"Steve, the only talk out there is know your seller and supply chain. No one is saying anything about who is dropping the bad stuff on the street."

"No one is saying anything about those who have died from the bad heroin. That's hard to believe, why are they so hush hush over this? No wonder the guy is still able to sell his bad stuff."

"Well, Jordon they are a bit afraid to talk 'cause their regular seller might find out they been going elsewhere with their business. They don't want to risk the loss of their connection for the dope."

Smith and Weston were thankful of the information and asked Zack to keep his eyes and ears open to the streets for more info. They would be back frequently to get more info. They took off to the Detox Centre to question their witness again, hoping to get a bit more info on the guy doing this. They got to the Centre and enquired of her room number at reception. They went up to her room and knocked on the door before entering.

Weston called, "Hello Ms. Elizabeth Cardinal, it's Detectives Smith and Weston. We're here to ask you some questions. Are you up to answering some questions?"

"Ah, yeah sure come on in. I did provide answers a couple of days ago though."

"Yes, we are aware of that, but we thought you might just have info you did not realize you have by asking questions again. I'm Detective Steve Weston. My partner, Jordon Smith."

"Hi, nice to meet you, wish it was a different circumstance, but ok."

"So where did you usually make your drug buy, and who was your regular seller. Now, I don't need real names, you're not snitching, we're just trying to establish habits, and why the change of habit."

"I usually went uptown to the mall across from the arena. I would meet up just in the food court with my dealer, I would greet his collector first, and give the collector money, then he would pass the seller, and the seller would bump into me and drop my buy into my bag. That's how it would work. We picked the food court as it's always busy, so no one suspects."

"This is where you have always gone to do your buys then? And this same routine, nothing about that had changed?"

"Yes, same routine same buy. He would be there every day, anywhere from ten in the morning to six at night. Usual business hours."

"So, what changed in your buying of heroin? Less funds, closer dealer, what got you buying the last batch?"

"Well, Steve, I heard there was a new guy on the street. The word out there is he is selling to pay for his sisters' habit. I guess we hear that, and we think 'brother' equates to safety. Anyway, I found out the seller could be found by St. Michael's, in the park across the street. I sat on a bench and he sat next to me, offered me to share his chips. I would pass my money behind the bag of chips with one hand and take the packet with the other hand, with a few chips. The guy looked normal to me. He seemed meeker than the usual seller, but he said he had his guns hiding, so no one could hurt him."

"So how did you know what bench to sit at?"

"It was the bench in front of three trees, with a red paint strip on the back of it."

"Was there anything else about this buy that we need to know?"

"No, I don't think so, the guy seemed nice, but his drug killed my boyfriend. I feel so bad about that. I have to live with that the rest of my life."

"Believe me when I say this, Elizabeth, he saved your life. Stay clean in honor of his life. I'm going to give you my business card, it has my number and Jordon's number. You can call us if you think of anything that could help us. Also, even if all you need is to talk yourself out of doing drugs, we will be there to listen. Thanks for all your help, you have been a big help. We catch this guy, and your boyfriend will be smiling from heaven. Thank you, Elizabeth."

The two men left her room and decided to head to the park to see the layout and assess the activities. They needed to figure out how they would approach this the best way to ensure an arrest safe and quick. They drove around the park then they got out and walked across the park toward the church. From the church, they looked at the park, and just watched the activity. Then they saw, someone sit on the bench they thought was the right bench. They waited to see what would happen. Just as they were going to give up, a thin small frame man sat down with her. Then he pulled out a bag of chips and the exchange happened. They looked at one another and nodded. So, they waited till all of the exchange concluded, and then waited to see the directions the two took when they left. Their luck of waiting paid off. The woman was walking away towards them, so they turned to walk in the same direction, and hopefully stop her along her route. They had to be sure not to be seen by the seller.

"Excuse me, miss, I couldn't help but notice you at that bench. I'm Detective Weston and my partner is Detective Smith. Don't run, we are not going to bust you, we just need to talk to you."

"Geez, you're the cops. I don't have to talk to you, get lost and leave me alone."

"I think you're going to want to talk to us, since we just want to save your life."

"What the heck are you talking about?"

"Did you just make a buy of heroin? "Because if you did, you may have bought the killing kind."

"Neah…not from that nice man. He just gave me a deal, at cost."

"Yes, that nice man. Haven't you heard the word on the street, he's selling arsenic laced heroin. Would you mind coming down to the precinct, we will test it. If it's pure, you can have it back. If it's laced, you will be alive."

"Oh sure, then I get down there and you arrest me. I'm not stupid. What is this, your new technique to arresting?"

"No, Ma'am, I can assure you it is not a new way to arrest. Let's just say a fellow addict named Elizabeth is trying to save your life. Her boyfriend died a few days ago using the heroin she bought from this guy."

"Elizabeth Cardinal?"

"Yes, that is who I am talking about. She's in Detox, trying to get off the drugs. She feels responsible for his death. She told us about the buy she made."

"Ok, so I go with you, and you test the stuff. I get to leave no matter the outcome?"

"Yes, you are correct. Thank you for helping us out."

So, she went with the two detectives. They walked to their car, trying not to be noticed. Smith and Weston opened the car door for the lady, let her get seated, and they drove off to the precinct. They got to the precinct and turned in the heroin for testing then went up to the squad room. There, they offered the lady some coffee.

"Would you like some coffee, looks like it was just made. How about you, Steve, you want a coffee?"

"Yeah, I'll have some coffee, thanks Jordon."

"Do you put anything in your coffee, miss?"

"Yes, two sugars, and a little milk, Jordon. My name is Kim Fields, by the way."

"Well, it's nice to meet you, Kim."

"I'm just going to talk to the captain. I want to let him know where we are at so far. Hey, Captain Shepherd!" Steve called out as he knocked on office door before entering, "We got intel on the seller of bad heroin."

"You do, why haven't you brought him in yet?"

"Captain, we just got the intel, and a cooperative witness with evidence. She agreed to come in and help us as long as we don't press charges. I took the sample straight to the lab."

"Well, that's great, but when do you plan to bring this killer in?"

"Captain, I have a plan; I just have to get this witness to cooperate in a sting. Give Jordon and me a chance to set it up. Trust me, when we arrest him, he won't get off."

"Ok, I will give you two a chance. You bust this guy, and we can keep the streets safe!"

"Ok Captain, thanks. You'll see, we got this." Steve left the captain's office. He went to his desk, looked at Jordon and said, "I have a plan. We are going to set up a score for this heroin. Are you willing to work with us, Kim?"

"Will this keep me safe and out of trouble?"

"Yes, it will. Heck we will even take you to the Detox Center if you want to kick the habit."

"Ok, what do I need to do?"

"Well, you need to set up another buy, but no sooner than you would normally. If he asks questions, because he is going to wonder why you're still kicking, you tell him the cops busted you before you could use. That will keep suspicion off, I think. Then you make the buy and take off or hit the ground while we swoop in and arrest him. We will arrest you too, but we will kick you once we have him. We will still need you to testify about the sting. Now, you don't have to do this, we can get a female undercover cop, as this could prove to be dangerous. It's up to you."

"I will do it, I am in, and yes I will kick the habit as well. Especially if the test comes back for arsenic. I figure you are the angel God sent to save me."

"Ok, this will make for a quick take down." Just then Weston's phone rang, he answered, "Weston here, yes! What's the result? Oh really, ok, then bag and tag Killer Heroin case." He got off the phone, and he looked at Kim, and said, "It was heroin and it was laced with enough arsenic to kill a small group of people."

"Oh! Wow! I guess I should be thankful to that Elizabeth chick then."

"So, are you in?"

"Yes!"

"Alright then, but listen, you have to be focused and aware of your surroundings. When we give a command, we expect you to follow it, not freeze and panic. Do you tend to panic in a violent scene?"

"No, I tend to get riled if I'm threatened. I will fight back."

"Well, I don't want you to fight back. It will either be a command of get down or jump right or left. Just simple words to follow. But if it all goes south then fight back. I don't think he has any guns surrounding him. He is working alone. No one would want to help him murder druggies."

Kim Fields was a tough lady, she stood five foot eight and had broad shoulders and was very muscular. She seemed very healthy for someone using heroin. This made Jordon suspicious.

"Excuse me, can I ask a question before we go out and set this gig up?"

"Yeah, Jordon go ahead, ask away."

"Well Kim you seem quite healthy and fit. Why would you be using heroin? You haven't used since we picked you up, and I am not seeing withdrawal symptoms. What gives with that?"

"Well, I am a university student and the weekend was coming up. I like to have it to party, it's mostly recreational use. Although, I do get cranky for a few days after, as I feel I need a tweak, but I resist. That's why I said I was going to quit, not worth the risk of dying, just to have fun."

"Oh, ok, but you know everyone starts out doing recreational until one day, before they know it, they are addicted."

"Ok, now Jordon's curiosity is settled. How do you feel you will do in this sting?"

"I think I can handle it. I will listen and I will be fine. I can do this, don't worry."

"You ok with us doing this, Jordon? It won't work if there are any insecurities about the sting."

"Yeah, Steve, I am fine, I just had my question to ask. It's been answered and I am satisfied with it. So, let's go bust the guy."

So off they went to set in motion their plan. They drove to the area of the pick-up and they let Kim out of the car before getting to the park. She started to walk to the bench, hoping the man would still be selling.

Kim paced herself to get to the bench, giving the two detectives time to get in place. She reached the bench and looked around, then slowly she got close, sat at the bench, and waited to see if the man came. She was watching her surroundings, and realized it was just her and the two cops hiding, and this small man walking up the path to the bench.

He sat down and said, "I see you're back. Kind of soon, isn't it?"

"I got picked up by the cops soon after I made my buy. They took my stuff, then let me go. Mistaken identity they said."

"Well, do you want to share some potato chips then?" The man pulled out a bag of chips from his coat and opened it and offered her the chips.

Steve and Jordon saw that, and then split up on either side of the man. Kim slid the money to the man's hand and reached in the bag. She felt the drug packet and took it with her left hand. She said thanks, and slowly ate a few chips, then slowly got up to walk away from the bench.

Steve popped out and said, "Freeze, police, you're under arrest!"

The man jumped up and pulled a gun and shot at Steve. He didn't see Jordon, who shouted, "Freeze, get down, Kim!"

Kim laid down on the ground as the man turned to shoot Jordon. Jordon shot the man in the hand holding the gun. He went down dropping his gun. Steve was fine. He put handcuffs on the man. Read him his rights. Then he radioed for EMS. Jordon went to help Kim up off the ground, she seemed fine. But said she felt sick.

"I don't know but, I rarely get sick from excitement, I feel awful." Then her eyes started to flutter, and she got wobbly on her feet, and went down to the ground,

Jordon yelled, "We got one down!" He asked, "What did you do?" He was upset. He thought quickly and remembered seeing her eat a couple of chips from the bag. Jordon shouted, "He spiked the bag of chips, the son of a bit…...Steve, he dosed her." He was holding her on the ground, her mouth was frothing, and she was getting sick. The EMS could be heard coming, and he said, "We are going to need a second bus. She is going first; he can wait."

Steve radioed for a second EMS team to come. The first team went to Kim.

Jordon said, "She may be a victim of arsenic poisoning. You have to help her please."

They began working on her immediately; they began an IV therapy with ringer lactate, Dimer Val Capral and succinic added, as instructed from the hospital. They rushed her off in the ambulance. A second EMS team had arrived to treat the man's gunshot wound. They loaded him on the ambulance and went to take him to the same Emergency Department. Steve accompanied him, and Jordon finished up his statement there. Then got his car and went to the hospital.

Jordon arrived at the hospital and found Steve. He asked, "Do you know how she is?"

"I am not sure. They gave her stuff to make her sick. I gave them the bag of chips to test. They said if it's a mild poisoning, she will be fine in twelve hours. They have to make her sick to expel the poison. We can't see her for some time, hours, as she will be busy reacting to the treatment. The doctors think she may not have ingested enough to kill her, but they are being extra cautious. The guy is in surgery, they are fixing his hand. You did damage to his nerves and tendons."

"I am happy if she is ok. She was only trying to help us arrest this guy. I was only aiming at the gun; he was willing to shoot and harm. He will be fine. You read him his rights, so he will be fine.

Do you know if the captain will be coming down to the hospital on this shooting? I think I saw IIA in the ER looking for info."

"I haven't talked to Captain Shepherd yet. I think we will be ok with IIA, but we will have to request a car unit with uniforms for our suspect, as we will likely have to give up our weapons. I gave the suspect's gun to the uniforms that arrived at the scene, so it's bagged and tagged already."

"Oh ok, I am just worried about our witness and are we going to be in trouble for a civilian acting as our agent?"

"No, she volunteered. It will be ok; our captain knew our plan. We will be fine, just relax. The more nervous you look; the more suspicious IIA will get."

"Alright, I will relax," Jordon promised. "I'll let you do the talking on this case, ok?"

"Just breathe," Steve advised his partner. "You are not in trouble, and you can answer their questions. It's all good. Why are you so nervous anyway, just because she got poisoned?"

"Well, I feel bad that she got sick and injured from our caper."

"You can feel bad, as I do, but don't feel guilty. We informed her it was dangerous. Just be glad she wasn't shot. She got sick but it's ok. She will live."

"Ok, sounds good. I will sit and breathe and relax."

Just as they finished talking, Steve saw the IIA officers coming up the hall. He kept his cool and greeted them introducing himself and Jordon. They were asking their questions, which were matter of fact asked, no dramatic expression just calm. Jordon handled it all with a calm professional response, as did Steve as well. Steve gave an update on the civilian involved, and the officers were fine with that. They asked for copies of their reports once written, and their weapons be turned over, and they were. IIA stated they would get back to the men asap pending their investigation. Steve thanked them and stated they would be typing their report once they returned to the precinct squad room.

Jordon asked, "Why did this guy do this?"

Steve answered, "He was getting revenge for his sisters overdose death. He wanted to clean the streets." That's what he said in the ambulance ride.

CHAPTER FIFTEEN

On returning to their squad room, Capt. Shepherd met them to talk about what happened. He asked a lot of questions and was very serious. He was concerned about the safety of the civilian and the suspect. He reassured them that they followed it by the book, and that he felt they did a good job. He was tough in his questions and Jordon was sweating it, but he kept calm and professional. The captain said to get their reports done and hand them in, as well he reminded them there needed to be copies for the IIA team. They went to their desks and began the long arduous task of detailing their reports. IIA came up to their squad room to turn over their guns. They said to the two detectives they were cleared in the preliminary investigation.

"We still need to question the two in the hospital, get their statements then wrap up our conclusions, but it looks good so far."

Jordon was informed his gun was needing attention, the IIA investigators serviced it, as it was close to likely misfiring. A memo would be sent to his in-box.

"Jordon, have you been skipping your gun cleaning lately?"

"Yeah, Steve, I have. We were so busy, and things were happening so fast, the time flew by. Sorry, I will be more diligent from now on." Jordon hung his head, feeling bad and embarrassed about his gun."

"So, let's get our reports done and then see if we can check out those apartments you spoke of yesterday."

Then there was a disruption in the squad room. Barnes and Wheeland came in with a woman, who was busy swearing, kicking, and screaming big and loud. The two detectives sat staring in wonder at what this was all about. They walked the woman into the interrogation room and handcuffed her to the table and closed the door. There were uniformed officers in the room and just outside the room. There was such a ruckus that it sounded like she was breaking the furniture and beating the room up.

"What was all that about?" Steve asked.

"She is the arsonist that we have been busy chasing to catch. This time she lingered at the fire she started. She is being charged with murder, and attempted murder times two, as two firemen were hurt this time. There was a witness at this last fire. We were having so much trouble catching her; she has been very busy setting fires all over the place," Barnes reported. He had to shout above the noise, then the noise ended just as he finished talking.

"It sounds like she did not enjoy your invitation to be in custody," Steve quipped.

"No, I would say she did not want to come to our playpen. I'd better go check on her and the room." Barnes got up to go to the room, and an officer opened the door, peeked out and said, "Darndest thing, she stopped and sat down, and fell asleep, Sergeant." Barnes went in the room to check, she seemed ok but she was snoring loud. He came out and stated, "We better have health services check her out, to make sure she is ok." Barnes picked up the phone and made his request, explaining all that took place.

"So, you have arrested a firebug. You solved the multi-fires case then, that's great, I think our squad is clearing off our case list quite rapidly then."

"Well, we arrested a firebug. Can't say it's the one we are after. We will find out if it is while we have her. She either confesses, or no further fires start while she's in our custody," said Detective Barnes.

"Well, we will have to hope so, she sure was strung out when she came in here," said Weston.

"Guess she needed a nap, after all that acting out, she did," quipped Jordon.

Then a woman entered the squad room and cleared her voice. "Hi, I'm Doctor Jansen, I am here to assess a detainee."

"Oh, follow me. She is in an interrogation room." Barnes led the doctor into the room. The doctor could hear the snoring and grinned but decided to check the woman out. She pinched her shoulder and called out, "Miss, miss, miss!" In the last call, she raised her voice into the woman's ear, no response. She checked the pupils and they were tiny. The woman was not reacting to anything the doctor was doing. The doctor decided to use a pin to assess her consciousness. No response to the poke.

"I think we should call for an ambulance and transfer her to the Emergency Department," the doctor stated, "She is non-reactive to stimuli, she needs to be checked for a physical explanation."

Barnes went to the phone and made the call right away. Then he went into the captain's office to inform him of what was happening. Capt. Shepherd came out of his office and went to the interrogation room. He shouted and the whole building heard it. No reaction. So, he agreed send her to the Emergency Department.

The EMS came up to the squad room and checked the woman out, then got her on the stretcher. They took her to Emergency, with Barnes in tow, for an assessment. They arrived at the Emergency Room and Detective Barnes explained how the woman was before she went to sleep once handcuffed to the table in the interrogation room. The doctor that checked her out worked with the other ER doctors, as they worked fast and steady to find any problems. The doctors were stumped; they did scans, MRI's and finally they did an EEG to determine brain activity. They even tried Narcan to see if it was drug induced. After all the test results were gathered, they sat down and determined she was having seizures, and they were grand mall, which does not demonstrate as a seizure. They determined the treatment and delivered it. The woman finally came round and was screaming once again. She was freaked out, demanding to be released. A doctor spoke with her, filling her in as to what has happened. She quieted down and gave her name.

"My name is Shirley McDonald. I live at eight twenty-four Spence Street. I did not know I had seizures."

Detective Barnes spoke with her, he informed her she was arrested for starting fires. "There are witnesses of you starting fires, miss."

"I can't believe I would do those things."

A doctor asked some questions, "Have you been in an accident, possibly a fall or a head injury, recently?"

Shirley said, "I don't recall any accidents. I don't even remember getting arrested or being near a fire."

The doctor asked, "Is there a family member or someone who lives with you that we can call and ask some questions?"

"I live with my roommate, Tammy; my family is up north in Thompson."

She gave her phone number and they called it to enquire. It was discovered she had been in an automobile accident and had a head injury. Then the doctor saw her CT scan; it showed some old swelling and bleeding of the brain with ischemia (death of brain tissue) right near the bridge of the two hemispheres of the brain. The doctor explained the pressure on the brain from swelling caused an injury that was subjecting the woman to seizures. He asked, "Shirley, have you been having strange dream states lately?"

"The strangest thing that has happened to me is waking up cuffed to this gurney and being told I was arrested. I don't even know what fires I started or how. How is this possible?"

"As a doctor I can tell you that your sleep was so sound from the seizure, it's possible you were sleep walking, and no one realized this. I will explain this to the officer, and I will make a report, but I suggest you stay here at the hospital so that we can run tests and assess you. If you are found to have been medically caused to start fires, it will clear you."

"Ok I will stay for tests; I am afraid to find out what is wrong with me. But I don't want to be a danger to anyone either."

So, Detective Barnes returned to the squad room, then began typing his report out, and the captain came out and asked, "So where is our suspect?"

Barnes smiled and sat on his desk and went into his explanation the best he could. Capt. Shepherd was stunned and said, "It's a wonder she had been walking around in that state and not ended up hurt."

"Well, I guess we will wait and see if any other fires are lit in the meantime. We may have not caught our firebug after all."

Smith and Weston got their stuff together and finished their report. Their suspect was brought in, booked for murder and attempted murder. They had decided to go check on their witness and see if they could do anything for her. They thought she should be done with all the treatment and resting comfortably in a room. They arrived at the hospital, enquired her room number, and went up to see her.

"Hey there, how are you doing now?" asked Jordon, with a smile.

"Hey, I am doing fine, thanks for asking. I thought the treatment was going to kill me, but I survived."

"I hope you are still willing to be a witness and testify. What a day this has been for you!" Weston stated.

"Well after going through what I have, I am more determined to kick the habit of doing party drugs. I could have died as well."

"Well, the dope you did buy was loaded with arsenic, so I think we have the guy hard and solid. We just wanted to check on you and see if there is anything we can do for you."

"Yeah, I was feeling pretty bad about you being poisoned. I am sure happy you're ok though," Jordon stated.

"Oh, that is sweet that you were worried. I believe I have been through worse. You would be shocked by the things I've survived. Knifing, Gunshot, a beating, not that much fun. This was fun, a little undercover work got the adrenaline going."

"Woah, Kim, this was dangerous, you need to realize that you had poor Smith sweating it when you collapsed. I hope you don't become a junkie for undercover work! Smith may have something to say about that!"

"Aw, that is so sweet, thank you, Jordon. See, us drug users are important."

"Well, I don't see you as a drug user. It was gutsy what you did for us, you have guts, Kim. When are they releasing you from this place?"

"I am waiting for my supper tray. If I eat and don't get sick, they said I can go home tonight. I'd rather go grab a burger and fries, but I guess they are being cautious."

"Well, how about we hang around and give you a ride home, the least we can do for you."

"That is sweet to offer, but you do not have to do that."

"We want to, don't we, Weston?"

"Of course, it's the least we can do for our star witness."

"Well, that is really nice of you. I won't have to walk home at least. I don't have cab fare; I blew my money today already."

"Oh yeah, I forgot, we were supposed to reimburse you on the drug deals. How much did you spend?"

"Well, I don't know if I can take your money, you could just have the city send me a check. I spent seventy dollars on the two buys."

"Hey, listen, if you want to wait forever for the city to reimburse you, suit yourself. But if you want your money right away, just let us reimburse you. We will get it back from petty cash, or on our paycheck."

Suddenly a nurse came in with a tray for supper and she plopped it on the table in front of Kim, who looked under the lid. It was Mac and Cheese, with beets and green beans. Her face scrunched up and she said, "How Gnarly."

Smith and Weston started to laugh and said, "That good, eh," simultaneously.

"Well, it's not laced with arsenic, but it don't look pretty. I guess I better dig in if I want out."

"Hey, eat a bit of each thing, and then we'll take you out for a feast, how does that sound to you?"

"It's a deal, if you mean it."

"I sure do. I would not kid someone who's been through what you have been through," Steve said.

"Ok I am digging in, and there is no flavor in this stuff. It's like someone cooked the flavor out of the food." Kim's face was scrunched up and she did not enjoy the food."

Jordon cracked up laughing, and Steve was right behind chuckling. Jordon thought Kim's expressions were cute. She ate a bit of each thing and then decided to stop eating. "Why'd you stop eating, Kim?"

"I would like to save my taste buds for some real food, Jordon. Think the nurse will say it's good enough?"

"I think it is believable. If you get dressed, she'll know you are good to go. We'll step out and give you some privacy."

Kim jumped out of bed and got her clothes out of the bag on the chair. She took her time, and then went into the bathroom and fixed herself up. She was excited about going out for dinner with the two detectives. She came out of the bathroom, opened her room door, and called out, "I am decent. You can come in."

The nurse came in and took a look under the cover of her dish. "Hmm, you did pretty good, how do you feel after eating?"

"I feel great, I am a little restless. I want to go home."

"Ok, I guess we can discharge you; you seem fine. But remember you are also kicking a habit; you may have some withdrawal symptoms for a few weeks. Caffeine and candy should get you through the cravings."

"Ok, I will remember that. I also know meetings will help me."

Smith and Weston could hear the conversation but stayed outside the room until the nurse left. Then they both entered and asked, "So are you free to go on your way?"

"Yep, I am a free bird. Let's get out of here before someone changes their mind."

They all walked out of the hospital, and got in Smith's car. He asked, "Where to, everyone?"

"How about Zack's for some great food? It's a bar and grill," Weston explained.

"Sounds great," was Kim's response.

Off they went chatting and laughing, Kim was not shy. She had a great laugh and really seemed to like Jordon. But she also was reminding herself that 'they were cops, and they were being nice, but what would they want with her, she's just a druggy.' They arrived at Zack's and ordered their food, she was introduced to Zack, and he was friendly as well. She had a sense of humor; she also was intelligent they found out as they chatted with her. Kim was really liking the attention they gave her. Then Steve said, "Well, are you done, is it time to take you home?"

"I'm stuffed, thanks for the dinner out. I really enjoyed myself."

Weston got up and went to pay the bill and Zack said, "No this is on the house. She helped fight crime, so it's my treat."

"Hey, thanks buddy, are you sure?"

"For the sweet lady, my friend, she earned it."

"Well, thank you Zack. That is really sweet of you."

"So, let's head out then," Jordon said.

They all got in the car and took off; Jordon was happy to have Kim sitting next to him as he drove towards her home. She lived in central downtown; it was what she could afford.

"I don't live in a great area downtown, but I like my place, and the neighborhood isn't too bad either," Kim said

"Oh, I am sure it's a nice place. Not all of downtown is bad. You live in the Wolseley area, don't you?"

"Yes, right in the center of it, it's quaint and old fashioned. I'm in a boarding house, I have the whole second floor. The owner lives on the first floor, and there are a couple other guys on the third floor. They are all nice people."

"Well, I am sure you have a great place. I would not worry."

They drove for a while and then they pulled up to a very large Victorian home. There were many nice large homes on this street. All looked to be left behind mansions, and it was very close to the park it all started with. "Well, here you are home sweet home. Thirty-nine Canora Avenue. I'll walk you up to the door. Is that ok, Weston?"

"Don't let me stop you from being a gentleman."

Jordon opened his car door and got out, then helped Kim out of his side. "So, it was great to meet you and get to know you, Kim."

"I haven't had a great time like today in a very long time, Jordon. I loved meeting you too. Thanks for taking me for supper and bringing me home. I guess I will be notified when I need to testify in court then. You and Steve take care of yourselves." Kim kissed Jordon on the cheek, and got her key out to let herself in.

"Hey Kim, would it be ok if I called you some time and we could hang out, go bowling or something like that? Also, I'm glad you are ok."

Kim had a huge grin on her face, and she said, "I would like that, that would be great. Just call me up. Take care of yourself, ok."

Jordon headed to his car with a bounce in his step and a huge grin on his face. He got in the car and turned the engine on. He turned to look at Steve, who had a strange look on his face. "What are you looking at me like that for?"

"No reason, just hope you don't hurt yourself with that big ol' smile on your face."

"It's not that big a smile! So where to, buddy? Your place or mine for a beer?"

"Well, I guess we could go to my place and you could tell me what you two said to one another on that porch."

"She just said she had a great day, one of the best she's had in a long time. Oh, and she also said we should take care of ourselves."

"Aaand, what did you say?"

"I asked if I could call her sometime to go out and hang out, maybe go bowling or something. She said that would be great. I like her a lot."

"Good, I'm glad, I knew you liked her as you were falling over her when she got sick. Just glad you had the nerve to ask her out."

"You don't think it's wrong, me doing that?"

"Nope, you would moon over not doing it. Just don't tell the whole office about it. There is always a jealous person in the crowd. Besides, it may not work out. Although I think there is something there between you two."

"Well, do I drop you off or what? We going to have a beer. What do you want to do?"

"Let's go to my place, we'll have a beer, popcorn and a movie."

"Ok Steve, we are on our way."

Jordon, drove straight to Steve's and the two of them got the popcorn ready and set up each a beer, then found a movie on the TV. They sat down and started watching. Steve's phone rang at that moment.

"Hello, Weston speaking, how can I help you? Oh hey, Captain Shepherd, what can I do for you? Yeah, Jordon is here. Did you want to speak to him? Oh, ok, I will pass that on. Ok, you want us in to chat, not work, you have some news to share with us. Ok, we will be in at ten in the morning, got you. Ok, goodnight sir."

"What's up with the captain, buddy?"

"Well, it seems he has some news to share with us. It is in relation to a case we worked a year or so ago. He said it involves a woman we helped; he thinks it is important we know what is happening in the precinct. There are new hires, and it might affect us. He's skipping church tomorrow morning to meet with us. Must be pretty important for us to know."

"I can't think of a case we worked on that could possibly relate to new hires and changes to our unit, as Captain Shepherd makes the hiring decisions."

"What case did we work that we helped a woman? I can't seem to think of any."

"Gee Steve, we have completed a lot of cases over the last two years. We've put a lot of people in jail as well. We even shut down some big international gangs along the way."

"Well Jordon, whom did we help that stands out to us, that might bring a new hire in for our team?"

"Well, there was that Sandy gal we helped, but she hasn't stood out for me."

"No, it would have been more important than that case, the captain sounded a bit pleased in his seriousness. We had to have made a mark in our cases with this lady."

"Hmm, I am drawing a blank, Steve, can't think of anything that was special."

The guys sipped on their beers and sat back watching their movie. It was supposed to be scary and it involved woods on an island. Some parts made them laugh, although they were meant to be scary.

Steve was laughing and saying, "These guys are idiots, they could have just stayed put and laid low with this massacre goon, waited till dawn and crept out to the boat to escape the Island."

"Hahaha, yeah they would have taken the path to the boat and rowed out a ways, then started the motor. Not too bright I guess on their part."

"Hahaha, yeah that's right." Steve stopped laughing suddenly, he looked stunned. "That's it! I think I know who our captain was talking about."

"Who is that? I don't get it we were laughing at the movie."

"Remember that woman, the tiny one, she didn't even stand as tall as up to your chin. She had a short name; she was under witness protection. We were camping at Eagle Lake. What was her name again? She did some drumming, spiritual chanting, and showed us how to fillet our fish. Jen Lee or Jan Lee, and she told us to call her Lee. You know she witnessed a robbery in her Pharmacy! What a strange little lady you would say."

"I vaguely remember a small fry; she was a spit fire, wasn't she. I think she was native. Oh, and yeah, she was testifying against the MS thirteen gang. Those two crooked cops that were after her from River City. She was run off road, we were on an R&R vacation. I lost it on you two going for a walk-in public, with a gang after her to kill her."

"Yeah, Jordon that was her. Was she called Lee?"

"I think it was DeeDee, and D for short and simple. Her friends and family call her D."

"I haven't thought of her in ages, she went straight back into witness protection after the trial was done. We shut down a large part of their crimes. And we stopped the human trafficking scheme they had. We helped the U.S. with their case. I think she sent one note to Zack's for us and her recipe for Poutine. The captain passed on a couple of messages, and then we never heard from her."

"Yep, she was a pistol that one. But the captain said it was also about a new hire. She is so small, she's a kid! If she is a new hire, they will eat her up and spit her out, we told her that!"

"I can't see her as a new hire, must be someone else. She left her mark no doubt, but she is too small to be a hire. Well, I better get home and get some sleep. We are getting up early but at a decent time for a Sunday. And he's not making us work tomorrow then?"

"Nope, you know you can stay and crash on the couch. I don't mind, we can have another beer. Hey, remember that was at the time we were constantly bickering. Captain called us the bickerson's, ha, ha, ha, we pranked him and scared the crap out of D. Gosh, that was so funny."

"Yeah. I could stay if you want. I'll get us some more beer then." Jordon got the beer, set it on the coffee table, then went out to his car and got his overnight bag, then came back in and sat on the couch. "You know what, if it were not for D, I wouldn't be keeping an overnight bag in my car. I hated the tag team we played when doing witness protection duties."

"I hear you. Have to be prepared for the overnights. She was one cool and calm victim for what she went through. If she were not so small, I would have considered dating her, you know that Jordon."

"Well, you're six two, what's a four foot nothing to do. She is not that short, but your neck gets sore having to look down at her as you talk. I liked her she was spunky. She also could follow directions, no drama. But she was damaged pretty bad by the gang members. I felt for her as she testified, she had no life thanks to them. I am glad they are doing a lengthy sentence though."

"Yeah, when you think back on the time, we spent protecting her it was an adventure. We did not get our rest that vacation, but we had a pretty good time with her."

"I wonder how she is doing these days. We should ask the captain to send a message to her asking how she's doing these days, let her know we were thinking of her."

"Jordon, you sound like she is in your heart the way you say that. Does every female victim steal your heart?"

"No, I came to like her while helping her, remember how she made us smile, and she didn't have to do anything, but be herself. What a strange little lady she is. Remember that."

"I do, and you kept saying that as well. I literally thought she was going to attach herself to your arm at some point. She really came to trust you and like you. Although you kept hurting her feelings every time you spoke your thoughts."

"Yeah, I know, and I felt bad for a long time because of that. She was nice and sweet. I did like her, and I missed her for a long time. Like I think I am missing her again now that we are talking about her. You know when we left her at the end of our assignment, I was sad. Then we got the poutine, and we laughed, but it felt good to get it. Who would have thought it was so popular, every restaurant has it on their menu now?"

"Well, she was a good joe about us, we did give her a hard time, and she took it in stride, didn't she, Jordon. Remember that cop that came right into our squad room to grab her, he couldn't catch that little bean she was so quick and small. I joked about her fitting in the drawer of the desk. It was funny, but she was upset with my joke."

"Well Weston, you didn't make it easy for her, you had her running behind us all the time. I was enjoying it watching her not complain as she ran with her two strides to our one stride, ha, ha, ha. Well, she was a great little doll. She wanted to be a cop so she could carry a gun. As if her little hands could hold it and fire! Ha, ha, ha."

"I guess we should get some shut eye. Then tomorrow we will find out who the captain was talking about. Night Smith."

"Night Weston."

CHAPTER SIXTEEN

A New Case

Overnight both guys had vivid dreams about DeeDee McPhail, their fishing and hiking and the escapades with hiding and protecting her. She had indeed left buried memories of her on both men's minds. The following morning, they got up and made breakfast, and got ready to go into the office. Weston's phone rang and he answered it.

"Weston, how can I help you? Eric, nice to hear from you. What's up, brother? Oh, supper tonight, I think we could make it. Six o'clock sounds good. Jordon is here; we were about to go into the office. I will let him know. How's school going? Oh yeah, I see, well, that sounds great. Ok, six this evening, we will be there thanks. Bye for now." Weston hung up the phone and said, "We've been invited to our first official family night dinner at Eric's mom's place."

"Ok that's great timing, should be fun. We will have to remember the Trivial Pursuit game. So, let's clean up so we can go to the office."

The guys cleaned up and then took off to the squad room to find out just what was up from their captain. They got to the precinct, parked the car, and walked up to the third floor and into their squad room. Everyone that worked the third precinct was there for the meeting. They greeted everyone and their captain and sat at their desks.

"Ok, everyone is here so let's begin the meeting. We have been given the go ahead to initiate 'Operation Nardelli Take Down.' We also have two new undercover agents that are being added to our group of Special D's. This operation is about shutting down Nardelli's illegal operations in River City. We are putting some officers deep into his operating system. We want to close the illegal gambling houses and his female trade workers. We will get all the ladies out of his control, and free. We are going to find out how he tricks them and keeps them under wraps. This will be a dangerous undercover operation for the two detective agents we already have working inside Nardelli's ring.

"I want to introduce you to the two of them now. We have Detective Peter Austin, I snagged him from the RCMP. He is already sewn into the ring, and today I want you all to get to know him, so that if you see him, you don't pick him up. Back off his case if he is working. But back him up if he is in trouble. He will fill you in on his signals. Now we are working with the U.S. Securities Commission, the FBI, the RCMP and Canadian Securities as well. We may end up having a few meetings like this from time to time, just to keep everyone up to date. Also, we do not discuss this out in the open for public ears, or other cops. Our usual four uniformed cops will be informed, and they know this is top secret. Now, some of you may know the other detective undercover. We have her from the Canadian Armed Forces and Security Commission. She is best known as D. Her undercover name is Cindy Bishop. D, come on out here and meet the group."

D came out from Captain Shepherd's office smiling and with a tiny giggle at the same time, she waved at everyone. It got quiet in the room. Here was this tiny lady, she looked great, but was not very big at all. Smith and Weston looked at each other, and smirked saying in unison, "Neah, this is a joke, right Captain?"

"She isn't big enough to be in high school, Captain," shouted Detective Wheeland."

Then the other detectives began speaking their minds: "she's too small, she looks like a nun, or the cousin in the family that everyone protects."

Capt. Shepherd heard all of it, then said, "Men, I know she is a might tiny, but she is in deep enough to infiltrate the human trafficking of the ladies. I do want you to think of her as the little cousin in the family that you protect. When we drop in and bust Nardelli, we will arrest her too. She will go down heavy with the rest. If this works out, meet the newest detective on our force. She is special ops. She has had extensive training, so trust her."

D was excited to be there. She dreamed of the day she would meet up with the guys once again but on an even playing field. D was fit, and Smith and Weston were just staring at her as they were shocked. They looked at one another and their captain. And her. There was so much chatter in the squad room no one could hear anyone.

"Smith, do you believe this?"

"Weston, I do, and it's crazy!"

"Quiet down everyone. Quiet!" the captain howled.

D spoke up, "I am in at one of Nardelli's cocktail lounges and restaurant; both as a server and an entertainer. Antonio Nardelli keeps a close eye on me. He has me as his number one server and hostess for his private parties. He gets me to pick the girls that best fit his needs. Let's just say, I proved to him I can take care of myself without a weapon involved. I proved that to him the first night I was hired. If you need me to, I will prove it to each of you."

The room was very quiet when D finished saying what she had to say. The men were all asking her questions and talking with Detective Peter Austin. He was handing out file copies of the operation information. When he reached Smith and Weston, he had a grin on his face, and introduced himself.

Then all of a sudden, Smith said, "I remember you; you were the officer who met us at the airport when we landed with D. So now you are working this case? Nice to meet you."

"Oh yeah, I also remember you. So now you are working with us. What do you think of your partner D in this case?"

"D is very capable, Steve; she has proven herself over time. This undercover operation is exhausting, and she has kept going and kept it together over time."

"Well, she had some health issues when we worked with her. Has she been ok with it all?" Jordon asked.

"Yeah, she used that to get on the good side of Nardelli. He is actually protective of her. She is very diligent in looking after her health, no drama with it. She doesn't look to piss anyone off, so she is cautious with her health. When Nardelli takes her to the private parties, he has been known to double check with her that she has her meds and enough for the night. As well he makes sure she has healthy meals, he's kind of like a father in a way. It worries me, if he finds out she is betraying him, he would likely be very cruel to her. Only concern I have in this operation, to be honest. D is lovable; that's how she wins everyone over. Nardelli is a cruel controlling man. The reason he is not married."

Jordon had a concerned look on his face with the last statement, otherwise he was pretty proud of D and how far she has come. "I guess she got her wish to be a cop then."

"Well, I still don't think she could fight her way out of a paper bag personally," Steve said to both men.

"Oh, don't sell her short, she has mastered self-defense, she's a little tornado, when it comes to hand-to-hand combat," Peter said.

"Wow really? That's fantastic," Jordon was very happy to hear that.

"You say hand to hand, but those people all carry, don't they? Once they've had their fun with her, they'll just shoot her, won't they?" Steve countered.

"Well, she carries a pistol and, as long as they don't find it on her, she is ok, but if they find it, it's like any other cop, then it's up to her to think fast and solve the problem." Peter countered Steve's statement.

Suddenly D came into the conversation, "Hi Smith and Weston! It sure is nice to see you guys again. I am sorry I didn't keep contact, but I was busy being trained and going to classes, so that I could be a special ops cop, like you two are." D had her infectious grin going and she was quite pleased to see them. "How are you two doing?" she asked.

"Well, I think we are still trying to process everything from today," Jordon responded.

"Oh, I am not trying to process anything, I just think it's insane and suicidal what you're doing," Steve said with a tone of anger.

D lost her smile for a moment. She said, "I have done all the training and tests you have done and passed with flying colors. I don't think it insane nor suicidal that I am doing this. I listened the day you said that if I join the force, they will use me and spit me out. I know and realize that. I also know if I can save some women from trafficking, I am doing ok then." D looked at Steve so seriously that death rays could have been shot at him.

"Hey, we are all on the same side of law enforcement. Let's not lose sight of that, ok everyone," Jordon said.

"Yeah, until the day it gets bad, and she needs rescuing. I can foresee that happening, no question about it," was Steve's input.

"Well, trust me, I am not going to put myself in that position. I've come too far to mess this up, I remind myself daily. Lucky for you, I am not reporting to you anyway. My check in partner is Dave Barnes, so you do not have to sweat your little head any, Steve. So nice talking to you two as always." D was not happy and walked away, then approached Capt. Shepherd to great him, he was pleasant and welcoming.

"Captain Shepherd, I hear my check-in partner is Detective Dave Barnes. Could you introduce me? I would like to get to know him."

"Oh, D, I was told to hold off on that as there was a discussion on how confident he was with his role. I was told Austin would look into who would be your check-in partner."

"Oh, that's disappointing to hear. I heard we would have made a great pair as brother and sister- in-law. Darn it."

Just as she finished saying that Peter Austin came up to her and said, "Come and meet your new check-in partner that I found for you."

"How come you didn't tell me he backed out of his part? Now I need a new cover, I suppose."

"It'll be ok, your cover does not need to change. It may even fit in better. I just need to talk with him and check and make sure he agrees to do it." He walked over to where Smith and Weston were standing. D was mortified, wishing, "God no, don't pick them," then she thought, "They won't do it, as they disagree with it."

"Hey, is it Jordon Smith?" Peter held out his hand to shake as he introduce himself, "Peter Austin. Can I ask you to speak with me in Captain Shepherd's office?"

"Sure thing, what's this about?"

"Well, it's confidential, you cannot tell anyone about what I am asking you to do."

"What about my partner? I don't keep secrets from him when it comes to the job."

"I am sorry you cannot. We can't afford a leak in this operation. I picked you as you know D well enough to sense when trouble is near."

"Oh, I think you should pick my partner if that's what you need. He's no nonsense and can tell if D is getting in trouble."

"I understand better than you know. I just observed him tearing a peace out of D over this operation. I don't need someone knocking her confidence out just as it gets a lot tougher in the game. Would you be willing to be her check in partner? You meet with her twice a week, delivering her our instructions, and you deliver her expressed needs to us in turn."

"I can't say yes. I'm sorry my partner would need to know or he would suspect something is up. We work better as an honest pair of me and thee."

Peter Austin was disappointed then called D over. He explained the situation to her and said that he had decided to go back to his commanding officer for direction. He told Jordon, "Don't go anywhere." He picked up the phone, spoke with his commander and there was quite a discussion. He got off the phone and then went to Capt. Shepherd to fill him in on the changes and then Capt. Shepherd turned and called for Detective Steve Weston to come into his office. Steve had a feeling this was not good. Weston looked at Smith and frowned.

"So, what is going on here, and don't tell me they are pulling you in on this farce of an undercover operation."

"Weston," the Captain barked, "you will be respectful, and you will listen with respect. These officers have put a lot of time and effort into 'this' investigation. It's your partner who refused to go into it without being able to tell you, so listen up." The captain was irritated and he did want to cooperate with the Federal Security Commission.

Peter Austin began explaining, "We need a check in detective for D. He would act as a brother-in-law, who has been living here for some time. He would meet up with D for lunch twice a week to exchange updates in the investigation. We are hoping to make a raid on the Nardelli's in a few weeks. D has an assignment to get photos of the books. As well, she gives us addresses of the houses that she hosts the gamblers at, and brings the girls to for hosting the party. She keeps an eye on them to ensure no one goes missing on her watch. I asked Jordon if he could act as that check in detective and he refused when he heard he could tell no one of his duty. I am now hoping he will say yes, and you will say nothing of this to anyone."

"Well, he was smart. You guys are insane putting her undercover in this operation. What if it goes south all of a sudden?"

"Weston," the captain barked, "Be respectful. You're not getting a choice, say yes and shut up."

Jordon was stunned and afraid to say yes, but more willing to do the job now that his partner was included. "I will do it, but I need more info as I said before. I want to be committed to the role, and be safe so no one gets hurt."

Weston just said, "Do you have files on all the players. You included Austin. It's easier to problem-solve on the fly when you know the players involved. Predictability is important."

Austin was surprised, "You've done a few of these undercovers, I think. I can give you all the info and intel you want. And you and your partner can discuss between the two of you, and no one else."

"Sounds fair, and if I think there is something wrong, I can let my partner know and he will let your contact know. That way you know, and we can avert a disaster."

D just sat there listening to everyone, and her smile got bigger. She knew she would be ok with the operation when Steve gave in. "Thanks guys, I appreciate the help you are giving."

Weston turned and glared at D, "You just better be on your toes, and be careful. I'm not losing a partner in this deal. I don't like losing any good officers in any undercover."

"I assure you, Detective Weston; she has been trained by the best. You will see, she is all business, and no ego. But you can't go around shooting her down like a jealous brother. She has done well so far in our undercover operations."

"Can I ask how many has D done over the past two years, because we know it's only been two years since her testimony of what happened to her," Jordon asked.

D answered, "I've done five completed operations and one aborted operation. The aborted was because a rookie got caught in the midst of the operation, and we had to get him out safe."

"You say that so matter of a fact, how did he get caught up in it?" asked Weston.

"The rookie figured out who the collar was and saw an award; he got anxious and got caught snooping. He would have been killed had the boss not said something when he did. I was able to get word to my check in and we dumped the operation and sent in the regular cops to find the rookie."

"Well, I guess you have an answer for everything. Let me ask you who was the intended Boss man?" asked Steve.

D looked at Austin then Steve, "Nardelli, he was the intended, and we were not as far in as we are now. As far as Nardelli is concerned, I was not able to get a decent job since he let all of his girls go, he felt bad and took me back on. I have served him devotedly and he acknowledges that. He treats me with respect. I get my days off on Sunday and Monday. I have his men pick me up and drop me off, unless I am shopping or at an appointment before work. He will even send a ride for me if he knows I have an appointment."

"Ok, so you are special to Nardelli. What happens if he finds out you're a cop? How you going to get out then?"

"He will not find out unless someone blows my cover. Well, Jordon, you going to do the job?"

"Do I have a choice? I guess I am in since you included my partner."

"Alright, we meet for lunch at Georges noon on Monday and Wednesday each week. I live two blocks from there, I walk there and back before my shifts start at six. I usually get there a half hour ahead, so I can chat up the girls. And just so I don't shock anyone, I smoke at work, then I can step out in the back lane to drop evidence for pick up."

"So, is that good enough for now? I think D can head home; she can call a cab. She knows the number. I will get you guys the files to read. They cannot leave the squad room, and if you are fast readers, I can run by and pick up the files later this evening."

"Well, Austin, I am good with that, but we have a family dinner tonight at six. I may need time tomorrow to read the files. Can you pick them up then? I will lock them in my desk?"

"Sure thing, Steve, and Jordon, I will give you the files with the numbers you need, as well as your role should someone ask you."

"Ok, let's get on with things. It's two forty-five and we need travel time home. You ok with all this Jordon?"

"Yeah, Steve, I am good with it all. How about you? You ok with all that's happening?"

"I am fine with everything now that I know everything. No fast-talking federal agents are going to be pulling the strings on us."

CHAPTER SEVENTEEN

The guys sifted through the files and discussed everything. They picked through every little piece of information that there was, they made notes of questions they had that were not answered or found to be explained by the information they had. Steve was thinking of things that could go wrong and trying to come up with solutions for those things. Steve was worried about D, she was too trusting, and he felt these feds were using her.

D, who was now Cindy Bishop, left the precinct, walked two blocks and called from a payphone for the undercover cab driver. She went home to her Wolseley Avenue Apartment and then she relaxed. She was careful watching her surroundings, while she was out at the meeting.

Smith and Weston finished all the readings of and making their notes. Then Weston locked up the files in his desk. He told Jordon they would go over it in the morning, and that he could meet with Cindy Bishop for lunch. The guys took off as it was four thirty and they needed to get ready for the family dinner.

"Do you need to go home first, Jordon, since we have time. Do you need to get anything for the dinner?"

"No, Weston, I'm good, I'm going home tonight so I will be good. How are you feeling about Cindy Bishop now?"

"I am not happy. Someone is going to get hurt, and I think she is going to end up in trouble."

"Well, don't you think you should trust the training and she is very smart, don't forget that."

"I know she is book smart, an intelligent lady, but also naïve to say the least. She trusts too much. That's why I think she'll end up in trouble."

"I see a much tougher little lady than I remember from the past, she did not back down when you challenged her. She must have overcome her PTSD; she isn't shy about what she's doing. I think you should give her a chance."

"I am giving her a chance. I wanted to shut it down as soon as I heard what they were doing. She was informative so that's why I am giving her a chance, but I want to go in prepared, do you understand me? You need to be prepared to cover without blinking any questionable issues that come up."

"Ok, I hear you, I already feel better having read all the files, and knowing who is involved in this sting. Who knows, we may even find all the missing and murdered women that have been disappearing."

"Now, see that is what I am saying, you are too far ahead in what you intend to accomplish, all admirable, like that rookie. But we need to focus on Nardelli."

"Ok then, we will stay focused and I will be the best check in detective she can have, how's that?"

"Alright then, just know your surroundings and anticipate any issues, and you two should be fine. We need to stop at my place, I need to get the game and some wine for dinner."

"How about we park and walk over just to stretch our legs before dinner?"

"Ok then, we will do that. I think I'll cut some fall flowers from my garden as well for Mom."

The guys went back to Weston's and got ready for dinner. Weston went out to his green house, and he cut some flowers to make a small bouquet for Mom and the dinner. He then went into his pantry and grabbed a bottle of wine, then looked for the trivia game. He had gathered everything. It was five thirty so the guys started to walk to Mom's place.

"First dinner invite to Mom's, should be fun. Eh Jordon?"

"Yeah, I wonder what she cooked up for us? I am hungry, we missed lunch today."

"Hahaha, you and your stomach, Jordon! Too funny. Then you'll eat well no matter what is being served. I see the new assignment has not deterred your appetite."

"No, should it? Am I thinking wrong on this assignment? I am hoping it goes well. I think it's time to see Cindy do well for herself and be strong."

"All right then, we will see and help her accomplish that goal. So here we are - feed time for you," Steve laughed as they got into the elevator. They got up to Mom's place and knocked on the door.

"Hi strangers, long time no see. Glad to see you, come on in, sit relax." Eric had answered the door.

"Wow, it smells great in here, is that pot roast I smell."

"Yes, Jordon it sure is, you seem to be able to identify anything through smell."

They all exchanged hugs and greetings with Mom. It did feel good being back together again. Steve gave Mom the flowers and the wine for dinner.

"I like what you've done with the place it seems so homey and cozy. So, Eric, how have you been making out at school these days?" asked Jordon.

"Well, so far so good, mid-terms are in two weeks. I am passing so far; my teachers are happy with my work. I have made some friends, and I am happy."

"Well, that's great news, and the studies, they are not too tough then?"

"No, it seems I have a strong grasp of science and math this term."

"They are thinking of advancing Eric into University entry level course if his marks are high in his exams this term. Wouldn't that be great," Mom stated.

"I would have my first-year university done by June and I would graduate High School at the same time."

"Hey Steve, we have a genius in the making here, isn't that something," asked Jordon.

"Oh, oh yeah it's great, we'll have to get a tougher set of questions for him from Trivia." Steve was in thought somewhere else when Jordon spoke up and drew him into the conversation.

Eric's mom was curious and asked, "Where were you at, at this moment? It's like you were miles away from us. What's bothering you, Steve?"

"Oh, it's nothing really, we just got a new assignment at work that's all. We were reading the files this afternoon, and I guess I got all caught up in it. Just thinking, I'm sorry, but I am quite pleased with Eric's accomplishment."

"So, when do we eat," asked Jordon.

"Well as soon as I set the table I guess."

"Let me help with that. As Jordon missed lunch today, he may be too weak, so I'll set it to save him energy, hahaha."

"Oh, very funny, Steve! It was a good thing we did eat breakfast. Since we went in thinking it was just a meeting, and we ended up working."

"Well, I plan to ask Shepherd to give us time owing. I am building up some days for a getaway. And we may end up needing it sooner than I thought."

Steve finished setting the table then sat down. Everyone sat and Eric's mom said grace, then they dug in after a harmonious 'amen'.

"Wow, this roast is so tender it melts in your mouth, Mom," Jordon said.

"It's very good, I must say, and the gravy, wow just sets off everything," Steve stated.

They were just so happy eating, there was barely any conversation during the meal. Everyone was smiling, except Steve, He was in deep thought. He remembered when they first met D, she was a kind, and caring soul, but terrified of her situation. She was so afraid of her own shadow. He remembered how she clung to Jordon's shirt. He remembered her recounting what had happened to her and her friends, and work buddies, her pharmacy being blown up, a friend dying, how she fell apart and sobbed in his arms. He was remembering how hard it was for him, he was helpless in comforting her. Steve went very deep into his memories. All he could think of was D as a fragile little lady, finally he came back to the present with Jordon shouting.

"Steve, are you done eating? Can we take your plate? Do you want dessert? Come back to us!"

"Oh yeah, sure I'm done. I am full, thank you. Would you like me to wash the dishes, then we can play Trivial Pursuit?"

"Ok, but Mom made apple pie for desert with ice cream, don't you want some?"

"No, I am full. It was a very good meal, Mom, I thoroughly enjoyed it." Steve got up and kissed her on the cheek and started to get ready to wash the dishes.

"Steve, are you sure there is nothing wrong? You seem so far away and distant. What's bothering you dear?" Eric's mom asked.

"Nothing's wrong, I am just remembering a case Jordon and I were on a couple of years ago. It was a dangerous one, we all got out of it ok, but we had our difficulties. I know I shouldn't be reliving the past, as it all turned out ok. I am fine though, Mom, nothing to be worried about, believe me."

"Yeah Mom, he is just thinking how hard it was to control all the players involved, and how hard it will be for him, because he can't control everyone in the assignment. He just has to learn to trust others to do their part. I think it's easier said than done, right partner?"

"Yep, you're right partner, it's a hard lesson and it will be hard to watch it unfold for me. I like to be in control. I have to learn to let go and trust. I don't think you remember how scared that little lady was, when she did not know what to do, or how freaked out she was in the woods."

"I do remember, West, but I also don't know how she did after we left her with the prosecutor, and all the time in witness protection since we last saw her. I am choosing to trust what these other professionals are saying she can do."

"It sounds like there is a great deal of conflict going on here, as well as some feeling of responsibility for someone you care deeply about, Steve," was Mom's thought on what she heard.

"I guess we both care too much, but Steve can be like a dog with a bone. That can make someone second guess what they are doing and make a mistake."

"I get what Jordon is saying, let it be and see what shape it comes out as," Eric said.

"Ok then, let's get the dishes done for Mom. She can sit and sip some wine if she wants to. Then we will play our game. I just want to set my thoughts on something else tonight, ok everyone?"

So, the three guys did the dishes and cleaned the kitchen. Then they pulled the game out and played for a couple of hours before they realized how late it was getting. So, Smith and Weston called it a night, thanked their mom for a great dinner and for being a good listener. They walked back to Weston's place.

"You want to stay over, or are you good to drive, Smith?"

"I'm good, I will pick you up in the morning around seven thirty."

"Sounds great, have a good night, see you in the morning.

Jordon left to go home and Steve went into his apartment. Steve had an awful time sleeping and ended up awake more than half the night fighting off his negative thoughts, and he knew they were negative and would not help anyone. Finally, around four thirty a.m., he got up had a shower, and was making breakfast for himself and Jordon. He ate then cleaned up what he could till Jordon got there. He fed Jordon and started putting stuff away.

"You're not eating, how come?"

"I was up super early, bad sleep, so I ate earlier. It's all good, not to worry."

"Ok, as long as you are good for work today, not too tired."

"I can catch up with a nap at lunch while you are busy eating and chatting with D. I was thinking about Nardelli, he hides his criminal funds through his fashion designs. He is quite successful with his fashion design work. I think at one time, his criminal activity paid for his start. Now he is successful, he can hide his criminal funds with his fashion sales. I plan to ask Austin about this, they had to have figured it out and have already checked it out."

"Wow, Steve, you sure have made the dots connect. I was just thinking about that last night and this morning."

"Well, we should get going we have a big day ahead of us. You ready, Jordon?"

The guys left for work. They were driving and talking about the case all the way to work. Steve was discussing his questions with Jordon. He wanted to prioritize the questions, so they could get the best answers for the case. Steve was already formulating what he believed would be happening. All the files he read, he found that the rumors of human trafficking were more than rumors, and the city councilors helped Nardelli get away with his crimes. He believed they were still corrupt in helping him. He wanted to talk to Austin, as he thought it important to anticipate interference with the investigations. Steve asked Jordon if he thought he was crazy thinking that way, Jordon said no, because he agreed with Steve's summation in the case files.

They arrived at the office and went up to their desks, and Steve unlocked the files. They were there before the other detectives got there. But Capt. Shepherd was already there. He opened his office door and called Steve and Jordon into the office. They went in his office and Austin was there.

The captain said, "We are going to talk out some of our main concerns about this operation. I, too, have read the files and come to some conclusions. I need to run them by all of you."

CHAPTER EIGHTEEN

Smith and Weston looked at each other, then at Austin and then at their Captain.

"The fashion mogul, he has gotten away with murder in this city. It's played down, but we think he is using his fashion outlets to launder the criminal money." Steve was blunt as he spit it out.

"D can get the photos of his books, but he will likely in court be able to explain his earnings away via his fashion design and the sales. His business dealings are being watered down for money he skimps off the top." Jordon popped that off and surprised himself in saying that.

"Did you guys eat the files and digest them? It's like you all came loaded with your thoughts of what you learned. We have an auditor working on his tax files the past fifteen years. It does not add up and it does not explain the out of country payouts for workers that we cannot find. The city has been trying to shut down this investigation. They have some land deals and construction deals, money changing hands that is not adding up. They have no idea they are being investigated by the Federal Securities Commission. That's why we can't have any leaks. This Police Department is the only one that operates at arm's length away from the commissioner. Your captain has the say and no one has to be informed of the investigations that take place here. Your captain is who we approached. The Commissioner and the Mayor, no civic government official knows any of this is happening. Every one of the men in this department has gotten an email committing them to secrecy."

"Ok, you just answered a dozen of our questions, Austin. We have a slew of them written down. How is D going to find this information for you?" Steve had a stern look on his face.

"D has given us lots of evidence in her undercover work. She just doesn't know the big picture. Everything we've asked her to get, she has done. She has allowed us to develop schedules that are predictable and all the addresses we have, have either answered our questions of what happened to some women, or have told us Nardelli has tunnels and secret rooms in the homes where the gambling and trafficking are happening."

"But Austin, does D know this, or are you guys not telling her? She needs to know. If she figures it out on her own, she is going to get upset, and may slip up, either by panic or anger." Steve sounded very upset as he stated his opinion.

"I don't like her being in the dark," Jordon agreed with his partner. "I am her check in detective. Deceiving her is not fair. You were right, Steve, they are using her!"

"D knows we are deriving clues and answers from all the details we are getting from her; she knows we are building a bigger case from her intel. That's all she needs to know at this time, men."

Captain Shepherd shook his head, "I don't like this. An undercover cop needs all the info to be safe. Why haven't you sat her down and told her any of this? Does she not get to read these files, as we have done? I think this is reprehensible to say the least. I would not treat my undercover detective this way."

"Have you men finished the files; I can take them now."

"No, Peter I still have some info I need to read. Can I have them till the end of the day? I want to go over them to ensure I read things right. Would that be ok?"

"Yeah, end of the day. Do not let anyone else read them. We cannot afford a leak of any kind."

"Ok, well I better get busy reading so I can finish the files. I have to meet D at noon. Is there anything I need to tell her or is she just informing me?"

"We have no new info to give her. She knows her assignment this week. She should be telling you when she will look at the payroll book and taking photos. She will also tell you if there is another party for this coming weekend. By the way, you two will be on surveillance that night. She will tell us about the address at the next meet for lunch. Like I say, predictable."

"Ok, Peter, you have been very helpful to us, I understand better, thanks."

Steve shook Peter's hand and looked at Jordon and rolled his eyes. The Captain caught it but did not say a word. Smith and Weston went to their desks and sat down to read. Peter said goodbye to their Captain and exited the office. The captain came out of his office, whistled a quick note and signaled Smith and Weston to come back into his office.

The boys went into his office and Capt. Shepherd said, "Can you believe those idiots, they think they are smart. Now, I saw the wheels working. Fill me in, Steve. What are you going to do about this? I know you are not going to leave her hanging in the wind."

"Well first, I need to make copies of the files, then I need to find a way to meet D, without creating suspicion from anyone, and I have to hope she will listen to me. Now, I think I can use the copy machine in Ballistics. No one will be suspicious. The printer in the main office records everything to memory, we can't use it."

"I knew you would have an idea. Be careful, Steve, that you don't get caught. Not a word to anyone outside of these walls. Jordon, you fish around in D's mind - see what she is thinking and feeling. Don't upset her though. That would tip off Peter."

"I will, Captain, and thanks for understanding. I don't want D getting hurt." The guys started to leave the captain's office.

"I care what happens to that girl too. Feel free to come to me with your ideas on this operation. She's a sweet girl, and they are using her."

Steve was grateful he did not have to twist his captain to seeing it his way. They went back to their desk. Steve gathered up all the files, and was heading to the Ballistics lab. He turned to look at Jordon, "Spend time thinking about the conversation you are going to be having with D. Formulate the what-if's and the how to approach, got it!"

"Yeah, Steve, I've got it, and I think I've got my work cut out for me." Jordon was thinking about D, and he was worried she might think that he and Weston may be interfering with her case. He needed to be sure what he was going to say to her. But he also gave thought to the fact D has always been practical and realistic. Then he decided he was going to approach her with that same practical and realistic thinking.

Steve was busy making his copies of files and the staff was wondering what he was up to. They were watching him as he worked diligently, and he was organized. He knew they were watching, so he was telling them the Captain wanted the copies, so he could conference on the case and make notations, thus leaving the original files untouched. The staff seemed to have bought the story.

"So, Steve, the Captain is going to pick apart the case files, I take it."

"Yeah, Curly, he has some concerns, he wants to mark and refer to in his conference on the case. Rather than memorizing or rewriting, he would like to just mark his notes on the file. We are not supposed to alter the files, so we came up with the idea. Just don't say anything to anyone. The Captain doesn't want to start a trend. He's just under a time crunch, as it's an active case."

"Oh, we won't say anything. It gets so busy here, we likely won't remember about this. We don't have time for gossip on what we don't know."

"Thanks, Curly, I owe you."

Steve wrapped up his copying and started to head back to the squad room. He put away the copied files and stacked the originals on his desk for Austin to pick up on his way through. Steve's phone rang, he jumped as if being caught. Jordon chuckled as he saw it.

"Detective Steve Weston here, how can I help you? Yeah, hi D, how are you doing?" Steve was happy to hear from D.

"Hi Steve, I am doing ok, I just wanted to touch base with you. Everyone thinks I am shopping right now. I think I need to talk to you. I feel, or I think /sense, you are not happy with the situation. It's on my mind and I need to clear things up, or I won't be on my game and focused. Can we figure out how we can meet with no one knowing?"

"Yeah, we can do that, I am glad to talk to you. I am not upset though; I just need to know where you sense you are at in the case. Can we meet at Zack's upstairs or is that too out in the open for you?"

"Well, if I can enter from the back. I think there is a strip mall on the next street over, that I can cut through without being seen. It has a popular pizza joint there. I can place my order for home. I would just feel more confident if I knew we were on the same page."

"Ok D, we can do that. At what time can you be there? I will fill Jordon in, he's listening right now."

"There's no one else listening, I hope. I need to know it's between us, this conversation. Austin doesn't trust you and is very suspicious, which is what has me worried. I can meet you at say three or three thirty, would that be, ok?"

"I will be there at three and no, no one knows we are talking and you can trust the Captain. He is worried as well. He doesn't want to see you get hurt. It's just us three who have met on my concerns."

"Ok then three o'clock I will be there just a little after. I think I can disappear for an hour - not more though or my driver will get suspicious of me."

"Whatever you have to do to keep suspicions down is fine with me. Be careful, ok D. Talk soon."

"Bye." D hung up and was very nervous, but she was before she made the call, and felt better after the call.

Weston said goodbye and looked at Jordon. "I don't think you have to worry; she is thinking, and she is sensing something is up. She wants to meet; I am happy she trusts me. You can tell her that if you want at your meet today." Suddenly Weston went quiet. "Austin, are you back for the files?"

"Yeah, Weston I am. My commander wants them back in his hands. I hope you got to read them all."

"Yeah, and hey thanks, rereading some of them, I got a clearer understanding. You know Nardelli is using his fashion mogul to hide his criminal activity, don't you?"

"You figured that out, uh, good of you. We have been auditing him and trying to find the leak. We haven't found it yet. I expect D – Cindy - to come up with the evidence this week. We've got intel that says this weekend his house party will seal the deal on his holdings. He's going to have the girls model his latest fall season designs."

"I hope you're right, as I don't want Cindy getting caught off guard with her undercover work."

"Believe me the less she knows the better off she is."

"You do have an escape plan ready for her if she has to get out of the way?"

"Not to worry she will be fine, you will see. She knows to duck if bullets fly."

Jordon was shocked when he heard that comment and so was Steve, but he didn't flinch or react, he stayed composed and said, "Yep, Cindy does know how to duck." Steve was thinking he would like to kill this Austin guy and his pompous ass thinking.

Austin picked up all the files and started walking out the door, saying, "Chat later, guys."

Jordon looked around to make sure Austin was out of ear shot, "Do you believe that guy? He's going to leave D hanging in the wind."

"Oh, I believe it, but we will have a plan in place. D is listening to her instinct twitches. I think Austin is playing for himself and using D. He just proved it with his statements. We will meet D and fill her in."

Steve looked at the time, and said, "You should get going, Jordon, it's getting close to noon. I am going to head home and get my car, to meet D later. We won't take your car; we don't want people to get familiar with it everywhere."

"Ok Steve, I will see you later. I feel better already about this case, I am sure it's going to work out. See you later, buddy."

Jordon got in his car and started to drive. He was watching all around himself, he didn't want a tail, but he felt he had one so he tested that feeling by doubling back toward the precinct and radioing in about the tail. As he neared the precinct, he saw the car turn away from him. He made it look like he was going to park in front. Then he quickly took off with the tail out of sight and sped towards the meet. No further tail, but he put to memory what he noticed. He got to Georges and D was there. He went in and was greeted with a big hug from D. He was smiling, and he said, "You know when I left the office to meet you I had a tail. I ditched it, but you might want to take note of anyone following you. I think Peter has you on a tight leash." They both sat down at a table and placed their orders.

"You are very right; he is very suspicious of Steve, almost like he's jealous. He said that Steve's a hot head and I should not talk to him. I am not to trust him. Peter said that Steve will undermine me and get me hurt."

"You don't believe that though, do you?"

"No Jordon, that's why I called Steve earlier. But if you were being tailed, don't use your car later to meet up or they will know I'm up to something."

"Funny you should say that; Steve is heading home to get his car for the meet up. If I don't get a ride there with him, I will get someone to drop me off. Steve is proud of you. He is not mad. You are using your instincts. He made copies of the files to go over with you. He has a few concerns he wants to share with you. He thinks Austin is in this for Austin. And he showed up at the office to get the files. What he said, was really crass, and I did not like him much. D, you have to trust us, we don't want to see you hurt."

"That's why I am meeting with you guys later. But for now, listen. Nardelli called me today. He said he has a surprise for me tomorrow. I have to talk a new girl into going to the party, someone at the club is interested in her. The new girl is my roommate. She is eighteen, new on her own and innocent. I will talk her into going, but I need to keep her safe too. Her name is Alexa Knox. She is five foot six, long dark brown hair with blond highlights. Tomorrow, I am going in early as I am going to take photos of the payroll books. I will put the camera back in my locker and I will drop the key in the back lane by the door. That's the info you can pass on, and the party is at one-forty-three Wilmington Avenue. It will get underway at eight thirty, and we are wearing his fashion clothes, so I can't tell what we will look like. He has a bunch of fashion moguls coming to the party. They will be bidding on the designs for the patterns. Their bids are their buy-ins for gambling. I am hearing rumors that this house has tunnels to other houses in the neighborhood. That's how people will come and go, so when you are sitting with Surveillance, you need to watch the comings and the goings. If we disappear, we may be taken to any one of those other homes. I would make sure there is a team of uniforms hidden on the next block over. The florist we use is Pembina Floral Designs just in case a few bugs are necessary. I can repeat that info later today if you need. Ahh, here is our food. They have the best burgers, bro, that you have ever had."

Jordon said, "I doubt they beat Zack's, but I will give them a chance."

The two of them were smiling and eating. Jordon was enjoying the food and D was happy to have her best friend at her side.

"You know when you guys had to leave me, I cried for a couple of days, I was lost. I kept your shirt to hang on to. I am sure you must have felt my pull. I missed you guys so much. It took everything I had not to come looking for you two. When the verdict came down, I sobbed, I was so happy they were going away for a long time. I felt a relief I had been waiting for, I was no longer their captive. When I was moved to Vancouver, I decided to work with Secret Service. I went through military training, and police training. They taught me a lot, but so did you and Steve."

"Why did you, as we told you they would just use you like Austin is using you."

"I missed you so much I thought if it kept me busy, I would be better off. And I wanted to deal with my fears and PTSD. For the most part I got over them. I still thought about you guys, but it was to ask, 'What would they do in a situation?' I remembered how you guys got me home safe to testify, and it was no easy task. I've also learned there are a lot of crooked cops, and politicians in the town."

"Well, I am glad to see you in one piece. I wondered what happened to you when you stopped sending messages."

"I was told I couldn't send anymore; Austin has been stuck to me like glue. I've tried to get him reassigned; they won't do it. He would love to control my entire life. He was upset when he found out I volunteered for this assignment. I figured it would separate us almost immediately, but he decided I made the right move."

"Well, I will tell you, I will talk to Captain Shepherd. He wants to keep you on our team when this is done. I will let him know about this."

CHAPTER NINETEEN

They both sat and enjoyed their lunch they both agreed the burgers were really good. They talked about things that happened in the time they had been separated and they laughed at some stories, and got serious about other stories. Both decided they missed one another.

"I wish I'd had the courage to have told you I was really falling for you, but I thought you would have thought I was too young for you."

"Well, how old were you when we met, I thought you had to be at least thirty."

"I finished High School at thirteen and graduated from Nursing School at seventeen. I had the car accident, and finished Pharmacology at twenty-two. I was twenty-three when we met, I'll be twenty-seven next summer."

"I only admitted to Steve today that I was interested in dating you, but you were so small, I wasn't sure we would last."

"Well, if I get the opportunity to hang around here, maybe we could find out about size being a problem." D giggled her quiet giggle and Jordon laughed. He missed hearing that giggle.

"We had better keep our wits about us for now, as you are in a serious position right now. I want to be sure to get you out of it safely."

D looked up at that moment and then her expression changed, as she saw Austin enter the restaurant. "What are you doing here, we are not to be seen together," she whispered. "Wow! Look at the time, seems we just started catching up. I need to get going, Jordon, I still have errands to do. Can we do lunch again, and finish catching up?"

Jordon, turned, looked, and became annoyed, and then quickly agreed with D, "Sure Cindy, we could get together later in the week, I'm glad I found you."

The two of them hugged and D left. She was walking quickly to get home and away from Austin. Jordon turned and asked why Austin had showed up. He was annoyed.

"Are you trying to endanger D, or are you just stupid?"

"I didn't know you guys would still be here. You don't have to get in my face about it."

"Well, from now on when we meet up on the days we meet, you don't show up or I may have to shoot you, got it." Jordon was not kidding. He paid his bill and left. He went straight to the precinct and didn't care if Austin followed him. He was pissed. He parked his car in the service garage. He told the guys to search his car for any kind of bugging device and remove it. He would be back at the end of shift and that they should just keep the car in the garage.

Jordon saw Detective Barnes leaving and he ran up to him, "Hey Barnes, can you give me a ride to Zack's? I have a meet up there, and I don't want to be followed."

"Sure Jordon, jump in, be glad to help you out."

"That's great, thanks!" Jordon hopped in the car, then got on the radio. He asked to be patched through to his partner, and the dispatcher obliged. "Weston, I am heading to the upstairs for a ten forty, arriving in the Barnes ride. Will catch you there ten four."

"Ten Four, Weston out," was the response.

Barnes laughed and said, "What was all that BS about anyway?"

"I wanted to let Steve know I would meet him at Zack's upstairs, and not bringing my car. I did not want certain ears to know where I was heading."

"Well, if this is in relation to Cindy, I totally understand. That Austin guy needs to get a better life, he is obsessed with her."

"You noticed that did you. Can I ask you to talk to Captain Shepherd about how things went with you and Austin? I have a feeling he would be interested. The guy is dangerous for Cindy. He showed up at our meet up, really rattled Cindy. He doesn't care if he blows her cover."

"That is what I figured just listening to him. When Steve got all mad, I thought, 'That's who needs to handle Austin'."

"Well, thanks for sharing that. We weren't sure if we were making a big thing out of nothing. The captain needs to know discretely though."

"For sure buddy, I will get back to him before end of shift."

"Oh, can you go to the back lane for me?"

"Sure thing, buddy. See you later then, you guys be careful. If you need anything, just ask. I got your backs."

"Hey, thanks Barnes. I really appreciate that, so does everyone else that is involved."

Jordon got out and headed in to Zack's and up the stairs. It was only two-forty-five, so he knew he would have to wait a few minutes. He decided to call down and order a pot of coffee and three cups. Zack would oblige. He knew these guys only used the upstairs when it was very important. He brought the coffee himself.

Jordon was pumped and upset and chomping at the bit to inform Weston about the meet-up. He was sure Weston would have a solution for the problem. Then it hit him. Find out What Austin is driving and have his ride grounded. He would talk to Weston about his thoughts. Jordon was very worried about this case making it. Maybe Austin didn't want it to happen, then he could keep D to himself, or maybe he wanted the credit for the sting, for personal gain. There was a lot to think of. He heard steps coming so he sat down and tried to relax. It was Zack, he was bringing the coffee.

"Weston is in the back lane watching for D and making sure no one is watching," Zack said, "D is really here?"

"Yep, the three amigos are back together. But you can't tell anyone, she's undercover."

"Oh, your secret is safe with me. And my staff all know what is seen here, stays here. That's the deal or they aren't seen here no more."

More steps were heard coming up to the room. D came in followed by Weston. D gave Zack a big bear hug, "It's good to see you, Zack." D had a huge grin and a silent giggle her usual trademark.

Weston came in and joked "I suppose you want a hug from me as well Zack, hahaha."

"Ok, so we are together, how are you doing now, D?" asked Jordon.

Weston spun around, "Why what's happened why are you asking her that Jordon?"

"We had our meet, we were talking and about forty-five minutes into the meet Austin came walking in the restaurant, for no reason. I left immediately; I practically ran home. I was mad," D stated with some hostility.

"Yeah, I was pissed too. I told Austin on meet days, he is not to come near the restaurant at any time or I'd shoot him. And I meant it. He had some nerve. It's like he was hoping to blow her cover. He is too involved with D. He needs to stay away. He also followed me when I left the office. I back tracked back to the office, he stopped following me. I took off to the meet up afterward. We have to do something. I ditched my car in the service garage. I am having it checked for bugs. Barnes gave me a ride, we talked. I asked him to report to the captain about his concerns, and to not repeat it. I just wanted to break Austin's neck!"

"Well, he isn't here now, so let's sit and talk, alright." Steve appeared annoyed but kept calm. He put the files on the table and told D to read them. She sat down and started reading the intel that was gathered. Zack had already gone downstairs. Steve waited to assess how D reacted to what she was reading. It was very quiet.

D looked up and at Jordon and then at Steve, "He must think I am a complete idiot, the way the reports are written. No wonder he would never let me see what he wrote. I was giving him all those details, and he was busy telling me that the Commander would be irritated with all the extra details. He told me he would write what was important, and the rest about which I needn't worry. I kept telling him it's the fashion industry the money was going through. I mean look how big his name is in the industry, He's known worldwide. And today, he shows up. He tells me don't talk to Smith and Weston; they are dangerous. God, I'm an idiot."

"Hey, you're not an idiot. You managed to get a lot of clear evidence; you are a key witness. You know that, right? You are smart. You contacted me for this meeting. You know what you're doing. I am just sorry I cut you short on credit. But I know that Austin will pay for this deception. Just we need to stay focused on this week and the next few days of the operation. Has he said when they wanted to do the raid?"

"I think he wants to do it this weekend, Steve. But he has not said anything yet. I expect to hear from him tonight. Once he gets the info on my meet up."

"Ok, give me the details on the meet up."

D told Steve everything and Jordon was listening again as she gave all her intel to them. Steve was amazed how she could cover so much information.

Then he asked, "Didn't you already photograph the payroll books the last four pay weeks? It's all in these files. Why is he sending you in again? Isn't it dangerous if you get caught?"

"Yes, but he kept telling me having consistent two-week reports was important for evidence. It doesn't matter. I snuck into work and took the pics today. I have the film to give them tomorrow night."

"Well, how did you figure that you could do it today?"

"Connie from the band, he's my back up drummer and is still learning some of the hard numbers. He is slow on the triple repeat, three quick beats three times. A climb up and return to climb."

Weston had a confused look in his eyes, as did Jordon.

"Ok, I was hired as a waitress and entertainer, I sing and drum in a band, that's my entertainment. I performed overseas for the service men in Kandahar. Connie is learning to take my place to free me up to sing up front. We switch off every two to three songs. I wanted him to practice, and I snuck off to the office, took the pictures, and got back on stage. No one missed me."

"Why does that not surprise me. Tell you what, anyone know you went and took pictures?"

"No, I did it myself when Connie called me. It was a thought spur of the moment. The club is not open on Mondays, and it's simply for restocking and cleaning. But I know the payroll girl has the books there for Monday and Tuesday, on Pay week. She has specific days for each club."

"Ok, you are not going to be able to take pictures tomorrow. He'll be disappointed, but I want you to give me the film, and I will have it developed, I have a guy who is discreet. I don't trust tomorrow. I think he is doing stupid things to set you up. That way, he will make a mistake, and something happens to you, he was just tired and made an innocent mistake. Your next meet up will be here at Zack's, in this office. Can you take a bus to get here?"

"I think I can, I'm not too familiar with the bus routes."

"Tell you what, I will meet you two blocks over from your place, I will pick you up, and Jordon will get here undercover for the meet up. We will go over everything, and then we will do the raid Saturday night. We will finalize the signals. I will have all the men we need. You just have to promise me you will keep safe."

"Ok Steve, I will keep safe, and I'll keep Alexa safe as well. If Austin wants to do the raid, are we still doing it as if he called it?"

"Yes, you have been at this for too long. It has to stop. Captain Shepherd will agree. Now you better go get your pizza. Do you want a ride home?"

"I don't know, maybe if you drop me off two blocks over so no one gets curious," D grinned and had her little giggle back.

"I am pretty sure I will blend in with my wreck."

CHAPTER TWENTY

D left to get her pizza and hurried back for her ride with Steve and Jordon. She was all smiles and giggles. Then she reached in her blouse and pulled a roll of film from her bra. "Before I forget here are the photos I took. I hope they turn out. I also took film of some blueprints that were sitting on the coffee table out in the open. I didn't waste time looking to see what it referred to, I just figured bonus shots."

"Ok thanks, good work. So, you get some rest, and be careful tomorrow. Do a good job and keep your nose clean. And D I'm proud of you I really am."

The car came to a stop. D gave Steve a kiss on the cheek and Jordon a small kiss on the lips. "Thanks, so much guys, I am happy to be working with ya's." She smiled and giggled. Then started walking to her place.

Steve started to drive away, "Hey, doesn't that Kim live up this way, Jordon?"

"Yes, she does. I thought of that earlier today, when I went to Georges, I prayed she did not show up there when I was with D. We were heavy into serious talk."

"Yeah, and that kiss she gave you just now tells me something else is up Smith."

"You caught that did you! I didn't expect it, she initiated. I told her we need to keep on our toes with this case. We can't afford to be distracted."

"Might do good to remind her at the next meet up. Should I drop you off to get your car?"

"No, I will call the Service Garage to keep it in protected. You could drop me off at home."

"How about we go by your place? You get some stuff for overnight and then we can get some pizza and beer and go back to my place for the night."

"Alright, sounds like a great plan."

So, the two guys drove to Jordon's and parked. Jordon got out and ran up the steps to his apartment, let himself in, and flipped the light switch on. He walked in and felt strange then someone from behind hit him in the head. He went down on his knees, he spun around and blocked the next hit, and flipped the person who hit him. He went into hand-to-hand combat; it was so automatic. Then a lamp went flying and smashed against the wall.

Steve heard it and sprung out of the car, he ran up the stairs to check on Jordon, and the person took off down the stairs knocking Steve over. Jordon came running out and saw Steve falling. He went to help Steve up, and asked, "Did you see who it was?" Jordon was holding the back of his head but was confused as to why the blitz attack. Steve got up and asked Jordon if he was ok.

"Yeah, I'm alright, but why would anyone do this?" Jordon was looking around his place nothing was missing or ransacked. He was puzzled.

"I think I know what it's about. D and Austin is my guess as to who it was that hit you." Steve was checking Jordon's head. He had a gash. There was a pry bar off in the corner. "You may need stitches, Jordon, he split your head."

"I didn't pass out; I'll get my first aid kit we can tape it up. I am ok. We know my head is tough."

"I think you need stitches, Jordon." Steve was concerned.

"How long is the gash, and how deep is it?" Jordon was trying to rationalize not needing stitches.

"I would guess it's two inches long and I can see skull bone. It's deep."

"I will be fine; I hope D will be fine. I'll grab my stuff for the night and then we can get our pizza and beer."

"Ok, but you are bleeding quite a bit. It needs to be closed."

"Steve! I am not going for stitches. That's it. Do you know how to sew or use butterfly stitches? That's the only way I will do it."

"Ok, just settle down. No yelling. It raises the blood pressure and causes more bleeding. You got any ice to put on it?"

"Yeah, I do I'll get it. I have to call D's; I need to make sure she is ok."

"Well, just sit still for a minute let me work my magic."

Jordon sat and picked up his phone, it was dead. "He killed my phone the dirty son of a-"

"-Ok, I am going to close the cut, and then we can race to my place. We will check on her. Just relax, buddy. I don't know what this guy's end game is, but he is really getting under my skin and pissing me off. He's been a weasel since I set eyes on him."

"I am pissed too; he comes in my place, and he attacks me. Why?"

"He's insecure, he saw how D looks at you, he's jealous. But we will fix his wagon. There butterflies are done, get your stuff, and let's go."

The guys took off and then Steve asked, "Jordon, do you have D's number with you?" Steve pulled over to a payphone and stopped.

Jordon jumped out of the car and started to dial D's number. It was ringing and no one was answering. "No one's answering, where is her roommate?" Jordon was panicking.

"Just relax, Jordon, maybe she's in the shower. Get in the car we will swing by."

Just as Smith and Weston were arriving at D's place, there were black and whites stopped outside. "The roommate must have called the cops."

Weston was out of his car to ask the uniform what was happening. Smith was running up to D's apartment.

"So, what's happening here anyway?" Steve flashed his badge.

"Break in and assault with a weapon. The guy got away. The girl is out cold. We called EMS they should be here soon."

"Ok, thanks for the info." Steve dashed into the building, following the uniforms to what must have been D's apartment.

"Jordon was calling Cindy's name. "Cindy, come on wake up!" She was on the floor and moaning like in pain. "Cindy! Wake up. What happened to her, Alexa?"

"I don't know. I came home and some dude came running out of the apartment. He knocked me over. I came in and found Cindy crumpled on the floor. I called nine-one-one Then I got a cloth to wipe the blood off her face. She hasn't woken up yet."

"Do you know who the guy is, a guess will do?" Steve asked. He was checking for D's pulse and checking her breathing. "Jordon, her pulse is weak and thready, and she is only breathing shallow."

Jordon was doing a body check, trying to see if anything was broken. He got to her ribs and her body winced in reaction. "I think she's got a broken rib, or at least a cracked one, and she has a bump on the back of her head kind of like mine with an indent and blood. Where is that ambulance?"

"Take it easy, buddy. They are on their way. This is the far end of town. It takes a few minutes to get here." Steve was trying to reassure Jordon.

At last, Cindy was coming to and thrashing around to fight her way free. "No! No! No!" she hollered, swinging her arms but when she felt pain she curled up in a ball. She then realized the assailant was gone and it was her two friends. She turned and looked at them, eyes tearful, nose bleeding and asking did they get the guy. "How is Alexa? Is she ok? I'm sorry, he caught me off guard from behind. I don't even know how he got in here."

"Shush, quiet Cindy, just breathe easy. You're going to be alright. Breathe nice and easy," Steve was trying to calm her. Steve was very angry though; he knew something like this would happen and it's not even the case she's working.

"Alexa's ok, she called the police and ambulance. She was great, she gave you first aid, she did everything right," Jordon was trying to calm her and reassure her that her roommate was not hurt. He turned to Steve, and he said, "I want an all-points bulletin on this Peter Austin for attempted murder, break and enter, with a weapon."

The uniformed officer standing there heard this and went to put it out on the radio. Steve started to protest but Jordon grabbed Steve's arm and said, "No, let them put it out there, get him off the streets we will deal with evidence after the fact."

"Has anyone called the CSI unit to come out yet?" Steve wanted to know. Then he started asking about evidence disturbance. The paramedics came in and started to assess Cindy. They got her on the stretcher and said she needed medical attention. Jordon said he was going with her.

Steve said, "You go, I will meet you at the General, is that where you are taking her." It was confirmed by the paramedics. Steve stayed till the attending Detective could arrive and take over.

Steve filled in Detective Wheeler from the third division. He reassured Steve they would investigate thoroughly. Then Steve took off. He thought about his buddy and small friend. Thinking no one has eaten, he picked up a pizza and beer, then he stopped at Zack's. He asked Zack to take it to his place for him on his way home after he closes up for the night. Zack obliged him. Then Steve sped off to the hospital to see how Cindy was doing. He found an anxious Jordon pacing up and down in the waiting area.

"How is she doing do you know?"

"They had to put a chest tube in for her to breathe, a lot of blood came out of the tube, Steve. They haven't said a thing since, she went for an MRI, the doctor said he would fill me in asap."

"Ok, so we know she is stable. They didn't say go home or anything to indicate it would be a while till they know anything," Steve said to Jordon.

After waiting for what seemed like forever a doctor came out asking for Miss Bishop's family. Both Steve and Jordon stood up and said, "yes," at the same time.

"Family?"

"No, she has no family. We are like brothers to her; we are Detectives Smith and Weston. How is she?"

"Well, we have her chest draining, and she's breathing better. She has a broken rib, and it punctured a lung. When the chest stops draining, we'll pull the tube out to see if the lung seals and expands on its own. She has a severe concussion; her skull was fractured. We stitched it up and we are watching for any bleeds. She also had a broken wrist, we've put a brace in place rather than a cast, as her I.V. was established on that arm before we knew it was broken. She has a lot of bruises, and her cheek bone is broken, we reset it while resetting her nose. Her face looks bad, but it will heal fine. We have applied an ice pack to her face. She is heavily sedated. They are taking her to her room for the night."

"She has to stay overnight then?" Jordon asked.

"I would generally keep her for a week to monitor, but she said her brother is a medic and she had a job to go to that was important. I will not release her if she worsens. So, which one of you is the "Medic", so to speak?"

"I am doctor," Steve spoke up. "I was a second-year intern when I dropped out of Med School."

"Ok, you know she is a diabetic, right? We have to watch for infection and other complications. If she can eat and drink without assistance, and if she can use the facilities well on her own, I will consider releasing her into your care. But I want an MRI first thing in the morning to be sure no swelling of the brain is happening. She is lucky she is alive. Someone didn't want her to be."

"Ok, thanks doctor. What floor will she be on?" Steve asked.

"She will be on GD-four that is the old building wing, you can go up and wait for her."

Both Smith and Weston thanked the doctor and left the E.R. area to go to the fourth floor and wait for D to be in her room. Jordon paced like a nervous nut, he was shaking from nerves and anger. Steve was talking to Jordon in a soft calm voice to relax him. It was hard as he had his own anger to deal with. Then they both saw D come off the elevator on a stretcher that looked gigantic to her small frame, and it upset both men at the same time. They waited to be told she was settled in her room.

Suddenly as they waited there was an alarm that went off. They looked down the hall to see what was happening. There were nurses and doctors rushing into one room and a cart rushed in the room. The guys did not know what code blue was, but it sounded bad. Jordon was getting very anxious and paced even more. Then he saw a nurse heading their way.

"Bishop, Cindy Bishop family."

"That's us we are here for her, is she ok?"

"Oh, she is fine. She rolled over to sleep on her side and set an alarm off as her chest tube was kinked. Follow me. Please do not tire her, she is scared, and was asking for Jordon, just don't let her turn on her right side, she can lay on her left, but the chest tube needs to be cleared to drain. She is on a morphine pump for pain. Here is her room, four- twenty-six."

"Ok, thanks a lot we will be careful." This time D was on her left side, and the nurse adjusted her tube. The guys came in quietly but spoke softly, calling, "D?"

"Hello, I am here," she called out, and when they got in her sights, she smiled slightly. "Hi guys, I am happy you're here. Sorry for the trouble. How did you guys know I was in trouble? I know you're not psychic, but when I was attacked, I was wishing you were there."

"I was attacked in my apartment," said Jordon, "Weston had to tape the cut on my head. I am sure it was the same guy that attacked you. Do you remember the time you entered you're home?" Jordon asked.

"I know I walked back to my apartment when you dropped me off, so shortly after four."

"Well, I got hit on the head at around five thirty. Weston came in when he heard the commotion. That's when I got worried about you. So, we got to your place around six. You were out cold for a couple of hours."

"Yeah, and that gave Austin plenty of time to hit both of you. I am hoping he doesn't try to hit me, as I have Zack delivering a pizza to my place."

"Oh, I am sorry I wrecked your supper tonight. I am hoping they take the tube out tonight; it's driving me crazy. But I am in pain so if I start crying, don't worry, I am just in pain."

"You do know you are on a morphine pump, you just push the button by your hand, and it delivers your pain medication, so just push the button. Don't try to be a hero." Jordon didn't want D to suffer.

"Austin deserves to rot in jail as far as I am concerned, he hit me in the back of the head so hard I literally felt my skull crack and heard it. It was a weird sensation with pain. I went down, and he was punching me and kicking me. I had no chance to fight back, I feel so stupid." D was crying and her nose and face were hurting, she wasn't taking a breath. She set off the alarms.

"D! Breathe nice and easy, in and out slow and easy, focus on breathing not on what happened," Weston snapped and then instructed softly. He felt bad but wanted her to relax.

The nurses came rushing in to check on her, they asked if she was ok, she nodded yes. "I noticed if I cry my face hurts and I can't breathe."

"Then darling don't cry, and please use you're morphine pump, we want you to be comfortable. And if you are going to set off alarms, your friends will have to leave!" the nurse snapped.

"No, no, no, I want them to stay. I am scared the guy that did this is loose in the city. Please?"

Then Capt. Shepherd came in the room "What's with the please? I came to see how our little lady is doing?"

The nurse looked shocked at the captain. "Little lady! She's just a kid!"

Then there was laughter. D looked cross; she did not like to be referred to as a kid.

Weston was chuckling and said, "Ok kid, the gig is up. Now the nurses are going to get tough on you. You've been ousted."

"Steve, you don't have to laugh so hard, really, I know I am small, but I am not a kid. I'm twenty-six, the nurse can put that in my chart. But I still want Jordon to stay by my side. I am too scared."

"Oh, so I am chopped liver here am I?"

"No Steve, you are welcome to stay too. Then I will feel double protected."

"Well, missy, if you are not getting your rest, they will both be out of here. I cannot have a patient not getting her rest, and she will not get out of here very fast either."

"No, no, I will rest, starting now."

"Oh, I think I will ask you to go on your back, the supper trays are coming. You missed it and we requested one for you. We want you to eat, so we can monitor your body functions."

"It hurts when I am lying on my back." D turned over on her back. The nurse straightened the chest tube, then raised the head of the bed till D was in a sitting position. The color she had left her. She was very pale but did not complain.

Capt. Shepherd stated, "I am putting uniformed guards outside your room and at the hospital entrances. Security is doing a sweep of the hospital, checking all nooks and crannies to find this Austin. If we find him, he is going to be locked up, so you don't have to be afraid D. Smith and Weston can stay or go home to rest. We will have you covered. We have photo ID for the hospital staff. We won't let anyone get close to you."

"I would like to stay on this case, Captain," Jordon stated.

"I also want to stay on this case, Captain," Steve said.

"There is no covert case. Cindy's injuries will prevent her from going to work."

"Like heck, it will. I am out of here tomorrow morning, noon at the latest. I am back on duty at six in the evening, nothing is stopping me."

The captain appeared surprised by D speaking up and so forcibly.

CHAPTER TWENTY-ONE

D pressed her pump button as her last statement was a painful demand. She hoped no one noticed. It made her feel dizzy and nauseous. She held strong, not to gag as her food tray came.

"Oh boy, what is this stuff? I was going to have a perfect pizza earlier this evening. Now I am looking at Brussel sprouts, wieners heated up and cold dry fries. The coffee is cold, I don't want to sound unappreciative, but could I order a pizza please? I'll even pay."

Steve spoke up and said, "Hold on, let me make a call to Zack. If we are staying here tonight, I will get him to bring the pizza here." Steve made his call, went to the vending machine, and got pop from it. He came back to the room, and D was looking grey. He asked, "Are you ok, D? You look like you're going to be sick."

"I feel shaky, and I feel like I'm going to be sick. Hand me my purse, I need to test my sugars." She got her bag and began the process; her sugars were two point one. She grabbed her glucose tablets and started taking them, but it made her gag. "Can I have the garbage can? I might have to heave ho. My sugars are too low, the taste of the tablets are making me sick."

Steve went to get the nurse as he was worried.

"Ok everyone, clear the way." The nurse came in. She asked, "What did you get for a reading? I have a glucose push IV, spit the tabs out." The nurse connected her syringe to the IV and D spit the tablets out as she vomited in the trash. It hurt like the dickens, she hurt all over. D put her head back and closed her eyes. It felt like the world was spinning out of control.

Cindy, as she was known, was dry heaving, and not liking it one bit. The Nurse was asking, "Cindy, are you still with us?"

Cindy nodded. "Yes, but I feel awful. Everything is spinning, my guts are twisting, I should never get this low."

"You should start feeling better soon, I gave you a bolus of Glucose via IV."

D nodded and just laid back her head and kept quiet. She figured she'd wait and feel better in a minute. Her color improved only slightly, and the nurse checked her vitals, she was happy with it. She kept checking D and watching the changes. D felt foolish having a low blood sugar but had other things on her mind.

"I am sorry for making everyone race around. Thank you for the glucose. I will eat the cold fries till the pizza comes. And I will drink water to help myself. But not the Brussel sprouts." D gagged as she said the last part.

"Sweety, if the food is making you feel sick, don't eat it. You have about fifteen to twenty minutes to eat; you may feel sick again when the glucose hits you. It will be a rush. There was enough for a six-foot heavy weight. I am just sorry the food took so long." The nurse felt bad, and she saw D as a kid not an adult because of her size.

Then Zack appeared with the pizza and some wine. D was chewing crushed ice, and the guys were thankful for food.

"Thanks Zack, you are a life saver," Jordon said.

Steve jumped in and took some slices out, and placed them on a paper plate, and he said, "You're just on time." He put the pizza in front of D, and then put the diet soda with a straw alongside the food. Steve was trying to act normal, but he was concerned.

"Thank you, Zack you're a life saver." D started to eat and was happy. And she continued chewing ice chips to quench her thirst. She didn't want to drink her pop to fast, due to creating possible gas. She chewed slow as her face was in pain and kept her eyes closed and head back. She was trying to rest at the same time as eating. It was quiet in the room; everyone was enjoying the meal. Capt. Shepherd had excused himself as he needed to check on the investigation.

"So, Steve do you think Peter has been waiting for you at your place?" D asked.

"D, he'll be waiting for some time. He is likely watching your place, waiting for CSU to leave and you to come home. I have officers checking each place and monitoring to catch him should he show. Your commander is aware of everything that's happened. He feels bad that he was so well manipulated by Austin. The military is looking for him."

"They didn't cancel the operation, did they?"

"That depends on your recovery. Even if you are stable all night, do you think you could handle working with a broken rib, and facial/head trauma?"

"I will do it, no matter what happens. As long as I can stand and walk, we are going forward. No one is crapping on my cornflakes."

Capt. Shepherd came rushing in the room, "We have Austin! Everyone clear the room; D has a visitor coming to her room. Nardelli is coming in to see Cindy. Her roommate told him what happened when he called. Nardelli's men caught Austin and gave him up to the police. Everyone out. D, can you handle the visit?"

"Yes, for sure. I am good." D straightened herself out and tried to look normal for her boss.

"There was a knock on her room door. She called out, "Come in, oh hi Mr. Nardelli! What are you doing here?"

A man who was tall with long styled white hair, and well dressed in fashion and in good physical shape came in the room. "I vanted to see my favorite girl, she vas banged up I heard." He spoke with an accent, as he was European. "Are you ok, my dear?"

"I am going to be ok, Mr. Nardelli, I might not get out of the hospital for work tomorrow night. I need the chest tube removed and my head was cracked."

"Oh, look at your pretty face, zhat man vas a nazty pieze of slime. You don't vorry about vork. I vill take care of you."

"I didn't want to disappoint you. I got the drummer to be able to play the numbers you wanted so I could be up front singing. I wanted you to see that. I am sorry about this and that crazy nut. The police gave me protection overnight because he's on the loose."

"My men found him, ve took care of him, the police have him now. You stay in hospital till you are vell to be let out. I hope before the veekend though. I have girls coming into town this veekend, I vas counting on you to train them. I know Alexa agreed to help vith the party, so I have a gift for you to vear vith a special outfit I designed just for you."

"Oh, well thank you, Mr. Nardelli, that is nice of you."

"Call me Antonio, please."

"Ok, Antonio thank you, you are very kind to have come to see me. My first visitor outside of the police and my brother-in-law.

"You have a brother-in-law, I thought you had no family?"

"He found me, we just reacquainted ourselves today. My sister left him. He doesn't know I work for you; I don't want him knowing much."

"Don't vorry about me telling him anything. Your secret is good vith me. Here is my personal card, you call me and let me know how you are healing, ok."

"Ok, Antonio I will do that. I will get lots of rest, thank you for caring."

Mr. Nardelli kissed D gently and said his good-byes, then he slowly walked away and out of the room. The guys and Capt. Shepherd came out of hiding and into D's room.

"Good job, Cindy, you kept it all together, and he still wants you to host, so the case is not a wash yet." The captain was pleased and Steve was proud of her.

"Yeah, and I am tired, I have a huge headache as well." D laid back her head on the pillow and closed her eyes. Then she realized she had a remote control for her bed and lowered it a bit. She was feeling the room was spinning and wanted to rest.

Capt. Shepherd left to check on the arrest of Austin, he said good-bye to everyone. A guard was left at D's doorway. Jordon dragged a chair over to sit next to the bed and sat beside D, he was going to see that she got a good rest. Steve just sat quiet in the room; his eyes eventually closed as did Jordon's. D slept soundly and was trying to turn over on her right side which set off the alarms, and Jordon shot up to look, so he woke D up and had her turnover onto her left side and he placed the chest tube so it would not kink. Jordon was relieved D was fine. He sat and watched her fall back to sleep; she was holding his hand, a sense that she felt secure came over him.

It was a quiet night, no problems were noted, D was stirring and sleeping very restlessly, she was thrashing and moaning. Jordon tried to wake her up, he thought she was having a nightmare. As she would not wake up, he called for the nurse.

"Cindy Bishop, wake up," the nurse shook her and pinched her shoulder. She was listless, the nurse called for the attending physician, she was concerned. She kept trying to wake Cindy, and no luck, then all of a sudden, Cindy was seizing.

"What's wrong with her," Jordon asked. He was horrified. She was frothing at the mouth, and not awake, but vibrating.

"I am not sure, but I think her brain may be swelling," the nurse said, then she called a code white for emergency staff to come to the room. The nurse told Steve and Jordon they had to leave the room. The doctor entered her room, and then started barking orders for medication. The cart soon came to the room, and all of the staff were working quickly. There was a lot of activity around D. Jordon got very worried, He was praying she would be ok. The doctor came out of the room and he asked Jordon, "Is there anyone who can speak for D at the moment?"

CHAPTER TWENTY-TWO

Jordon thought for a moment and then said, "The Government of Canada, I guess." He asked, "Why, what does she need?"

"Her brain is swelling and there is pressure on the skull, we need to surgically relieve it."

"Well, do it!" ordered Jordon.

"I need authorization by someone responsible for her care."

"Well, will I not do; I care about her and do not want to lose her." Jordon said with an anxious worried voice.

"We are employed by the Government. Can't we answer that for her?" Steve spoke up.

"I am not sure if that is ok." The doctor would have loved it if he could have accepted their word.

Then the nurse came running down the hall, "Her Commander is on the phone, he has given permission for surgery."

The doctor was relieved and said, "Get her ready. I will get an operating theater for her." He raced down the hall to get things done.

Jordon stood at the doorway to her room, and the nurse said, "You can come in and sit with her till they come get her, then you will have to wait in the waiting area till her surgery is done."

Steve stood in the hall and was worried about his buddy and his little lady friend. As the nurse left the room, Steve snuck in quietly. D lay very still in the bed, intubated and on a respirator. Once again, she looked very small and fragile to both guys.

Jordon was upset. He could feel his opportunity to get to know D just slipping away.

"Just trust the medical staff here. They are well trained and knowledgeable She will come out the other side doing ok," said Steve. Just then the transport staff were there to take D to surgery.

"D, I will be here waiting for you, you are in good hands, hang in there, D," Jordon whispered in her ear.

Jordon watched her being wheeled away. He was scared he might not see her again. It was killing him that she was going through all of this. He walked down to the waiting room and sat down. Steve followed and then started to pace. He was worried but, did not want to admit it.

Jordon spoke up, "Sit down and wait. She'll be awhile."

Steve sat down. Hours went by, and the guys eventually fell asleep, no one disturbed them. Soon there were footsteps heard coming up the hall, then there was an aroma stirring the nose of both men. Steve opened his eyes first then he nudged Jordon awake. It was their Captain and the Commander; they were standing there looking at Smith and Weston holding coffees and doughnuts.

"Heard anything yet?" asked Capt. Shepherd.

Jordon shook his head and said, "No."

Steve looked at his watch, he said, "It's been four hours, we should be hearing something soon."

The Commander said, "Well, while we wait, let's think positive and plan the weekend. We have an in for taking this guy down. I think we should make some tactical decisions."

"Commander, forgive me if I turn you down. Since it was your own guy on the inside that was missing marbles and you didn't notice it, I really have no faith in your planning," Steve stated.

"If it hadn't been for your man, we would not be here, worried," shouted Jordon.

"Guys! I expect respect and cooperation with regards to the operation and D," the captain barked.

"Sorry, Captain," both guys said.

Steve was concerned that after this brain surgery it might be too soon for D to resume her cover, and he expressed that with calmness and respect.

Jordon expressed he did not want D involved in the operation, as he felt she might be killed. He feared for her life.

The captain stated, "Ok, maybe we wait till we know something, and if she wants to move forward, we will make the plans, last minute. Smith and Weston are good with plans on the fly, and they are successful. I have faith in them."

The commander agreed and was apologetic to Smith and Weston. "Believe me Austin will be dealt with harshly. And credit will go to the right people."

"I, or we, are not worried about credit to the right people, there is a young lady here that he almost killed, and she is still fighting for her life," stated Steve. "If she goes undercover here, and gets hurt in the raid, it could kill her. Do you know her injuries and understand that?"

More footsteps were heard coming down the hall. "Jordon Smith is he here?" a nurse called.

"Yes, I am right here," Jordan responded, as he jumped up.

"You can go in and see her. The doctor is there waiting for you."

Jordon ran down the hall and into the room. He was quiet as he approached her bed. "Is she ok doctor?"

"She is fine. She came through with flying colors. She will need a day of rest, but she will be fine. I took her chest tube out in the surgery, so she should recover well. She has a drain tube in her skull for any further bleeding, but there should be no more bleeds."

The Commander, Captain Shepherd, and Weston arrived in time to hear what the Dr. said, and smiled with relief.

"Jordon, you are here, that is great," D stated. "I made you my designate, so no more worries."

Jordon pulled a chair up beside her bed and sat and held her hand as she fell back to sleep. He was relieved and couldn't help but smile. "Thanks doctor, I appreciate what you've done."

"That's great news isn't it men?" asked the commander.

"Jordon, of course we are going to wait until D wakes up and is feeling stronger, before we revisit the operation," said the captain.

"Ok, Captain, that's fine, and I will be giving it serious thought," Jordon said with authority.

Steve was quiet in the room. He put his hand on Jordon's shoulder, and said, "It's all good buddy, she will be fine."

A few hours went by. The captain and the commander had left. It was getting close to noon and D was finally waking up. She saw Jordon stayed by her side, and they were holding hands. Jordon had nodded off. D sat up in bed.

Steve was quietly pacing. D said nothing, just sat there smiling and quiet. Steve turned around, as he could feel someone watching. He saw D sitting there smiling and he quietly went up to her and asked, "Hey how are you doing, your color is good."

"Well, I feel fine. Why? I had a good sleep. You guys should go home and get some rest," D was concerned and looking at Jordon sitting on a chair sleeping.

"We will when we are sure you are ok and doing well."

"I slept well right through the night, no disturbance at all. My head hurts but not as bad as last night. I will be fine. There is a guard at my door. You two could go get some rest."

"You just woke up from brain surgery, are you sure you are, ok?" Steve was asking with concern.

"What are you taking about? I was tired last night and fell asleep. I didn't go anywhere," D smiled and giggled. She did not remember any of the night before.

"Hey, you're awake now," Jordon stated. He was happy to see D awake and was happy to hear her giggle.

The doctor came in, and asked, "How is my patient today?" He started to check D over for her recovery.

"Doc, she doesn't remember any of last night," Steve stated.

"What's he talking about doctor?" D asked, as she noticed the doctor was testing her reflexes and her right side felt weak. "What's wrong with my right side? I can't lift my arm or move my leg."

"That will all return when your brain swelling is gone. We did surgery last night to relieve the pressure on your brain and stop the bleeding. It's normal to have a weak side afterwards," the doctor stated.

D was upset and scared because she was paralyzed on one side. As well she could not understand that she didn't remember what happened. She looked up at Steve and asked, "What happened to me last night? I don't remember."

"You started having seizures late in the night. They raced you into surgery, as the pressure in your brain was excessive. You were in surgery for hours. When they brought you up you greeted Jordon, then fell asleep." Steve was worried and was afraid D would freak out. He went over to soothe D, but Jordon was hugging her at that point.

The Nurse came in to check on D and ask if she had any pain. She assessed her vital signs, and checked her pupils, she stated, "We will be doing frequent cranial checks on you, Cindy. You can let us know if you are in pain. You no longer have your morphine pump, so we will give you analgesics as you need them. Your chest tube has been removed. We will be assessing how your breathing is as well. We will be getting you up and walking. When your IV antibiotics are finished, we will remove the IV. You should be discharged in two days."

"Well, here's your coat and hat, don't let the door hit you on your way out!" D said in shock.

The nurse laughed, and said, "We don't keep healthy people longer than necessary. Doesn't mean you're as good as new, just you can recover at home the rest of the way."

"My right side is weak, and I can't move my leg, how will I walk?"

"We will have a couple of hospital attendants help walk you, you will regain the use of your right side quite quickly," the nurse responded.

Jordon was squeezing D's hand as he was worried for her.

She looked at him and said, "You're squeezing pretty tight there, Jordon."

"Oh, sorry, ok," Jordon said as he released his hold. "Guess I am tired and didn't realize my strength. You are going to be ok. I will make sure of that, ok D."

"Ok, you two will have to get strong and think seriously as to what you are going to do the next few days," Steve said.

"Steve, I am going to recover that's a priority, I don't know why you are so serious."

"They are going to want to know if you are going undercover!"

"But I just had surgery," D said with surprise.

"You heard the nurse; you go home in two days. I am not trying to be mean, but the reality is the Captain and the Commander are going to want to know. I need to know so I can plan."

"Steve, I think you need to give D a chance to take a breath, see how she feels in a day. So much has happened in the last thirty-six hours. I know you're not being mean, but I am being honest," stated Jordon.

"I'll let you both know in a day; I want to see how I do today." D wasn't going to rush her answer to Steve. She rolled over to take a nap. So, the guys spoke quietly about the what-if's and should-not-do's. A few hours went by, and the dinner trays came by.

So, they put her tray on the table and woke D up. "It's time for your walk, Cindy." The attendants barely gave her a chance to wake up and were helping her stand next to the bed. "Here's your house coat, we'll help you with it and get you going, work up an appetite."

D was not sure about this. She was leaning to her right and thought she was going to fall over. They held her up and encouraged her to use her legs. "This is just your first try, Cindy. We won't let you fall. You may need a walker or a cane, we will decide that later. Just let us know if you think you will pass out." D made it to the doorway of her room. They turned her around and walked her back. "Tonight, you walk the stretch of the hallway. And then we will see how you do." D made it back to her bedside.

"Let's do that again," she said, "It felt not too bad." She was smiling and confident with them holding her up.

They did it one more time, then told her to sit up to eat. She did and stayed up in a chair into the evening. D ate her meal. The guys left to get some rest, as they knew D would be busy with walking that evening. They picked up her meal tray and left her sitting in the chair, away from the bed and the bathroom.

D decided she could get to the bathroom on her own then to the bed. She used the over bed table to lean on, it had wheels, and she used her own leg power. It took a bit of effort and skill not to fall or let the table get away from her. She was on the toilet huffing and puffing when the attendants came to walk her.

"How did you get in here? Are you crazy? We are supposed to assist you!"

D grinned and giggled, "I used the table, not bad eh?"

"Not safe you mean. No using furniture unsafely to walk. We brought you a walker to use, but we are to be with you as you use it in a safe manner," the attendant stated very firmly.

The grin left D's face, and she responded, "Ok."

They showed her how they wanted her to use the walker. And she started to use it but was hanging on to the walker while leaning over it. "No Cindy, you must straighten up and walk balanced. Or the walker will take off on you." They held her straight, not leaning, and then they had her using her legs to walk. She did good with their help but could not get all her weight down on her right side yet. "You're doing great Cindy, you will get there, tomorrow you will be stronger, and you will do fine."

D was tired and asked to get into bed. So, the attendants helped her, and reminded her to ring her bell if she needed help for the bathroom, they would come and help her. D said she was good and thanks. She laid there for a moment and in no time she was asleep. She slept through the whole night soundly.

D woke up early and rang her bell to get up, she wanted to freshen up and get ready for a day of getting released. She was determined. She was going to do everything they expected. She was on a mission. The bell kept ringing, D thought they must be busy with other patients, so she moved the walker closer to her bedside. It was a reach, but she managed without falling off the bed. She got her feet over the side of the bed. She slid down to the floor to stand up. She then tried to straighten up and move to the washroom. It was no easy feat, but she was determined. She almost tipped over a couple of times, but managed she made it to the bathroom, and did what she had to do. She also freshened up. Now to get back to her bed she thought. She was tired and did not notice others in the room. She started to get turned around to head out of the bathroom, she was hanging on to the wall and walker, almost fell but saved herself. Then she looked up and there watching her were Smith and Weston. They had silly grins on their faces.

They both asked simultaneously, "Need any help?"

"Nope, I got this I think." D continued to move along, then the attendants showed up. They were mad she got out of bed on her own. "You never answered my bell in a half hour, I wasn't going to have an accident. I am standing quite straight."

"So, you want to fall and stay longer?" one of the attendants said.

"No, I was careful." But D was losing her focus and was slowly falling to one side, her weak side. The attendants held her up and got her back to bed. She climbed up on the bed and said, "If the bed wasn't so high it would be easier for me to get in and out of bed."

The guys were smiling and chuckling.

Jordon spoke up, "D, you need to learn patience and to wait."

D looked at the guys, "I want to go home, and get back to work. I don't want to just sit around. The only drawback is my right sided weakness. I am determined."

"So, you have decided, I take it, that you want to do the undercover operation."

"Yes Weston, I do. I am determined not to waste all the work I've done so far. I want to close this and then deal with where I go from here."

"Ok, D but you have to be safe in getting well. You cannot afford another injury while convalescing here at the hospital," Jordon piped up and said.

"I will be patient, and I will wait for assistance I promise you."

"Ok, then can you tell me if you remember what Nardelli was talking about he has girls arriving for you to train, when he visited the other day?"

"Steve, he has girls from other provinces and cities as well as states. He may even have some from other countries that he is using as models for his fashion show on the weekend. At least that is what he tells them, they are going to be models. Some are, but some don't fit the criteria, they go home with the buyers. I don't know what is done to them at that point. That's why I am worried for my roommate, Alexa."

"When he talks about you training the girls, what does he mean, D?"

"Well, Jordon, I am expected to help them wear the fashion design he assigns to them. Then do the make-up and hair so they look like models. The ones who stay with him, I show them their job at the club. I find out if they have a special talent by befriending them. This makes them saleable to his clients. That's all I know, I don't know how much or what currency gets exchanged, but there are many prominent figures at these gala parties."

"So, are there any other things we need to know?"

"No there is nothing else I can think of. I only know the dressing rooms, the main ball rooms of these houses. I've never gone upstairs in any of the party houses and I only have heard rumor of secret rooms, halls, and tunnels. The tunnels connect to other homes that some of the guests arrive through. I see them in the ball room but do not how they get there. The files, that you have read, may give you more of an idea." D actually had thought of an idea. "Actually, now that I think of it, I should call Mr. Nardelli and let him know how I am doing."

"Hold off till the doctor assesses your progress. Maybe you will have a better idea of when you'll be discharged."

"Ok, I will, now I need to have a rest, I am tired from thinking, ok guys."

Both Smith and Weston nodded that it was ok for D to have a rest. Weston was working his plans out in his head. Smith Looked at Weston. He could see the wheels spinning in his head, formulating the plans for the take down. The two of them easily knew what each other's thoughts were, they had a special connection.

CHAPTER TWENTY-THREE

D worked hard on getting released from the hospital that entire day. By evening she was using a cane and doing quite well with it. She was released and sent home. She was looking after her eye that was still swollen, and the bruises on her face, using her grandmothers ways to eliminate the bruises. Mr. Nardelli was aware she was home recuperating. He was calling every few hours to check on her. His latest call found him telling D that he was postponing the party to the next week, then she could rest and be in better shape. D made a call to update Smith and Weston.

"Hi Steve, it's D. I wanted to let you know the party has been pushed to next weekend. Antonio wants to give me time to heal. He will still have his usual party for gambling this weekend, but the big mover one is postponed. I just wanted you to know. I am doing fine, getting around in my apartment, Alexa has been helpful. She is even helping me with my exercises to strengthen my leg and arm. Yeah, I have a return appointment for tomorrow at the hospital to see the neurologist. They will take the shunt out of my head. Nardelli is sending a car for me to go. I don't think I need any help just now. I am doing pretty good."

D spent a day just moving about in her place, the next day she went to her appointment, her doctor was pleased with her progress.

He stated, "You can work but light duty for the first week, and then gradually add the tasks for three weeks. I will see you in a month at my office. The nurse will give you a card with the date and time. Take it easy, don't rush things."

All D heard was she could go to work, and that's what she told everyone. She went to work the next day for just a few hours, to get her legs working. She also rehearsed a little to see how strong she could sing with the band.

"Cindy, how are you doing now, how do you feel after a few hours?" Mr. Nardelli was asking. "Don't push yourself too much. Your voice is pretty strong, not full out, but strong when you sing."

"I'm feeling good, a bit of dizziness and headache, but good. Tuesday, I should be right as rain."

"Well, if you get dizzy or your headache gets bad, you sit and rest, I don't want you getting sick trying to work," Mr. Nardelli was a bit concerned in his voice. D was just happy to be able to work her cover.

After a few more hours, D decided to head home for a deserved rest. One of Nardelli's men drove her home. She was glad, as she was very tired. She got to the steps of her apartment block and suddenly realized she was having trouble with the stairs. Once she was in the apartment, she realized she was done, no energy left. She sat on the couch and did not move. Consequently, she then fell asleep.

After some time had gone by, Alexa was trying to wake Cindy up. Alexa, was worried about Cindy, and finally shouted in her ear, "Cindy!"

D woke up startled, "Oh Alexa, oh what time is it? I must have dozed off. I was exhausted after working."

"I've been trying to wake you up to eat the past hour. You had me worried, I thought your sugars crashed or you relapsed. I phoned Jordon, your brother-in-law. He's on his way over."

"You gave him my address? I'm fine. I don't need anyone worrying about me. I was just so tired and climbing the stairs did me in. I am sorry I worried you. I will get up and get something to eat."

"Well, Mr. Nardelli sent over some dinner for you and me. I already ate, I was getting hungry waiting for you to wake up."

"Oh, that was sweet of Mr. Nardelli." D was trying to get up off the couch, but her legs just were not working. "Alexa, could you help pull me up, my legs seemed to have fallen asleep?"

Alexa had Cindy's arm and helped pull her to her feet. D waited till she felt stable before trying to walk, then a knock on the door came. Alexa went to open it, it was Jordon.

"Is she up yet?" He was concerned.

"It's ok, Jordon, I am fine." D was moving slow; she was hurting in the ribs and on her right side.

"You did too much today, it's too soon for you to work I think."

"Jordon, I am fine, just a little stiff, and I am going slow and careful because my legs fell asleep. I am tired, but a good tired. Please don't worry so much."

D sat down at the table and started to check what she had for dinner. It was a fruit salad and cottage cheese, and there was a cheesecake for dessert. "Mr. Nardelli sent this; I will have to thank him. I really didn't feel like cooking tonight."

Jordon was relieved that D was ok, and Alexa felt bad for calling him. "Cindy Why was it so hard for Alexa to wake you up?" Jordon wanted to know.

"I was so dead tired when I got home, I reached the steps and realized my body was so tired I struggled for twenty or so minutes getting up the steps. I sat on the couch to catch my breath and I guess I fell sound asleep. I feel better after the rest I had."

"I should think so, Cindy, you were snoring at one point. I was worried you would not wake up."

"I Think I was just tired after four hours of work, and that was not serving or anything, just rehearsal, and walking around the club. I am off tomorrow, I can rest up, and I will see Jordon for lunch, right?"

"How about I pick you up for lunch tomorrow, save some of your energy."

"I will walk over to the next block, getting some exercise, and you can pick me up. We don't have to go to Georges if you don't want to."

"I will talk to Steve and see if he wants to see you too."

"Ok, sounds like a plan. Now, don't worry about me so much. I am tougher than I look believe me," D patted her hand on Jordon's as she said that.

Jordon got up and was going to leave. He turned around and gave D a kiss, then said, "See you tomorrow then."

D was gob smacked, as she smiled and said, "Tomorrow then, alright."

D finished eating, while trying to figure out what she was feeling. His kiss went through her like lightening, and she felt good all over. She was not sure what to think he meant when he kissed her. D got up from the table, and cleaned the place up. She took a shower and got ready for bed. She went to bed and sat up and read for a while then fell asleep.

The next morning D got up and got ready for the day. She fixed herself up and was humming away as she did her work out for strengthening. Alexa had left for the day to go visit some friends so D knew she could just take it easy. She left to go meet Jordon, and it was Steve and Jordon together. They were going to talk about their plan D figured. "HI guys, how's it going? What a great day it is, sky is blue, and the sun is shining. So where are we going for lunch?"

"Hi D, we are doing ok, how about you? I thought we would go to Zack's and talk strategy for this week." Steve gave D a serious look and D took note of it.

"I am fine and happy to have a great day off." D looked at Steve and then Jordon. Jordon was not smiling, nor was he frowning, he was just stoic, that had D worried. Jordon got out of the car and let D in to sit between the two men.

"Do I need to be worried about something, 'cause you two look so serious and a bit like someone did something wrong?"

"We had a serious discussion, and no you need not worry, D. You are fine. We will talk about everything when we get to Zack's."

"Ok then. Sounds reasonable, I guess.

The ride to Zack's was quiet. No one spoke. It was killing D; she did not feel any harmony, and she was thinking all kinds of things were wrong. Then she wondered did Jordon tell Steve that he kissed her and that's what was wrong.

They got to Zack's and all of them got out of the car and went inside. Zack saw D and gave her a big hug, "I am so glad to see you upright between the goal posts, little lady."

"Thanks Zack. I am happy to see you too."

D waited to see if they were going upstairs or what the guys were doing. Then they turned and went upstairs so D followed.

The door closed behind them and then Steve got loud, "So you want to tell me what's going on between you two?"

D was gob smacked and did not know what to say. She looked at Jordon and then at Steve. "Nothing is going on as far as I know it or understand it. I have been focused on things, and I would like to say there may be something, but I think that would be getting a head of myself. Jordon?"

"I told Steve what I did yesterday when I went to check on you. I was worried about you overdoing things, and I was relieved to see you were fine, then I kissed you!"

"Oh, ok so what's the problem here now? He was worried and relieved, and he kissed me. Tell me, Steve, what is wrong? We have all had a huge emotional juggle the past number of days so I think some slack could be cut here."

"Well, I am concerned that there will be unnecessary distractions here if you two lovebirds get started."

"Love birds, are you serious Steve? No one has proclaimed their undying love to the other. Look you two guys are important to me, and if one of you is worried, I am going to get distracted, I can tell you don't worry."

"Well, I thought it only fair to tell Steve what I had gone and done."

"Woah, woah, woah, only fair to tell Steve. Look, we are not going to get into this now, it's personal, and I think it's between you and me, Jordon. You haven't given me any info on your personal feelings, and I am not going to get into how I feel about all this right now. It's inappropriate for conversation."

Then the door opened. It was Zack he had a tray of food and brought it in. "Ok I have a Greek salad and Poutine here for D. I have burgers and Poutine for the guys and I have two beers and a wine. Bon appetite!"

So, they all sat down and started to eat. D was quietly praying then started to eat. She wanted to know how Jordon felt, but really she wanted him to tell her personally not just blurt it out in front of Steve. So, she took a deep breath and sighed. This was not turning into a beautiful day after all.

"What's wrong? You just gave a big sigh. What's up?" Steve was worried now.

"Nothing up, down or wrong or inside out. I just took a deep breath and exhaled the negative. I meant nothing by that, ok."

"Ok, I get what you mean no one wants negative energy. I am just worried about everyone."

Jordon looked up at Steve as if to say don't say anything.

D noticed the look then said, "What's up? There is something wrong and you guys are not telling me, what?"

Weston was looking a little antsy and unsettled. Smith was looking like he was holding the dam from busting open. "Well, there is something else, I don't want you to get upset or panic, but Austin is out of jail."

"Steve! I didn't want you to say anything," Jordon protested "It's not for her to worry about."

"He's what? Why, why the heck is he out and how the heck is he out?"

"The Federal Government and the armed forces got him out. He is in MP guard protection in the hotel till he goes back to Gatineau for his court martial."

"And when were you going to tell me this. Why is everything secretive between us? Why can't everybody trust the other person's reaction. It just means we have to be extra careful and have eyes watching for our safety. Did you guys think I was going to lose it and panic all full of drama?"

"Yeah, kind of, that's why I thought Steve should not say anything, that I could tell you when we take you home."

"Oh… I see and that's when Steve asked what's up with you and you had to tell him about kissing me. I get it now. Little D will take the news better from you, my big strong guy friend."

"I wasn't really thinking that way. I just thought you do trust me; you cling to me. The news might be better coming from me, that's all."

"Well, Austin is out loose, but he has MP guards. That's not that scary. But I have news for you two," D was smiling and had a giggle. The guys looked confused. "I am not the Drama Queen here. It's Jordon who is the Drama Queen!"

Steve burst into laughter, a full hardy laughter, and Jordon was caught off guard. D was giggling.

"Ok, ok, let's just take it easy. I am not a Drama Queen. I am a Drama King," Jordon said quietly then laughed.

They all finished their lunch and then got down to business. D asked the guys if they had given any thought to bugging the floral arrangements for the party. Steve was a bit surprised that D asked as he hadn't remembered speaking about the floral arrangements. During the ruckus and confusion D had forgotten what she had said to the guys. She said she thought it would be good to bug the flowers to hear what exchanged during the party for evidence. Steve agreed and made note of that. Then they spoke about the raid signal. D had a laser light lighter. She said she could go to a window and flash it two times to signal all clear, three times for trouble. They spoke about what kind of trouble could come up from all of the party people and from Nardelli's men themselves.

"You need to be careful no one figures out you had something to do with it," Steve wanted D to know, as they might shoot her at the last second.

She said that she would let herself be arrested. The meeting ended with some kidding around and Steve being quite pleased how D was handling the case. Then it was time to head home. D was tired and was looking forward to having a nap. She knew she had the rest of the day to herself. So, Steve drove her home. They stopped a block over.

Steve asked, "Do you want to walk from here or can we take you to your door? I see that stairs are still a problem for you."

D thought about how exhausting the steps were the day before and said, "You can take me to my door, thanks." She didn't admit she was weak, but instead allowed them to help her. When they got to the apartment block, Jordon jumped out and helped D out of the car. He walked her to the steps and helped her up the steps and walked her to the door.

"D, I'm sorry I put you on the spot, I didn't mean to. And right now, I just want to hold you tight and kiss you goodbye, but I realize I don't want to risk your safety or cause distractions. I'm just glad you are getting better."

"Jordon, yesterday you kissed me. I did not expect that; it threw me a bit as I wasn't expecting the feelings that came with the kiss. The time to talk will be after we close this case. We need to keep sharp and our wits about us. Just know you rocked my world for now." D opened her apartment door and this time looked before entering.

Jordon was smiling and pulled D back and he hugged her and said, "I hope the rest of your day is good."

"It will be. I am sure of that. Now you better get going before Steve honks his horn." Jordon gave her a kiss, and D felt herself melt. She fought it, and said, "Goodbye," and closed her door. Then D went into her bedroom to lie down.

Jordon jumped in the car and Steve said, "Did she have trouble with her door?"

"No, we just spoke briefly about the kiss and about staying focused."

"And…What else did you two say?"

"D said that how we feel is for a later day to discuss. For now, we focus on the case and close it."

"Well, that's smart of her so why are you grinning so much?"

"D said that I opened feelings in her when I kissed her yesterday but the time to talk about that is after we finish the case. She said, 'Just know that you rocked my world.'"

"Well then, she has a head on those shoulders, and she is using it. You need to use yours too. To think I got mad at her! It's you Jordon, you need to wake up and smell the coffee."

"I am awake. I lost my focus when D got hurt, but otherwise I have been focused and, in some ways, I think D sees I am drifting and reminds me to focus. I can't help it. She snuck in somehow and grabbed hold of my heart, buddy."

"I think D has that effect on everyone she meets. She got into my heart as well, but I know I need to keep a clear level head. So, buddy, you going straight home today or are you going to hang out with me?"

"I have some chores to do. I need to do my laundry or I am not going to be easy to be around!"

"Ok then, I'll drop you off and maybe you can come on over for supper and a movie."

Weston dropped Smith off he waited a few minutes before taking off just to be safe. There was no commotion, so Weston drove off. He got home and decided he would cook a meal instead of ordering out. He checked his fridge for beer and decided to run out and get more beer for the evening and the week. He got back and checked his scalloped potatoes; they were almost done. He checked his pork chops and flipped them; they were looking good. He turned the oven down and he decided to have a shower and then he would change into sweatpants for the night. He wanted to be comfortable. it was a few days since he was last so comfortable. He also started some laundry, to catch up. He was not too behind but decided to be a head of the game. Both Weston and Smith were great at housekeeping as bachelors. They give all bachelors a bad name in keeping house. Weston took pride in his home. He liked to be neat and tidy.

From the door came a knock and a "I'm here" call.

He yelled out, "Come on in," as he was coming from the back of his place.

It was Smith he was dressed in casual clothes and had a go bag with him.

"Smells good in here, what did you fix?"

"Pork chops, scalloped potatoes and corn. I did not feel like take out tonight. I found a couple of good movies on, Halloween scary like movies. Should be entertaining."

"Yeah, make the girls scream and the guys smile."

The guys enjoyed their dinner and movies.

D woke up from her nap. She had a bit to eat while she wrote down thoughts and hummed along. Then she got her guitar and she played what she had written. She was pleased with her new song. She thought she would get the band to hear it and see how it sounded with other instruments. D began doing her strengthening exercises, and then sat and watched a TV movie. It reminded her of time she spent with Smith and Weston. It was a very good memory and brought happy tears to her face. The movie ended and D went to bed for the night. She was happy to know she could go to work in the evening the next day. She had some great thoughts of Jordon and fell off to sleep.

Smith and Weston watched their Halloween movies, laughed at some parts, and discussed others. They decided the movies were not that great - just blood and gore, no scary parts to really make note of. Once the movies were done, they cleaned up the dinner dishes, and the kitchen and then called it a night. They wanted to be their best for their shift, and for the evening. They were hoping to peek in on D at her work.

D woke up nauseous and sore. She tried to climb out of bed but was suffering from vertigo. She thought this is not good, she needs to go to work. She managed to get up and take an anti-nausea pill and went back to bed to ride it out. By two in the afternoon, she got up. Alexa was up in the kitchen.

"Well, good afternoon sleeping beauty. I hope you slept well."

"Oh, I slept after I took some Gravol. I woke up with vertigo - worst feeling to have. But I think I will make it to work. How about you? How was your day and when did you get home?"

"Oh, my day was great, my family was happy to see me. I got home around ten last night, you were already sleeping."

"What family do you have and where? I thought you were alone here."

"Oh, I call them family - just a bunch of friends from back in the school years. They all came into town to see me. We went out for a special dinner, it was great. They want to meet you, I told them all about you, they want to meet the spitfire that takes care of me." Alexa giggled and D laughed at that, as it sounded funny.

"Meet me! That is funny, but maybe we can get together over the holidays to meet and get to know them better. I would like to meet your friends." D smiled and giggled.

D made herself some tea and some dry toast to get her started for the day. Then she started getting dressed for work and did up her hair. She came out of her room looking very nice, and asked Alexa if she was ready for work.

"Yeah, Cindy I am ready for pick up."

D was picking up her papers for the song she wrote for the club. She was tidying up as she was too tired earlier. "I'm sorry I wasn't up earlier to pick up and clean in the apartment, Alexa."

"It's ok, not the end of the world we will get it later. The place looks fine."

"Our ride is here, let's get going."

The two ladies left the apartment and got in the car for their ride to the club. D was worried about her vertigo and made sure she had her Gravol pills with her. She had decided she would not make fast moves and she would try to take it easy for the evening. It was early in the week so the club did not get overly busy. They arrived at the club. D was excited to share her song with the band. Mr. Nardelli met the ladies at the door. He was greeting everyone as they came in.

He saw D and his smile got big. "Vell, how is my girl, Cindy? I hope you are doing vell, but I don't vant you to vork too hard either."

"Good evening, Antonio. I am pretty good, but I do have some issues with dizziness. I thought I would try to work, but not overdo it. I wrote a new song so I am going to see if the band can play it tonight. If it works out and is thought to be good, we will perform it Saturday."

"A song, how lovely that is. I look forward to hearing it. I have your dinner in the fridge in the kitchen for later. I vant to be sure you stay healthy. You be sure to say something if you are not vell at any time tonight. I have the new girls in the change room. You go meet them."

D went to meet the young ladies. She greeted them and learned some did not speak English, they spoke Spanish. She found out Alexa spoke Spanish, so asked her to communicate with the ladies. D handed out the outfits for work to the ladies, and they changed into them. D explained it was mostly drink orders they took but many customers would eat a meal. "Get the order, turn it in at the bar, they will give it to the kitchen."

She made sure each lady was paired with a regular waitress to learn. D was thinking that they had a few Spanish clients so it should work for training. She went back to Mr. Nardelli to report how she worked the training assignments. He was pleased and said the customers will like the new girls' looks in the club. His plan was to send each lady to a club of his should they stay after the fashion show. D saw the band come in, spun around fast and got dizzy. She grabbed a chair to balance herself.

"Ok, D, slow down you will be fine," she told herself. D went up to the stage and took her time up the steps. They were difficult to climb. She showed the lead guitarist her music, and they tried to play it. She sat at the piano and he played the guitar. They went through it a few times, then she added the lyrics. They played and sang through it. Once they got through it completely, D had a grin and was happy with the sound. "Alright, that was great. We will play it at the end of our first set tonight." She then went to exit the stage. D paused and took the steps carefully - her right knee wanted to give out. She was met by Mr. Nardelli, who said, "That is a beautiful song, Cindy. You sit down for a few minutes; I see the stairs are still a challenge." He pulled a chair out and sat D down to rest.

"Thank you, Mr. Nardelli, I appreciate the kindness."

"I need you well for Saturday, so take frequent breaks, please. I am glad you refer to me as Mr. Nardelli. I don't vant the ladies to lose respect to me."

D sat for about ten minutes, and as the girls came to her with questions, she could answer them. It was working out well. Then the band cued her, so she got up and headed to the stage. She was happy to be there and working. So, D looked around as she realized there was no drummer. Her heart sunk as with her wrist in a brace, it would not be good to try drumming.

"Where is our drummer?" she asked.? No one knew, so she got the microphone, and said, "Connie we need you on stage." D waited a few minutes and one of the bar tenders went to look for him. D was relieved when they brought him in from the back lane where he had been smoking.

"You need to be on time with the band or Mr. Nardelli will not be happy."

Connie said, "For sure, sorry."

So, he got on the drums and the band cued up for the first song and they began.

D was playing keyboard and singing. She was smiling and looking around the club to connect with clients. She could see a lot of the regulars and a few new faces. Then she saw one that was familiar, but was surprised. She wondered why he was there. She was belting her song out - the "Arms of an Angel" (a Sarah McLaughlin song) an easy smooth song not to taxing for her, then she saw the other familiar face come in. She was really surprised and then got self-conscious but kept performing.

Both Smith and Weston had showed up for the show. D continued the performance with an upbeat faster song that many preferred, it got her huffing and puffing a bit.

So, when they finished that song, D got up and said, "Ok, we will slow it down some with this love ballad from the eighties by Anne Murray, and it goes like this, 'Could I Have This Dance for the Rest of Our Lives'. She was singing it sweet and smoothly not missing a word or note. She moved around the stage a little. The lead guitarist was on a violin, and he played it so well D was melting. She loved the song and the band sure knew how to play it. They sang a few more with D up front.

Meanwhile Smith and Weston were getting a feel of the land and enjoying the music. It wasn't their style, but D was good, and they agreed about that. They watched what was going on in the club. It appeared all good and normal activity. While they realized the new ladies had been paired with the staff. This they figured was the human trafficking they were trying to stop from happening. So, when D finished the set, she handed the drummer the music, as she realized he was not there when they discussed it.

He looked at it, it wasn't tricky or anything, he just didn't know about it.

D introduced her new song, 'Jessie,' explained it was dedicated to Jessie, and it told the story of a young lady traveling out on her own, making friends and choices. She said, "I do hope you like it. I wrote it last night and it just came to me in a flow."

She turned to the band: "One two three four,

"I only knew her as Jessie,

she had a short journey in life,

she went through her journey,

as a positive light,

touched each person's heart, bringing in light.

Her name was Jessie that's all I knew.

She was small and an angel with eyes so blue.

We fell in love with Jessie,

the first time our eyes met hers.

Her name was Jessie and God just knew

her heart was good and light so true.

God saw her struggle, but she stayed so true,

the light she shined to me and you

touched our hearts and our day got bright.

Her name was Jessie and God just knew,

the angel with eyes so blue,

he called her home from me and you.

We only had her for a year or two.

We named her Jessie and loved her true.

Her name was Jessie, a little girl so true.

Her name was Jessie, a fighter for love so true

D finished the song, then thanked the crowd. They clapped and cheered and that's how she knew they liked her song. She went to leave the stage suddenly feeling a bit dizzy. Her lead guitarist seemed to know. He helped her down the few steps to the chair at the table.

Mr. Nardelli was thrilled with the song and praised D about it. He was proud of 'his Cindy' as he called her. Then D got up and went to the bar and got some club soda; she was quite thirsty. She was thanking people as she walked through the club. Then she came across Smith and Weston. Steve pulled a chair out and signaled her to sit.

"You weren't kidding when you said you could entertain the troops."

"Well, thank you, I appreciate the compliment. What brings you guys by here?"

"Well, we just wanted to see what the club was like and get the feel of it. What's with getting walked off the stage and sitting right after?" Steve was concerned.

"My vertigo, it's got the best of me today. And my knee wants to give when I do a few steps. I am ok. Mr. Nardelli is making sure of that. Jordon, you are quiet. Are you on lockdown?" D grinned and giggled.

"Who is Jessie? And I want you to take it easy. How did you know Jessie? Don't forget to have your dinner."

"Jessie is a story for another day, I am going to eat, as my supper is in the kitchen, and my sugars are good; I have been monitoring them. Thanks for the concern but relax, I am not jeopardizing my job. I should get up and go so Nardelli isn't suspicious about you two. See ya's."

CHAPTER TWENTY-FOUR

Then D got up and turned to go, she almost tripped but did not. She saw Nardelli coming her way, so she grinned and giggled, she said, "Just on my way to eat."

"Oh, good, my dear little lady. You go sit at the bar. They vill bring your supper. I vill join you at the bar to talk, ok."

"Ok, see you there soon, Mr. Nardelli."

D got to the bar and was tired. She looked at Dave the bartender and said, "I would like my dinner please and thank you."

Dave nodded and went to the kitchen and asked for it. He came back out and said, "It will be a few minutes. That song you sang was pretty good, you may have a hit with it."

"Well, thank you, Dave. How kind of you to say."

"You're welcome, Cindy."

Cindy ate her supper and enjoyed it; it was filling. She then drank lots of water. She decided to walk to the ladies room for a little break. As she passed the girls, she smiled and acknowledged them. She got in the washroom; one girl was in there, crying and upset.

"What's wrong sweetheart, is there anything I can do for you?"

"I no belong this place, I want to go home."

"What's your name, dear?"

"I am Theresa. I am from the States. I answered an ad for models and went to an audition. Then I ended up here, I have family. They be worried."

"Ok, I'll tell you what, I am going to the washroom. You wait for me here. If someone comes in, you say you are waiting to help Cindy, she asked you for help."

"Ok, I wait."

When D finished, she washed up, then she said, "Follow me." She went to her locker and got her cigarettes. Then she walked with Theresa holding her arm. She said, "Stick by me like you are helping me stand up straight."

"Why? Are you drunk?"

"No, I am sneaking you out to get away. I am handicapped; they all know that."

D walked her out to the back lane and then looked around. There were no workers outside. She turned to Theresa and said, "See the dumpster out in the dark there. Go to it and hide, stay in the dark. There are two cops inside. Friends. I will tell them to pick you up and get you home. Go." D shoved her to move fast. She put her cigarette out and turned to go back in, she was prepared to fall to create a distraction if she had to.

D saw some of Nardelli's men were looking for the girl, then she looked over at Smith and Weston. They were watching her. She was getting closer and then she saw the men coming towards her from the corner of her eye. Just as she reached the table, she faked a fainting spell. As the guys shot up to check on her, she whispered, "I'm faking. Go to the dumpster in the back lane. There's a girl, Theresa, she needs to be picked up and helped to go home."

The guys were pretending to revive her. Mr. Nardelli was right there. He said "Cindy, you ok? Cindy!"

Then D was coming around, and said, "Oh my gosh, what happened?"

Nardelli helped her up. "Are you ok? You passed out. You ate right? I think you should go home and rest, dear. You take tomorrow off, take it easy."

"No, I should be ok. I got dizzy; I was walking too fast. I can finish the shift, please!"

"No, I am sending you home. I vill get Ramone to drive you and help you up the steps to your apartment. He can make sure you get home safe. I vill call you Friday to see how you feel. Remember it's only been a few days since you vere in hospital."

"Oh, ok if you insist. Thank you, Mr. Nardelli! You are very kind to me."

"You are my little lady; I vill look after you for sure. You are very hard vorker."

"Ok let me change."

"No, you go now. I vill make sure you get your belongings."

D was happy to go home; that little bit of theatrics had tired her right out. Ramone took her straight home and helped her into her apartment. Then as though he had an idea, he asked, "You didn't help that girl get away, did you, Cindy?"

"What girl, Ramone?"

"The one I saw you with near the back door."

"No, I didn't I didn't know she left. I walked her to two clients she was afraid to meet. I introduced them and said they were nice men. Then I went for a smoke, I think that's what made me dizzy. Thank you for bringing me home, Ramone. Drive safe going back to the club."

D kicked off her shoes. It was easier to walk then. She made herself a pot of tea and sat on the couch, and just prayed and hoped she was not caught or Nardelli might not be too happy with her. D laid back on the couch and fell back to sleep. She woke up when Alexa got home from work.

"Cindy, you're awake? Mr. Nardelli is upset one girl got out of the club and left. How are you feeling now?"

"I just woke up to you coming in. I guess I wore myself out. I fell asleep in the middle of my tea on the couch. I am just exhausted. I don't know how or why, but just wiped."

"Well, it was a good shift, except for one body is missing."

"Are they sure one of the men did not grab her."

"Nardelli asked his men, he threatened them if they took her, they would pay heavily. Someone blamed you, but Nardelli would not hear of it. He slapped the man for saying that."

"Well, I do not remember taking anyone. I introduced a girl to two men, then went out for a smoke. That's when I came back and passed out. I think I'm going to quit smoking. Well, I should go to bed. I have a headache. I'm glad your shift was good, and that you are safe."

"Cindy, I noticed a couple of things about you. You seem to only smoke when at the club, and you worry about me at the club till I am off and home, what gives? Are you spying on Mr. Nardelli's businesses?"

"Alexa, what gives you that idea? I am appreciative of Mr. Nardelli. He treats me well and not like a possession. I worry about you like if you were my baby sister, is all, and at the club the men there get a funny idea about the girls. They treat the girls like possessions. I don't want you to get hurt at work or after work. Does that resolve you're curiosity now?"

"Yeah, I guess so, but you're friends with those two cops, and I know they are cops. What gives with that they worry about you so much?"

"Yes, they are my friends, I've known them for two years, and they are like my brothers. I love them like brothers, and they love me like a kid sister. They are protective that way. That's our relationship."

"But Jordon, he looks at you with love as a boyfriend. You look at him much the same except sometimes I notice a now's not the time kind of look."

"Ok, I am having feelings for him, and maybe he is having feelings too. But I figure I work at a club; he won't want a girlfriend that works at a club. I'm realistic, I don't pin my hopes on love. They care, and I love that, as well as I care. Please do not tell anyone at the club they are cops. Mr. Nardelli will be very suspicious of my relationship with them. Jordon is an ex-brother-in-law as it is."

"Ok, so you are not spying, and you are friends with the cops. I won't tell anyone, but I heard some of the girls discussing it. I will tell them it is a bad rumor."

"Please, but don't get into trouble, I need this job and so do you. We can't get paid as good anywhere else or taken care of as well. Now I think I am going to get some sleep."

D headed for her bedroom when there was a loud knock on the door. She went to answer it. It was Mr. Nardelli. D opened the door, surprised to see him. "Mr. Nardelli, what are you doing here?"

"I brought your clothes from the club. I vanted to see how you vere feeling."

"Well, that's nice of you, very sweet, but you could have sent them with Alexa. I am feeling a bit better. I fell asleep on the couch once I got home. I woke up when Alexa came home."

"Can I come in or do you have someone here?"

"Oh no, you can come in please; would you like a cup of tea as I was about to make some before bed?"

Mr. Nardelli came in and walked about the apartment, and Alexa said her goodnights to everyone and went to her room. Mr. Nardelli asked Alexa if she was sharing her room with anyone tonight.

"No, I have my own room for me alone."

"Oh, ok then, have a pleasant sleep."

D was getting the tea made and she told Mr. Nardelli to make himself comfortable. She was uneasy as to why he was there but decided not to react but wait and see of his intentions.

D brought the teapot to the table and went back for the sugar and creamer, then the cups. She figured her arm would not like the weight on it. D sat down and asked, "Sugar or cream in your tea?"

"One sugar will be fine thank you. I need to talk to you, Cindy. It is important. I vill not be angry if you are honest vith me, dear, but if you lie, I may be angry and not trust you anymore."

"What, is it Mr. Nardelli? You sound a bit upset." Cindy looked him in the eye.

"Vell, did you help to remove a girl from the club tonight or not?"

"I did not. I remember talking to a girl in the washroom. She had been crying about two of our clients. They were seated at the back by the exit. I told her they were good chaps. I asked her if it would help if I introduced her to them? She said yes we went to the two men I introduced them and then I went out for a smoke."

"You see I ask as everyone thinks you helped her, and I think she is here."

"No Mr. Nardelli, it is only Alexa and I here. I did not help any girl."

Nardelli grabbed D's wrist and twisted it, it was painful. He said, "You do not mind if I look for myself, do you?"

"No, I don't but you are hurting my wrist."

"I vill hurt more than that on you if you are lying!"

Mr. Nardelli then started to look throughout the apartment for the girl and any evidence of her. He even checked Alexa's room. D was worried and in pain. He threw her to the chair to be seated. "You see, Cindy, I know you are not hiding her, but people talk, and then others get in trouble because of that." He stared deeply piercing into her eyes.

D held her wrist it was hurting and bruising. She had tears in her eyes and said, "Maybe people are talking because you treat me kind of special." D kept looking at Nardelli.

"Vell, how do you think I should treat you? Should I make you come to vork tomorrow even if you are sick? Should I slap you around for causing suspicion to me?" He slapped her face. "Just how should I treat you?"

D was dizzy after the slap and started to dry heave from nausea. "I don't know what to say Mr. Nardelli. I respect you and am grateful for my job. I would not jeopardize that for anything." D was feeling sick and wasn't sure about his anger. "I will be into work tomorrow for six. Is that ok with you, Mr. Nardelli?" D was crying.

"I am sorry I have made you feel unvell. Have I? Don't ever lie to me or I vill make you pay for it. I don't like to be played the fool."

Just as Mr. Nardelli was about to leave, he got up and saw Alexa standing there in the dining area. "Alexa did I disturb you?"

"Yes, Mr. Nardelli. I had asked Cindy those questions when I got home. Her answers were the same, unchanged. I think she is right; the staff are jealous you treat her special, so they gossip, and now it has Cindy in trouble. I don't think it's fair."

"Well, I am sorry, Cindy, if I vas vrong, but I question the cameras as they cut out as you talked to the clients. It did not come back until your little fainting spell. From now on I am going to be vatching you and cracking the vhip on you, then the gossipers can be satisfied."

"I understand guilty till proven innocent. I will be into work, and I will work as hard as I can to prove I am a good worker. Goodbye, Mr. Nardelli. Have a good evening."

Cindy was not smiling or crying; she was just stoic. Mr. Nardelli was quiet and left the apartment.

Alexa stood in the doorway and said, "I have never seen him so mad at anyone. Are you ok?"

"Yes, I am fine, that's what jealousy does. He will be fine in a day or two. I wonder who played with the cameras. It could have proven my innocence. Someone is pissed with me being his special Cindy, I am certain of that. Now, I don't feel well. I am going to bed. I'll take a bucket with me. He slapped me, and I am still spinning. Good night, Alexa. Lock up please."

D went to bed and was vomiting; her head was hurting and spinning. Alexa locked up and felt bad but went to bed.

CHAPTER TWENTY-FIVE

The next morning D stayed in bed she slept, as she did not sleep well all night. She was having nightmares of her past, and she just needed to get some rest. She was a bit afraid of Nardelli's temper as well. Alexa knocked at the bedroom door to see if Cindy was ok. D said, "Yes, I am just sleeping."

Then Alexa came to the bedroom door and called to Cindy: "You have a visitor here. He wants to see you."

"Oh, just tell him to go away. I am tired and want to rest. I have work later!" D's bedroom door opened, and she asked, "What? What can't wait till I crawl out of bed?" D rolled over to look and it was Mr. Nardelli with flowers. She slid from the bed to the opposite side and said, "I will be at work on time. I promised you. I keep my word. Now please go leave me alone."

"No, I am not leaving till you accept my apology."

"Ok, I accept your apology, now go."

"I vant you to mean it not just say it!"

"Look you roughed me up last night. I am not going to forget that with a bunch of pretty flowers. I accept your apology; I can't say more than that. Someone messed with those cameras last night and I paid the price. Now go home or to work, I don't much care. I will see you at work."

"You don't have to come into work. I see you are not vell, I will see you Friday. You take it easy today, please."

"Ok, I will take it easy today. Now please leave."

Mr. Nardelli left the apartment, but he took something from under the table, it was likely a listening device. D did not care about the apology; she crawled back in to bed and fell asleep.

Alexa took note of Nardelli's behavior and thought she would fill D in when she got up. D got up an hour later, she looked a fright, but Alexa handed her a cup of black coffee and D thanked her for it.

"You know, Cindy, I couldn't help but notice Mr. Nardelli when he was leaving reached under the table and took something from it. I didn't see what it was, but I suspect it was a listening device."

"Oh great, he's listening in on us." D was not surprised in the least. "I guess from now on be careful what you say around the staff and him. I don't need a repeat of last night."

"I will watch what I say to everyone. I was scared last night I will admit it, but you stayed cool, and did not react."

"What could I do? It was my word against his, and you never win against the boss. I better get dressed. What day is it today? I am just lost."

"It's Thursday, Cindy, all day. The boss told you to stay home."

"I am not staying home I am going to work; I am going to show those lady's I am not special, and I know how to work. I am going to work everyone under the table. I'm just pissed off enough to do it too. They do not realize I take my anger and channel it." D got ready for work. She made some dry toast and had some tea just to have something in her queasy stomach.

"I see you are eating dry toast. Are you nauseated again?"

"Yeah, I better take a Gravol before work. It should last through our shift."

Alexa was a bit worried about Cindy but knew better than to challenge her when she made up her mind.

The two ladies arrived at work and Mr. Nardelli was surprised to see Cindy and he asked her what she was doing there.

Cindy answered while looking at some of the staff; "I am here to work, I do know how to work hard, and that is what I am doing here. Whoever thinks I am something special had better be prepared to outwork a woman with nausea and vertigo. Because that is what I will demand of the staff tonight. Everyone hear that and clear on that!" D looked around to be sure all heard her. Then she went to change into her uniform.

D got to the changing room and had to sit with her head between her knees. She waited a few seconds and got up to change. When she was done, she went to the washroom to throw up. It was rough and then she went out to the club. She saw staff setting tables and grabbed stuff and started setting tables. She used her anger to get the job done. Once the tables were done, she got the stage set. That was done plus the music was loaded onto the board. D went from that to ask what else needed doing. The bar keeper said, "It's all done sit and take a break."

D started thinking of what she could do next. She knew that if she sat still, she would likely pass out. She was about to become sick, so she went into the washroom and was sick.

Mr. Nardelli did not know what to do so he turned to Alexa to ask what got into Cindy.

"She is angry, and she said she would channel her anger energy into work energy. The thing is, she is sick, Mr. Nardelli, but she feels it's her integrity that is in question. She is really upset. I could not get her to stay home. I think she's afraid of getting fired, Mr. Nardelli."

"I vant her to slow down before she falls down. I need her for Saturday's party and show."

"I can talk to her, but I don't think she will listen?"

"You try, dear, you try."

D was coming out of the changing room, and she was seeing double. She realized she had pushed herself too far. "Alexa, I need a chair." As she spoke, she was looking at the double not Alexa.

Alexa grabbed a chair but was too late. D was on the floor. "Cindy, you need to take a deep breath and relax. You need to slow down. Mr. Nardelli is worried about you, Cindy!"

Mr. Nardelli was there, and he said, "I am going to call an ambulance. This is too much I can't handle this." He walked away to phone.

D was too slow responding. "No, no don't call an ambulance," she protested but then she passed out.

Nardelli called for an ambulance, but in doing that the police were also dispatched to the club. He told Alexa that an ambulance was on the way.

He got down on a knee, and he spoke to D, "Cindy, I wish you had stayed home. You've made yourself so sick this time."

Alexa said, "If you hadn't roughed her up last night she might have stayed home. Everyone insinuated she did something she didn't do; she couldn't defend herself. What was she supposed to do?" Alexa was concerned.

Cindy was coming round and started to fight her way through coming to. "No! No! No way, no ambulance!"

"Cindy, are you all, right?" Mr. Nardelli asked.

D was screaming: "Nobody touch me!" She was freaking out. She was out of it and fighting for air. She couldn't breathe and she was blue.

Meanwhile Smith and Weston had answered the call and were on their way to the club.

D tried to get up, fighting against Alexa who was trying to keep her settled. She was holding her chest, "I can't breathe, I can't breathe!" She fell and passed out.

Alexa put a jacket under her head and then put a coat over D to keep her comfortable.

Smith and Weston came in asking, "What has happened?"

EMS came in right behind. Mr. Nardelli told them, "Cindy was upset, she vouldn't stay home. She vanted to prove to me she is a loyal vorker, she vouldn't slow down, and rest, she just kept going till she got sick, she was vomiting and then came out, and passed out. She can't breathe vas all she vas saying vhile fighting everyone off her."

Weston said, "Must be an air embolism!" to the paramedics.

The paramedics worked on her and measured her oxygen saturation. It was seventy-six percent. They said it was likely a pneumothorax and her brain was not getting oxygen so she would be hallucinating. They cranked up the oxygen and rushed her to the hospital. The E.R. doctor recognized D and got the info on her. He figured air was trapped in the lining of the lung and the lung could not expand.

"I told this young lady to take it easy, and she does the opposite!"

The doctor made a cut in her chest and put a tube in, and the air came out. He then clamped the tube and stitched it in place. Then he sent D for an X-ray, her color was back, and she was breathing easy. The X-ray showed the trapped air in the lining of the lung. The doctor opened the tube, and the air was drained. Then they pulled the tube out and hoped the lining would seal itself while the lung was full of air. The doctor put D on bedrest for twenty-four hours and said he would reassess then. The doctor was hoping she did not suffer brain damage. He went out to talk with the police.

"Relax, she is fine, officers. She overdid it and the friction from her movement allowed the lining of the right lung to inflate. As it kept inflating the lung couldn't expand, she couldn't suck enough air in. She is on twenty-four-hour bedrest, and then I will reassess. I had told her she needed to take it easy if I released her. So now I will keep her till she can behave. I only hope she has no lingering brain injury from lack of oxygen. You can go in and see her, she is sleeping though. No excitement."

Smith and Weston went in to talk to D. They were a bit upset with her.

"What the heck is wrong with you, D? You were supposed to take it easy, then you go all John Wayne on everyone, scaring everyone? Do you not know what take it easy means?" As Weston spoke to D, he was getting worked up.

She was not saying anything. D knew she screwed up. She let Weston get angry with her and yell at her. She deserved it and stayed quiet.

Then Jordon stepped in and asked, "What were you thinking D, can you tell me that?"

"I, I was angry."

"Oh, you made that clear! What an idiotic excuse!"

"I was accused of being special," (D made quotation marks in the air) "being favored by Mr. Nardelli. I needed to prove I was a hard worker; I did not want those ladies thinking otherwise."

"And this would prove what? And don't say you are a hard worker, that's just plain stupid and moronic!" Steve wanted D to think about what she did.

"I am not a moron! Mr. Nardelli came over last night he was very angry, you don't know what he's like. I needed to prove myself."

"You let your ego get in the way and risked your life and this case," Jordon said. "What does that make you?"

"Well, I am ok, and I am not going anywhere. I am being made to take it easy." Trying to change the subject, D lowered her voice and whispered, "Hey what happened to Theresa last night?"

"She is fine, she is safe," Jordon stated.

"Hey, you don't get to do that, you can't change the subject, we are ticked off with you!" Steve yelled.

"What? You want me to say sorry, forgive me please. I lost my mind for a moment, I can't, and I won't. I will be out, and the case will be closed. I need to stay focused."

"You lost your mind…you lost your mind…you think? Do you think it's ok to lose your mind, and then say you need to stay focused! God you really are stupid!" Steve was still really angry with her.

D was quiet, and not looking at the two guys. She realized she had made a stupid move. The attendants came and got D to take her to her room. They told Smith and Weston they could follow to her room.

"No, we have to get back to work, she's smart, and she can look after herself." Steve looked at D angry and walked the other way to leave.

D was very hurt by that. She realized they Steve and Jordon had their limits. So, she was taken to her room and once the attendants got her in the bed and left, she was alone, so she cried. She was so hurt by so much and had not let herself cry till that moment.

A nurse came in and asked how D was.

D said, "I'm ok, I don't need anything. Maybe just some Kleenex."

The nurse stated she would get some if D would promise not to cry so hard.

D said, "I can't promise, I don't keep promises."

The nurse came back and said, "If you keep crying this hard, I may get the doctor to order something to calm you, it's not good for your lungs!"

D burst out in to full-out wailing; she was so upset and hurt that the guys had just left disgusted. She tried to stop, "I can't stop, I'm trying but I am so hurt, they called me stupid and a moron." D wailed hard and long.

The nurse said, "I am sure they didn't mean that."

"They just left and didn't even say goodbye," as D cried, all of a sudden, she couldn't suck in air once again.

The nurse called a code, and the doctor came, and he raised the head of the bed. He then ordered a sedative to relax D. He said, "We have to keep her calm."

The nurse said, "She's been crying since she got in the room."

"Where are the two cops who came in with her?" the doctor was asking.

"That must be who she means when she said they just left without saying goodbye. She also said they called her stupid and a moron."

The Doctor was shocked and said, "I will make some calls, but in the meantime, give her Ativan one milligram, every two to four hours when she wakes. That way she will lay still and not get worked up. I'll see if I can get them back here."

D had an oxygen mask placed on her face and she slept very peacefully, she was out cold.

CHAPTER TWENTY-SIX

D slept for some time. Mr. Nardelli came to see D. He had flowers and a card. He left them in her room with a note of apology. He promised to come back to visit, but said that he felt very bad that she got worked up to a frenzy and got sick. He left as quietly as he came in and D kept sleeping. Her breathing was even and every so often she would be sucking air as to catch her breath. As D slept, she started dreaming and having nightmares. She found herself waking up screaming in terror.

The nurse would run in and give her a shot to keep her calm, she would talk to D and reassure she was ok and safe, it was all just a dream. Later the doctor stopped by and asked the nurse if D's friends had stopped by. She said, "No, and no one has called. Her boss came and left her flowers."

"I guess they were really angry with her. I will try again, but this time I will call their Captain. He can send them. I don't want to over drug her unnecessarily. Keep up the good work, Nurse."

D pretty much slept all night with no more issues, but she was crying in her sleep. The nurse would check her every two hours. Then at five in the morning Smith and Weston entered the unit.

They spoke with the nurse, she informed them that D became hysterical, and had to be kept sedated. The nurse made it clear that D was hurt when they abruptly left "after calling her a moron and stupid. They never even said goodbye. That was verbatim. I have no idea what the issue is, but the doctor wants to keep her calm and quiet."

Smith and Weston smirked and thanked the nurse for informing them. They went to D's room and watched her sleep. They quietly talked about D and decided she never worked out her PTSD, not truly anyway. Jordon felt bad that D had got so upset. Then they could hear her crying, like a whimpering in her sleep as they looked at her.

At six a.m. the nurse came in with a needle. She checked D's vital signs then she woke up and said, "What are you doing and why am I here?"

The nurse said, "I am checking your vital signs, and I have more medicine to give you. Is that ok, sweetie? The doctor has ordered you be kept calm for your lungs. How do you feel?"

"Honestly? I feel sad and hurt, but I am fine I won't cry any more. I'm too tired."

"Well, that's good to hear, but I still have to give you your medication," the nurse explained.

Then Jordon came into D's view, and he said, "Hey there, how are you doing?"

"Hi! I'm sorry I made you and Steve angry, it wasn't my intention. I promise I will not act careless or reckless anymore, but I am not a moron or stupid. Don't call me that anymore, please."

"Hey, hey, don't start crying. We came back. We had a call that kept us from checking in. It's ok. We were angry because we could not help you. Just rest. Close your eyes and I will be here when you wake up, ok. Just relax."

D fell asleep and was quiet.

"Maybe we should get some of that shot for her to slow her down," Steve joked.

But Jordon didn't laugh, instead he reminded Steve, "She's had a rough life. Just be kind, that's all she needs right now, Steve."

D slept a long time that morning, she was exhausted. The doctor stopped the sedatives, as he did not want a buildup of drugs. He was happy to see her resting and thanked the guys for coming back in. "It's obvious she cares very much what your opinions are, she takes it straight to her heart, and feels the pain. I don't know her background, but I would say she has suffered years of abuse. Her PTSD is very apparent. So, I stopped her sedative. I am hoping today is a better day for her."

"Thank you, doctor, it's good to know you understand her. We will go easy on her. Thanks for calling us as well."

Steve was starting to feel like a heel that he had got so angry, and it just rolled and built. He was looking at Jordon and said, "You should have stopped me as I got angrier."

"Steve, believe me I was really angry as well! How would I stop you when I was feeling the same way?"

D was waking up and said, "Hey, keep it down partner, I am trying to sleep." Then she started to roll over and look toward the voices. She sat up in bed and said, "You guys came back? Thanks…I am so sorry for everything I did. I didn't mean to insult or hurt either of you. But, hey I am not a moron or an idiot, or stupid, and friends don't call each other that."

D had some tears in her eyes and wiped them away, and said, "I promised the nurse I would not cry. I have to behave myself if I want to be discharged this evening so I can do tomorrow. I need to find out why I couldn't breathe."

Steve said, "You mean you can't remember why you couldn't breathe? The doctor explained it to you last night."

"I don't remember at all, I remember seeing double and feeling dizzy, and then it was like someone was squeezing my lungs, and I couldn't draw air."

"You had a condition that the lining of your right lung was retaining air and the fuller it got, the less your lung could expand till you couldn't breathe. You were so worked up in a frenzy the friction of movement of your body triggered the condition. It also could have been the vomiting that didn't help. Your punctured lung was the culprit. That's why the doctor told you, you need to take it easy. They put a tube in and let the air out and then you were able to breathe. I believe that's how the doctor explained it."

Jordon said, "Yes, that is how it was said. All I can say is you must have been quite scared."

"It would be scary, as it would make me claustrophobic, and I freak out. My brothers locked me up once and forgot me. That's why I panic in closed spaces."

"You have brothers? You never talked about that before." Jordon smiled and got excited.

"I had brothers. I haven't seen them since I was twelve, when my parents died. I don't even know if they are alive."

"Speaking about alive or dead, who is Jessie? You sang about her."

"Well Jordon, it's a bit of a tale... Jessie is my daughter; she was two years old when she passed. She was a preemie and had a bad heart. She needed a new one but had a rare blood type, so they never found her a heart. She was a lively child and was not afraid of anything. I went to work, and my ex-husband fell asleep while watching her. She was playing in the yard. It was hot, and she got heat stroke. He didn't call her in. She had heat stroke. She died playing and not knowing. They couldn't bring her back, she was free." D was trying not to cry, she rarely told anyone about her daughter. "The song just came to me, I felt like Jessie was talking to me, that she was with me. You guys think I'm crazy, right?"

The guys had lumps in their throats. Jordon spoke, "No, no you're not crazy, just it's a sad story. And it must have been hard on you."

"That's why I am not married anymore. I was young, seventeen when I got married, I was too young for anything, let alone a child." D was crying, but not hard just softly. "Jordon, I didn't tell you to get sad. I was happy to have the thoughts I put into words."

"Now you know more about me. I have a lot of baggage; I don't know if anyone is able to deal with it. It's hard to make long lasting friends when I have to keep moving and changing my identity."

D lay back down and in came the breakfast tray. So, D sat up and was very polite and thankful. She ate the toast, had the tea and ate the fruit. She left the rest. She lay back again. She was out of breath; her oxygen mask was removed while she ate. She was quite tired and started to doze off in the middle of saying something.

Smith and Weston were listening, but she never finished. They wondered if the sedatives did that to her. She was short of breath while sleeping. The nurse came in and tested her oxygen level. It was low at eighty six percent.

"It should be at least ninety two percent," said the nurse. She put the oxygen mask back on D to get it up. D's breathing leveled out and was not labored anymore. The nurse left.

Then Mr. Nardelli came in to visit D. He saw the two detectives and asked, "How is my Cindy today?"

"She is stable, she had a good scare, and I don't think she will be doing any races any time soon," was Jordon's response.

"You are the two policemen at the club last night when I called for an ambulance."

"Yes, I am Steve Weston, a detective, and this is Jordon Smith, also a detective. We responded to the call. You're Cindy's boss then."

The men shook hands.

"Oh, good morning Mr. Nardelli. I am sorry for the trouble I caused you last night. I wasn't thinking right, I am sorry."

"I think we will go get coffees while you two visit," Steve pulled Jordon to walk with him.

"Good morning, Cindy, I hope you are feeling vell?"

"Oh, I am much better, thank you. And thank you for the flowers; they are beautiful. I am sorry I got so angry last night."

"It is all right, now I know not to make you angry, ha-ha. You scared me, I thought I vas going to lose you."

"No, I am ok, but when the doctor released me the first time, they told me to take it slow. I did not and then I worked myself up yesterday. I was sick and didn't take care. I got sicker. I promised the doctor I was going to behave this time. I won't be at work tonight, I am sorry"

"Vell, I blame myself too, I did rough you up the night before last. I didn't help matters. I made you sick when I hit you, didn't I, and I am sorry."

"Well, I guess we are two sad sorry people then Mr. Nardelli. I forgive you if you will forgive me."

"Oh yes, my dear Cindy, yes I forgive you." The two hugged and forgave each other and Mr. Nardelli was pleased. "You will be able to make the party, will you? You just have to be there; you do not have to work. I can get someone else to organize the models."

"I will do my best and follow doctor's orders to be there. Only if the doctor says it's ok though."

"Vell, that sounds very fair. I vill make it easy for you. I vill have lots of chairs around for you to sit. Do you think you vill be able to sing your song you vrote? The band can do all the other vork."

"I will ask the doctor if I can."

"I vill have a chair in the change room for you to advise the models, and organize their lineup, and Alexa can assist you."

"Ok, sounds fair. I will do my best."

"Ok, then you take care, and I will see you tomorrow at the house."

Mr. Nardelli left the room and Smith and Weston came in the room. They had a coffee for D. They were smiling, as it sounded positive in the room.

"D, why did you not tell us he roughed you up the night before last?"

"I could not call; I was sick when he left. I was sick all night. Then in the morning Alexa said it looked like he removed a bug from under the table. She got the feeling he bugged us to find out the truth."

"Yeah, well finding out too late that he roughed you up does not feel so great for us," Steve was concerned.

"He twisted my arm, and slapped my head, and threw me on the chair. He was mad that one of his girls went missing."

"He suspected you, did he? How? You created a distraction."

"He listened to the ladies gossip; they are jealous of me, Steve. They accused me of taking the girl. And when he checked the surveillance cameras, something happened as I went outside for a smoke; the cameras malfunctioned, so he thought I was guilty. That's why I got angry. My defense mechanism."

"Your anger is your defense mechanism?"

"Yeah, I channel that energy to fight or flight."

"You like to fight I take it."

"No, I always feel bad after I fight. I choose peace, not fighting. I feel bad when I get angry with anyone as it creates a negative energy, like yesterday, and I paid for it. Bad Karma."

"You are a strange little lady!"

D giggled and smiled, "I am not strange! I am likably different."

"Oh, you are little, and you have a lot of quirks, and you might be cute, but you are trouble," Steve said.

Jordon just winked at D when Steve said it. And she grinned and gave out a little giggle. Jordon teased he; "Well, I guess you are a spark of trouble to beware of then! I've taken note, beware of tiny spark! Could cause catastrophic explosions if triggered."

D made a face and said, "Now, let's not start the small jokes again, my feelings can get hurt." Then D laid down she rolled over to take a nap.

"Wait a minute, little missy, we need to discuss what is happening tomorrow. We need to make a plan."

"Oh, Steve I am tired, when I wake up again, please!"

Steve looked at Jordon and was confused. "She's the one that wants to break this case, and now she wants to sleep."

Jordon said, "Well let's let her sleep till lunch then we will have a serious meeting to discuss the plan." Jordon said it loud enough D heard him and let a little giggle out. Then she snuck out a "Thank You."

D did fall asleep, and she was tired. She slept when the lunch tray came, all the noise and she didn't wake up. She kept sleeping. Steve and Jordon had left to pick up their lunch and arrived to see D sleeping still. Steve checked her tray and saw she had not eaten. He shook his head and thought here we go, not watching her sugars. So, they ate and let her sleep a little longer.

Jordon said, "There is not much to plan, we went over it well on Monday and Tuesday."

Steve said, "A plan works when everyone can go through it correctly in a meeting. So, we should wake her up to eat and talk." Steve turned towards the bed. "D, time to wake up and have your lunch. D! Wake up we need to talk." Steve cranked the head of the bed up for D to sit up. She woke up and stretched and yawned.

"Is it lunch time already? I'm not even hungry yet."

"That's ok. We need to talk; we need to go over tomorrow's plans."

"Ok, ok, let's get this over with."

Jordon put her lunch tray in front of D and uncovered it. It was Mac and Cheese, with beets and coleslaw. D saw it and made a face, then was gagging like she was going to be sick.

"What are you actually going to be sick over the lunch?" Jordon asked

"Pardon me, I don't mean to do that in front of everyone, but I just cannot look at that food. I'll take the coffee, or tea that is on the tray, and the milk, and juice."

Jordon was removing those things and D said, "Just a minute, I'll eat the beets."

"Picky eater, are we?" Steve was laughing.

"I'm not picky. I made a deal with myself choose what you can handle, D, and keep your sugars leveled. Macaroni - that is soggy, makes me gag. It's automatic, I get sick. Coleslaw usually has too much horse radish. I can smell it; it reminds of the barns at the racetrack. I just don't want to get sick in front of you guys, that's all."

"You are one strange little lady!" Jordon just let that slip out automatically.

D ate what she said she would eat and drank her juice and milk. She sipped at her coffee, and found it was cold and tea - she made a face.

"Nothing like expecting to taste coffee and it's cold! Weak tea, yuck."

"How do you know what the barns at the racetrack smell like?" Jordon was curious.

"That's for me to know, and not you. I have things that are in the past and stay there. I am not a strange lady either. Let's get on with the plans for tomorrow."

"Can you honestly tell me you are full from that lunch?" Steve was concerned.

"I am as full as I can be without getting sick, in all honesty. So, what do you want to know about tomorrow?"

"Just a minute there, D. I am going to go get you something." Steve left the room and D said, "What is wrong with him? I ate and drank; can't he just be happy."

Jordon said, "Really, D, beets? They're going to keep you going till dinner. Let's be real, you need to have energy, and your sugars will not last till three, so he likely went to get you a sandwich."

"I am not a big eater. I would last till dinner, but if it were later, I might be in trouble. I don't like to complain." D reached for the card on the table and took it out of the envelope. She started to read the card. It said, "Get well, see you tomorrow at the Whelminton Avenue Home. I will never lose you, Cindy, you are my girl. The outfit I have for you is special. I will have the bidding high, you will be the last girl, I will not let you go or get hurt. Just get well! Mr. Nardelli."

"I think you need to see this card I was given," D handed the card to Jordon.

"We will make sure Steve sees this card as well." Jordon looked up and Steve was there. He put the soup and sandwich on the table for D, said, "Eat up," and grabbed the card to look at.

D opened her soup and unwrapped her sandwich. She started to eat as she looked at Steve. "I guess he wants to get paid for hanging on to me, without letting me go."

"Ok, so you know you need to stay in the open, no hiding as we need to grab you as soon as the sting starts." Steve had a serious look on his face.

"But just who is going to make sure they grab her in the melee of the evening?" Jordon was worried about D.

"I think I will arrange for Officer O'Reilly to grab and cuff her, straight off. D, you need to make yourself stand out ready to grab. Let him put the cuffs on you, and take you out of the place. Ok, you got that. We will do everything to keep you safe, D. You just have to promise us you will be where we can find you. I think we will bug the floral arrangements tomorrow in the a.m."

D finished the sandwich and soup Weston brought her and thanked him for it. He left the room and came back in with a coffee for each of them. She had a big grin when she saw it and said, "Thanks Steve a real coffee, you're a life saver!"

"Anytime D, if a coffee is saving your life, anytime." Steve had a grin on his face, because D had a grin and a giggle like a child at Christmas. A hard thing to resist. Jordon took note of his infectious smile coming out.

"Ok D, I think we will let you sleep; we have some paperwork to get done and we have to round up the officers we need for the sting. We will stop by at supper and see how you are doing."

"Ok, thank you Steve, I'll see you both later ok." D finished her coffee.

D lay down as she was tired. She actually thought she was quite tired and couldn't believe how tired she was. She was falling asleep and didn't fight it. The nurse came in to check her. She saw she was asleep and thought she would leave her be. As D slept, she began dreaming and was restless. She was dreaming of being choked and not being able to breathe or scream. She was thrashing and fighting in her sleep and woke up screaming, "I can't breathe, I can't breathe."

The nurse came running in and started to wake D, "It's just a dream, Cindy. Wake up it's just a dream."

D woke up and was holding the nurse tight and crying, "I couldn't breathe, I just couldn't breathe."

The nurse was comforting D: "It's alright, it was just a dream, Cindy. Just take some deep breaths, nice and slow. It was a bad dream, that's all. Ok you are doing better now?"

"Yeah, I am. I can breathe. Please don't tell anyone I had a nightmare, please?"

D was crying a bit, and the nurse gave her Kleenex and said, "If you start crying again and can't get it together, I will have to tell the doctor. I think you scared half the ward hahaha with your screams."

D giggled and said, "I am sorry if they ask."

"Ok, I will pass that on if you would like. The doctor will be making rounds soon and he will decide if you can go home tonight."

"Alright, that sounds great. I hope he lets me out. I have behaved and when I go home, I plan to rest and take it easy."

"I know you are trying hard to stay well, but I think after this case you are working on, you need to seek help with your PSTD. It is coming out strong. It could interfere with your work; it could cost you or someone else their life. Please get the help you need?"

"I will I promise. You are a good nurse. You know that I got the message, and I didn't have to be yelled at either."

"Oh well thank you, I just see it as sad you struggle with anger and remorse. Your focus would be so much better. And control of situations, would be better as well as judgement calls."

"Thank you for the insight. I do try to keep focused, and I know I let my anger control me, instead of my being under control. You know anyone I might want to talk to, who I could keep it confidential with?"

"I think I will ask the doctor to write you a referral. How does that sound, Cindy?"

"Sounds great, thank you, I am feeling better already."

D sat waiting in her room quietly and patiently, she was hoping the nurse would keep her word. And she was ready to go home. Mr. Nardelli came in to visit.

D smiled and said, "Hi." As well she thanked him for the get-well card and said it was sweet.

"You look very good Cindy, rested and healthy. Have you heard if they vill let you out tonight?"

"No, I have not heard yet, Mr. Nardelli. I will give you a phone call if I can go home, I promise. But I am going home and straight to bed to rest. I want the doctor to trust me. I want everyone to trust me. My behavior yesterday was inexcusable."

"You just have some anger issues, that's all."

"No, I have PTSD, and I need to deal with it."

"From vhat did you get the PTSD? I don't understand."

"My life has not been an easy one, Mr. Nardelli. I lost my parents at an early age. My brother abused me and dumped me at twelve. I got married young, it was a mistake. My list is too long to cover but trust me, if I suspect someone feels I've been disloyal, I will work myself to death to prove it, like the other night."

"My dear Cindy, I trust you, I love you, you have not realized that yet. Ve vill get you help to vork on that. I vant to look after you! You are like a daughter."

"Well, thank you, Mr. Nardelli, that is reassuring. You are sweet and yes like a father sweet. I will see you tomorrow at the party." D gave Mr. Nardelli a hug and a kiss on the cheek. She smiled and giggled as always. Mr. Nardelli said goodbye and he left. About a half hour later the doctor came in and visited D and was chatting and examining her.

She told him, "I promised my boss I would rest at home if I got out of here, I would be at his party, but as a guest, and he said there would be chairs everywhere for me to sit. He knows I need to rest. But he wanted to know if I would be ok to sing one song with the band. I just wrote it, and he likes it."

"Well Cindy, I will be honest with you, I wasn't going to release you, but the nurse told me about your conversation about your PTSD, I will write your referral for you. I think you lost sight of being seriously injured due to PTSD, and that's what got you in trouble. If you can keep yourself in a calm positive mind frame, I will release you tonight. First, I want to run tests for you, I've ordered them, and they will start when I leave. If they all come back normal, you can go home after supper, does that sound fair?"

"It sounds very reasonable, and I will go through them. I will pass them; I know I will."

"Just a minute, Cindy." The doctor looked serious. "There is one test, you may not want, but I need it to be sure. It's a pregnancy test. When you came in with your head injury and other injuries, the staff neglected the one test that is compulsory in the ER. We never checked to see if you were assaulted. I am sorry, the ER was very busy that night, and then you needed your brain surgery. Do you understand this, Cindy?"

"Yes, I do, I think, it is serious, but don't tell anyone please. No one needs to know this minute. It will create worry and doubt for our case. If I am, I will have to deal with it?" D was very upset with that piece of news but was willing to accept the test.

CHAPTER TWENTY-SEVEN

"Ok, I will get things started blood work first and then X-ray, and CT scan."

"That won't hurt the fetus if there is one, will it?"

"Do not worry about that for now, after everything you've gone through. We will worry about that later, ok? Ok, well here is the lab technician. Good luck dear."

The doctor left and he gave the go ahead to discharge Cindy. D fully cooperated with all the tests.

D asked the lab technician, "How long will it be for the result of the specific tests to come back?"

"That depends, are we talking the bunny dyeing or blood cell counts, that you want to know?"

"The pregnancy test, how long will it take to come back?"

"Not long, we could put a rush on it if you would like then. We need you to pee for us."

"Ok I'll do it now…Thanks for the work you do," D shouted from the washroom. Then came out and handed the sample to the tech.

D was a bit nervous thinking of what was not a planned occurrence. She decided to walk down to the nurse's station and talk to the nurse as she was feeling like freaking out.

The nurse saw her, and asked, "Is there anything I can do for you Cindy? I'll be going off duty shortly."

"Yes, please could you let the nurse coming on duty know, I want the result of the pregnancy test but in private, not in front of any visitors. I don't want to upset the detectives with this crazy problem."

"Sure, Cindy, I can do that. Are you ok?"

"Yeah, I am ok. I am going to go back to my room, as I know I have tests to be picked up for."

D thought about this unexpected problem and decided she would deal with it after the sting. She would just get the tests done then go home. She sat for a few minutes, had some tears, and the transport came to take her to the X-ray, then on to the CT scan. D thought about everything and she decided to take everything one moment at a time, one step at a time. Put her trust in God. If Austin did rape her, she would deal with it. She was having a few weepy moments at a time and told herself; "Once you're home, you can cry quietly in bed."

D was back in her room, she saw the X-ray it looked good, her lungs looked normal. Her CT scan showed her brain was good. It was just the blood work she had to wait for. A nurse came in and said she could go home after supper if she wanted. So, D got dressed to go but was waiting. She was looking out the window and pacing. Then she heard footsteps in the hall they were familiar.

Smith and Weston came in the room. D turned and smiled at them.

They asked, "You're dressed. Does that mean…?"

"Yep, I can go home, straight home do not pass go do not collect two hundred dollars."

The guys laughed and said, "Well I am sure we could stop for a decent supper for you."

"Well, I promised the doctor I would take it easy and rest."

"We will make sure you do, ok?"

Soon a nurse came in and saw the two guys, and she called D out of the room. She said, "Congratulations it's positive." D's heart sank. She walked back into the room and said, "Ok guys, let's go!"

But suddenly, D started gaging and dry heaving. She felt like she was going to be sick. She went into the washroom and vomited. She washed up and came out, and said, "Ok I am ready to go."

The guys were looking at D and asked, "What the hell was that all about?"

"I turned and came into the room too fast, got dizzy, and nauseous and threw up, I'm sorry."

"But your smile left after the nurse spoke to you, what was that and the vomiting?" Jordon insisted on knowing.

"Oh, I'm fine. The nurse reminded me to take it easy. I got a whiff of the trays; it's making me nauseous. Let's go before I get sick again."

"Alright, well, let's go the boss has spoken. We don't want to see her get sick again."

They left and walked to the car D was breathing in deep for the fresh air, it was cool and crisp, they opened the car door for her.

She asked, "Could I sit in the back, I want the window open, the air is nice and crisp, I love Fall."

Then Jordon said, "What? You don't want to ride up front?"

"Ok, I will sit up front." D got in the car, even though she was feeling sick, because she did not want to disappoint Jordon. D sat quietly but then closed her eyes and tilted her head a bit to alleviate her ill feeling.

Then Steve said, "D, you are awfully quiet, you ok?"

"Yes, I am fine, just tired. I had to go through a battery of tests before they agreed to let me go home." She kept her eyes closed as she spoke.

Steve could see that as he listened, "What's with your eyes being closed?"

"I am just easing my vertigo, that's all."

They got to Zack's and Steve parked.

"We are here. Order what you want. Poutine and burgers, anything."

D started to dry heave and she pushed Jordon out and said, "I'm going to be sick again."

She leaned against the car and was losing what was left in her stomach.

Jordon was concerned, "Are you ok, D? You seem pretty sick."

"I am fine, just hungry, I guess. Stop asking if I am ok, please!"

They all entered Zack's, and D went to the washroom to freshen up and wash up.

When Zack came to take the orders, Steve said, "We are waiting for D; she is taking a powder."

"What do you suppose is up with D? She has bouts of stomach upset and vertigo. You would think there is something up with her?"

Jordon was concerned, but Steve said, "It's likely nerves."

D came back and sat down with the guys, she was pale, no color. She sat across from the guys, so she was trying to look perky.

"You ok D, feeling better I hope?" Steve asked with a smile.

"I am fine. Geez, can't a girl get a break from the questions. I am fine. Not to worry."

Zack came by with Ice water, and D just downed the whole glass, and asked for a refill.

"Wow, you didn't get a brain freeze from that D?" Jordon was surprised.

"Well, I am just feeling a little warm and thirsty. It seems so warm in here. I need some cool air, order me anything." D got up and went toward the back door and stood in the cold air. Just breathing it in.

When she came back to the table, she felt a bit better, and sipped her ice water. "See I am fine, just a little flustered, that's all."

Steve said he was concerned, "Why are you suddenly always sick, you would think there was something up with you."

"I am fine, I need a good rest. It's my nerves is all. They will settle once I eat and relax."

Zack brought burgers and fries and said, "Oops, forgot the poutine."

D said, "Don't worry about it, Zack. This is fine, really. I am hungry."

The guys were stunned that D had said no to poutine.

"She's sick, I know it now, she's not eating poutine," Jordon said.

"I'm not sick for the thousandth time. I am fine. Hey, are we still on for tomorrow, no backing out, right?"

"As long as you are not sick tomorrow."

"I am fine. I passed all the tests at the hospital. The doctor would not have released me if any came back funny."

"Yeah, I guess you're right. We are on for tomorrow."

They all enjoyed their meal and for a little while at least D forgot about her test result and was joking with the guys, she seemed normal. She started yawning and asked, "Oh my, what time is it? I am yawning away; it must be late?"

"It's going on seven, hahaha, old lady!" Jordon thought it was funny, but he knew she must be tired.

"Well, I guess we should take granny home so she can get some sleep." Steve went along with the joking.

"Well thanks fellas! I appreciate the late dinner and the comedy," D smiled and giggled. They all got in the car and Steve drove D home; Jordon walked her to her door. He checked her place for safety, Alexa was there so he said goodnight to D and left.

Alexa said to D, "You need to phone Mr. Nardelli. He has been looking for you!"

"Oh yeah, I forgot to phone him, he must be worried about where I was."

"Yeah, he was upset. You had promised to call him, and you didn't."

"Ok, I am calling him now." D dialed his number and he answered immediately. "Mr. Nardelli, it's Cindy. I am sorry, I went out for supper. I was hungry, and the restaurant was busy, so I was a bit late. Yes, I am fine. My tests were good, I am free to go tomorrow, but I must take it easy. Ok, thank you I appreciate that, I will see you around noon then, oh one would be better. Ok, the driver will be here at one tomorrow. Thank you and goodnight."

"Alexa, you are going to be my assistant tomorrow, so you will stick close to me. We have to be ready to go at one tomorrow, I hope that's ok." D thought to herself for a moment and felt like crying again. "I'm going to take a shower, Alexa, then I am going to bed, ok?'

"Ok Cindy, have a good sleep. I am watching a movie then I'll go to bed."

D gathered her stuff and got in the shower. She started crying quietly but as she thought of the pregnancy, she got upset more, and was balling at the thought of being raped while out of it. D was thinking on a whole new level of how she was violated. She did not want this life.

She was bawling at this point and Alexa knocked on the door and shouted, "Cindy, are you ok in there?"

"Ah yes, I am fine, sorry I was just having memories. I'm a little emotional, probably just tired."

"Can I do anything for you, Cindy?"

"No, I will be fine, I'm almost done then I'll be in bed, thanks anyway."

D stopped crying and finished up her shower. She got into some cozy pj's and a robe, then took her stuff from the shower to the bedroom. There was a knock on her door. Alexa had a cup of tea for her. She thanked Alexa; thought of how sweet a gesture it was. She hugged Alexa and said goodnight. D went to bed and cried herself to sleep into her pillow. She woke up in the morning before her alarm to nausea and had to rush to the bathroom to be sick. She came out, went to the kitchen and got some soda crackers to eat, then a glass of water, and back to bed for a little while longer.

Alexa had heard Cindy and wondered what was up. She made more tea, and knocked on Cindy's door. "Cindy, I have some tea here for you. Can I come in?"

"Yes, Alexa, thank you so much that is sweet of you." D sat up in bed and Alexa handed her the tea.

"Cindy, are you sure you are fine, you're not pregs, are you?"

D started to cry, but said, "No, I am not. I think it's my nerves is all. Don't share those thoughts with anyone please!" D sipped the tea, it was soothing, and it helped D feel better. "Hey Alexa, thanks for the tea. It really helped. I appreciate those little things you do for me. You'll make a great assistant today."

"You are welcome, Cindy. I don't mind, you look after me, I look after you. Kind of a 'you and me' thing going for us."

"You are right. And tonight, I want you sticking by my side, ok, just to be safe."

"Cindy, can I ask you something in confidence?" Alexa said it quietly. D nodded yes. "I am not blind; I get the sense you are working undercover for the cops. Right?" Alexa whispered to D.

D answered as quietly as she could, "Would it make a difference in our friendship?"

Alexa smiled and said, "No."

D whispered, "I am a cop, you cannot say anything or let it slip ok? I am trusting you with my life here. You and me!"

Alexa hugged D and said, "Of course we are best friends." She went ahead and made some toast for D, and said, "I am just going to get ready, here's a pot of tea and some dry toast for those nerves."

The two ladies got ready to go, and their ride picked them up, and drove them to the house on Whelminton Avenue. D was so nervous and not sure how the evening was going to go, but Mr. Nardelli met the ladies at the car and led them to the guest house where all the other ladies were. He handed D a package and said,

"This vill help you organize. Vhen you are all ready, come to the main house. It looks like rain tonight."

D opened the package and found model cards all in order of showing and instructions to the models, so she got Alexa involved and they started organizing. There were makeup ladies to work with the models. Some of the fashions were very nice, and some were outrageous. D hadn't looked at hers yet, but was about to. She opened the garment bag, and she was wowed. It was a shimmering white to silver gown with a low cut back, it flared out a bit with a slit, not in the back but not on the side, it ran just behind the side of her body. The shoes were gorgeous, they were raised three inches. D got into it, and felt she looked grown up in it. Then the makeup girl worked on her, and the hair stylist did her thing. When all was said and done, D looked like a bride. Alexa was gob-smacked, and really was amazed how Cindy was transformed.

D said, "If your gob stays open any longer, you're going to catch flies Alexa!" as she smiled and giggled.

Alexa asked, "What is a gob?"

"It's your mouth, silly."

D wanted a good look at Alexa, she had a crimson red ball gown on, with a chenille crimson red scarf attached at the neck and shoulders scarf, and a low cut back. She looked beautiful and D told her so. Alexa had the works done as well. They all looked great in the designer fashions. D had them all line up in order and asked them to remember their order for when the modeling was to begin. Also reminded them to not overdo the beverages and food, and pace themselves throughout the evening. D told them to do Mr. Nardelli proud this evening and that they all looked great.

The ladies all went to the mansion and were escorted to a small ball room where they were to wait. D and Alexa were taken on a tour of the set up. The photographers were very busy with photos. Mr. Nardelli entered the reception room. He looked very handsome in his tuxedo, his hair was done, and he was wearing beautiful jewelry. He looked around and saw D. He walked toward her and greeted her.

"Cindy, you are very beautiful this evening. I told you I vould design a dress that vould make you look older. Alexa, you too are very beautiful.

"Thank you, Mr. Nardelli. It is very sweet of you to say. All of your fashions are very good. They are beautiful and flattering to all the models. I am left being gob-smacked at it all." D grinned and giggled as she finished.

"Gob-smacked? Vhat is that?"

"Jaw dropping, mouth stuck open in awe. That's all I mean."

"Vell, that is a cute vay to say it. Come, follow me for a moment, I vant to speak to you in private."

"Ok, Mr. Nardelli. What is it you want to tell me?" D asked as she was puzzled.

"Call me Antonio, tonight. I vant to adjust your gown, I can see the binding for your ribs. Do you think you could not vear it tonight?"

"I don't know, Antonio. I have a broken rib, and it's to keep it set in place. I would worry about my breathing without it."

"Ok, then I vill give you a shawl to vear over your back to cover it. It is all I vanted to say, you are so beautiful tonight."

"Oh, thank you, Antonio. I feel beautiful tonight."

CHAPTER TWENTY-EIGHT

D returned to the main room and noticed a few guests had arrived. She looked around and found Alexa. She signaled she wanted to sit for a while. The band came in, and D noticed there were a few extra members. She went to talk to her lead guitarist.

"Who are the extra guys? Where did they come from?"

"Mr. Nardelli hired a few musicians to play tonight. There is a violinist, a horn player, a percussionist, and a pianist. He said he wanted your song to be played well. He wants to see how it is received. He wants to record it; didn't he tell you?"

"No, Antonio did not say anything. I will act surprised, which won't be hard. Thanks."

D went back to sit down, and then asked Alexa to go check on the ladies and to tell them to be ready. D sat quietly admiring all of the beautiful flowers, and the décor. She decided to look out the window to see if she could see any surveillance. She did not expect to see anything. She noticed it was raining pretty hard, then she saw some lightning. D was not a fan of lightning storms.

"Vhat are you looking for, Cindy?"

"I'm not looking for anything, I am just noticing it's raining hard, and there is lightning. I hope the power doesn't go off, Antonio."

"Perhaps you should sit for a minute, and rest before we start the show."

D went and sat down. There were guests still coming into the room. They were coming out of the west room, a library. D stood next to a floral arrangement admiring it, then leaned into sniff, and said quietly, "Coming in from a west room, library." Then she went and sat. She thought if the flowers were bugged, they would hear that. D was having butterflies in her stomach because she was nervous. She had no idea how the cops would enter for the raid, or when.

Mr. Nardelli was calling Cindy to the front. Cindy and Alexa went to the stage, and he asked for the fashion show to start. He had a stool brought on stage next to the microphone. D sent Alexa to bring the ladies in order.

"Good evening, ladies and gentlemen, we have a beautiful fashion show for you tonight. It will be a silent auction to own the patterns of my styling," Mr. Nardelli stated. "I will turn the stage over to Cindy, my right hand."

Cindy cleared her throat to speak, and then stated, "Let the fashion show begin. Our first Fall celebration begins with Debra. She wears an orange taffeta, and channel gown, reminding us of falling leaves in a lively vibrancy. Welcome Debra to the stage."

"Next, we have Bonnie. She is wearing a bewitching hour black crepe pantsuit, with Italian leather boots and gloves to accentuate the outfit. Welcome Bonnie."

"Now we have a real special design being worn by Nicolette. It is playful and excites the senses, with the layered Fall colors, of silk, all the colors that develop in the full Fall weather, as they fall on the body in a sensual way. Thank you, Nicolette." She the model danced across the stage and looked like a fairy.

D continued through all of the models, and was down to Alexa. She cleared her throat and introduced Alexa as her assistant, and Alexa came on stage, and spun and walked playfully in her crimson colored ball gown. She was beautiful, D mentioned it and also that Alexa assisted with the fashion show.

Then D took the microphone and introduced herself as Cindy, and started to walk down the stage, spinning, and showing off her iridescent white to silver ball gown, and stated any woman would feel beautiful in this gown. Then she called all the models to come back onstage for one more runway walk to show off their outfits. D was hoping they got her description through the bugs. She was worried but kept smiling.

The models took their time showing their gowns. Then Mr. Nardelli thanked his models and his guests for attending his gala, he wished everyone a wonderful time and said, "Bidding closes in one hour."

D was surprised that there was only an hour to bid. The models were allowed to mingle and then they would change before the end of the evening.

D enjoyed a small bit of mingling and then Mr. Nardelli introduced her for singing her new song. D got up to walk to the stage, and she looked at her band and held the mic. She hummed a bit of the intro, then began singing. As she sang the words she was fighting choking up as it was stirring thoughts about her pregnancy. She had some tears rolling down her cheeks and started to increase the tones of her singing of the song.

She really liked the bands playing, it sounded so professional with the instruments mixing in. When she finished singing, "I want to thank the band and Mr. Nardelli for making my song sound so special. The crowd wanted to hear her sing some more, so she told the band that the next song would be "All of Me."

She belted it out, she was enjoying singing. By the time she had sung a few numbers, Mr. Nardelli signaled her to take a break. D went to Mr. Nardelli and thanked him for his added instruments to the band.

"You take a break now, I have a meal for you in the vaiting room, you can rest, yes?"

"Yes, I will do that, thank you, you are so sweet."

"I vill join you in a few minutes. My men are going to announce the vinners of the bids."

"Ok, see you in a few minutes."

Mr. Nardelli sent the models out to mingle. He went back out with them, Alexa stayed to the side.

"Find a way to stay close, Alexa, even if you hide behind the curtains. Be safe," Cindy said.

Mr. Nardelli came in to sit with D. He was wondering where Alexa was. "Vhere did Alexa run off to? Do you know, Cindy?"

"I am not sure, maybe to freshen up or something." D was eating her bits of fruit, cheese and crackers plate. She was hungry. She asked, "Did you want me to sing another set of songs, Antonio?"

"No, I want you to walk beside me as I talk to my guests. I want you to rest. Don't overdo it."

D was holding her side. She was having some discomfort; she wasn't sure if it was something she ate or just nerves. Then she heard noise coming from the other room. "What was that?" She looked at Mr. Nardelli surprised.

He got up to look and then said, "The police are coming in! Vhat are they doing here?"

D was shocked they were coming in before the buys were announced. She looked surprised to Antonio and he grabbed her arm and said, "Come with me."

They exited through a secret door behind a curtain. Alexa saw it and stayed where she was. She was close to a window; she could get out if she needed to.

D was being pulled along by Mr. Nardelli, and he was yelling, "Hurry up! Move it!"

D was running as fast as she could in the dress and said, "The shoes are hard to run in! Where are we going?"

Mr. Nardelli stopped and then took D's shoes off and threw them to the side, he grabbed her again, and said, "The police are busting in, they will not arrest me or you, I will not let them find you."

"Antonio, why would they arrest us? We have done nothing wrong!"

"They have been trying to get to me for years, they don't need a reason. Now move it!"

D was worried she was going to be stuck with Mr. Nardelli if she didn't get away. So, she was watching for her chance to break away, since she had not been arrested. They were in the tunnels. She didn't know her direction or anything.

Meanwhile up above, the police were arresting everyone in the main area that were betting and buying. There were a lot of city councilors on the take and at the event. They were protesting being arrested. The cops were telling them to tell their lawyers. Smith and Weston were trying to round up Nardelli's men and the girls. Then someone started shooting.

Weston got a bullet in his shoulder. He was in pain but shot the guy who shot him.

Smith ran to his side and asked, "You ok, West?"

"Yes, I am fine, just my shoulder." Then Weston saw O'Reilly with Alexa and yelled, "Where's D, O'Reilly?"

"I am trying to find her to arrest her! She disappeared."

Alexa was trying to tell O'Reilly where D was, but he was not listening. She decided to wait for the chaos to die down.

Meanwhile, Smith and Weston found themselves in a full out gun fight. They were hoping D had gotten away, but they doubted it.

D was trying to keep up with Nardelli. He was taking her through as many tunnels as He could to get away. They heard people running in the tunnels, then Nardelli stopped to pull his gun out, and he was ready to shoot. He was using D as a shield.

"Keep back or I will shoot!" Nardelli was ready to fight, then the cops came into sight. He shot his gun; D was trying to get away. He held her tight. The cops were blindly shooting, and D was hit in the abdomen.

"Ouch, oh my God that hurts like fire!" D screamed.

Nardelli screamed, "They hit you? No, you are no good to me." He got up and ran, he disappeared. Meanwhile, D tried to move away from the gunfire. Then she got hit in the arm as well.

D managed to hide and the cops ran past her. She was crying as she was in pain. She was pulling her gown up and pulled her pistol out. She wanted to be sure she had protection moving forward. She was feeling like she was in a war. A man came out of a corner, and he had his gun on D. He shot and missed. D shot back and hit. She went up to the guy, she wanted to see where he came from. She found a tunnel, and went up the steps. She carefully entered a home. She peeked in to see who was there. There were two of Nardelli's drivers and they were armed.

Then police kicked in the door and entered. They announced themselves and went to cuff the guys. D shot out of the house and was running in her bare feet. She heard yelling, "Stop or I'll shoot."

She thought it was Nardelli's men so she kept running she had no idea which direction she was running, but jumped over some bush. It was dark. She ended up falling down what seemed to be a hill, she heard someone call, "Cindy!"

It was a man so she got up to run, and ran right into the river. She was splashing and the current was sweeping her away. There were lights being placed on the river and she could hear: "Stop! Police!" and guns were firing.

The rain was so hard and heavy, she couldn't fight the current. She was calling out for help but was getting tired. Then she felt bullets hitting the water, they were shooting at her. D stopped fighting the current, she tried to move towards the shore. It was exhausting and she was getting hit with tree branches in the water and all sorts of debris that was floating on the river.

Her dress got snagged, and she realized she was not moving, and the current was trying to push her. D started to pull on her gown, pulling herself into where she was snagged. D was freezing and exhausted. She hung onto the downed tree that snagged her. She pulled herself up and decided to rest. She would try to pull herself up on shore later. Her shoulder was burning from a bullet, and her abdomen was on fire and feeling like it would explode. She knew she had been shot. D knew she was exhausted and didn't fight it anymore. She gave into sleep, even if awkward, she passed out.

CHAPTER TWENTY-NINE

Back at the mansion the police were rounding everyone up. Jordon was yelling, "Everyone look for Cindy! She has to be here somewhere."

Alexa finally got the attention of O'Reilly and told him, "She was wearing a white evening gown that shimmered to a silver color when the light hit it. She had a white shawl, and Mr. Nardelli took her in the tunnels. She came running out of that house on the right side of the street, then ran and jumped over the shrubs. That was the last I saw of her; the cops were shooting at her."

O'Reilly then began to worry, "They were shooting at her?"

"Yeah, I saw blood on her gown. She may be in the shrubs bleeding and in trouble. You need to tell Jordon and Steve; I think that's their names."

"Well, Steve is going to the hospital, and I think Jordon is going with a detainee, I'll see what I can do."

Alexa shook her head in disbelief. She was happy Cindy kept her safe, but she was worried about her friend and roommate.

Jordon came up on the opposite side of the police car, he startled Alexa. "Alexa did you see Cindy after the chaos?"

"Like I told O'Reilly, I think she ran behind that house. I saw someone in a white gown jump over those shrubs. There was blood on the gown and the cops were shining their lights out that way and started shooting."

"Ok, everyone start searching the riverbank. She went in toward the riverbank, she may be shot. Start looking! If you don't have anyone to book, go look, we need to find her it's cold and it's raining." Jordon was seriously worried now hearing Alexa say what she said. He was upset with the screw up.

Jordon went to the ambulance that had Steve. He said, "We have a lead on where D is. You go get your arm fixed. I will meet you there as soon as we find her."

Steve said, "Maybe I should stay to help find her."

"No, Steve, you go. Your injury looks bad. I will keep looking. She may be along the riverbank."

"If she fell in, she can't swim. She can't float, and the current is likely strong and would pull her! Get Air Search out to find her."

That shook up Jordon. He got on the radio and called his captain to get Air Search to come and look along the river. The Captain ordered Air Search to look as well as the Harbor Patrol to search the area. He asked for an EMS to be on standby should they find D.

The following morning at sunrise, it was cold and windy. The tree D was on was bobbing up and down in the waves of the river. She raised her head and looked around. She tried to get up and make her way to the riverbank. Her gown was twisted and tangled in the branches. She managed to beak the branches and tear a piece of her gown off. She got to the riverbank and climbed up it. She was exhausted, and laid there for a while to rest.

D heard a helicopter and looked up to see where it was. She thought she saw it, but was dizzy, and couldn't focus her eyes. D figured she needed to find a street to get on to be found. She knew that she would be seen better out in the open. D got up and tried to walk towards the bridge she could see. She got to the bridge. It was a train bridge. She was disappointed. The helicopter spotted her; she could hear the loud speaker.

"Hold it right there. This is the police, stay where you are, you are under arrest."

D was upset. "Why are they arresting me?" She started to walk along the bridge, and she was waving her arms. She thought maybe they didn't know who she was. D kept walking out onto the bridge. Then she heard, "Freeze! Police!" She thought they would shoot her. She was confused, she put her hands up and turned, she heard someone yell, "Don't Move!"

"I'm not moving!" D was yelling. She was staggering on the bridge, but she didn't know that.

"Freeze! Don't Move. Please stay still!" Jordon was yelling at D, and she recognized his voice.

D turned to look and tripped in the tangled gown. She fell and screamed, "Jordon help me!"

She dangled precariously from the bridge, and Harbor Patrol was almost there. Jordon was trying to get to D. Her dress ripped and she flopped into the water and was screaming. She was back where she didn't want to be. The current was pushing her along, but the Harbor Patrol scooped D up. They brought her to shore where the EMS was waiting for her.

D was a shivering drowned rat, that's how she felt. But she was happy to be in a warm blanket, and then the paramedic told D his name. He said, "We will get you to the hospital." Then the ambulance stopped, and she screamed, "Don't stop! They are after me, I need to get out of here!"

Suddenly, the door opened and Jordon hopped into the back of the ambulance. "Boy, am I glad to see you D!"

D was screaming and trying to get out of there, she wanted to get away. D was confused and in shock.

"We need to calm her down. I can't assess her injuries with her fighting us," the EMS said.

Jordon started to raise his voice over D's: "DeeDee, it's me Jordon! DeeDee! It's Jordon." He got up closer to her and switched seats with the EMS technician.

"Ok, we have a bullet hole in the shoulder, and one in the pelvic area. Her blood pressure is low, and she has a firm distended abdomen. Her oxygen level is low. D, we need to give you oxygen. Let me put these nasal canals on your nose, please."

D stopped fighting because she was too tired. She was not talking or screaming. She was just plain tired. She was shivering, and they started an IV to raise her blood pressure.

Jordon was worried. "Is she going to be ok?"

"It's hard to say. She's in shock, and was out all night exposed to the elements. Her body temperature is 88 degrees. She will soon start shaking uncontrollably from warming up."

"Will that be bad for her?"

"It may start her bleeding again. I don't know if the femoral artery is involved with the bullet wound."

"Well, we have to try to keep her alive. She is important."

"We will do our best, Jordon; we will do our best."

They arrived at the hospital and brought D in. The same ER doctor was there.

"Well, she lasted just over twenty-four hours!" He shook his head and asked, "What happened?"

Jordon gave a brief synopsis, and the EMS stated, "Low blood pressure and body temperature, out all night and exposed to the elements, as well fallen in the river. Two gunshot wounds, one shoulder, one right side pelvic region."

The doctor told Jordon to wait in the hall, as well told him his partner was in surgery. He asked Jordon if he knew if D had been assaulted.

Jordon said that he was not sure; he wasn't with her during the sting. This just made Jordon worry more.

The Captain met Jordon in the hall and asked him what he knew.

"I don't know much except we screwed up. D didn't get nabbed immediately; I have no idea what she's been through. Nardelli got away with her, except she has two bullet wounds. My partner was shot in the shoulder. I have no idea how he is. We screwed up the whole sting, Captain!"

"Now hold on there, Jordon! You did not screw up. Nardelli was picked up on a road two blocks over. You stuck to your search till you found D. No one screwed up. When all the players are well enough to talk, we will find out what happened. Everyone was busted and caught, except one councilor we found in the tunnels, dead. The coroner thinks it may have been a lady's pistol, so we know it may have been D."

Jordon paced; he was worried and nervous. He felt bad for his partner and for D. He did not know what to do. He was feeling like a failure.

"Here, Jordon, have a coffee." It was his captain's voice he heard. His captain had been and got coffees since they would be waiting for some time for news.

"I guess there will be an independent review for us as there was a lot of shooting last night."

"Yes, son, there will be, but I would not worry about that at the moment, unless it helps to take your mind off that little lady in there."

"It doesn't help, I wish it did though."

"I tell you what, you likely haven't eaten anything for a while. How about you phone that Zack and have him bring you breakfast? I'll buy."

"Ok, I will do that, but I warn you Captain, I have a voracious appetite."

Jordon went off to find a phone, he told Zack what had happened and ordered his breakfast. Meanwhile Steve was in surgery, and they found that the bullet had gone dangerously close to the heart. His doctor was going to have to put him off work for months for rehab. The doctor came out to tell Jordon and the Captain. Then he said he was going to check on Cindy and how her surgeries were going.

"Well, guess I will be down my partner for a bit of time, Captain. Steve will heal fast though; he hates being off work!"

"Well, he is going to listen to his doctors, and that will be my order. I want my officers to be all right when they are on the job," Captain Shepherd said that in his gruffest voice and he meant it.

The doctor went to check on the surgery of Cindy, and he learned they got the bullet from the shoulder. It seemed to have come from a thirty-eight. He had it sent to the police lab. The surgeon was working on the shot to the pelvic region. The bullet had ricocheted and tore through her abdomen. It tore her uterus, the surgeon repaired it, it cut her colon which was repaired, and the bullet was up against the tail bone of the spine. The surgeon had requested a spinal surgeon attend the OR; he was cleaning the wound but waiting. He said that he was also waiting for blood.

So, the E.R. doctor returned to the waiting area and informed the two people waiting to hear the news. "I hope you do not have any awaiting assignments for this girl, she will be off duty for some time to come. I don't want to hear about rushing to get better to get a bust done. She is going to be a sick girl, that's if they get the bullet from the spine."

The Captain thanked the doctor for checking on the progress, and so did Jordon. "I assure you there are no assignments pending. I am hoping to hire her, but she will not work until she has fully healed. I do hope she heals," the captain stated.

The E.R. doctor left the area to resume his shift. He was happy he would be done on his rotation soon.

Detective Steve Weston made it to his room on the fifth floor. He was sleeping, and Jordon was just sitting waiting to see how his buddy was. The captain had left to go back to the office. He wanted to finish up the investigation.

Steve woke up and was very sore. He asked how long he was in surgery.

"You went in at night to about one a.m., and it is two in the afternoon. Your wound was bad. Almost hit the heart they said." Jordon was restless but happy to see his buddy awake, although he did not want to tire him out.

"Did anyone find D last night?" Steve asked with concern.

"We found her around nine a.m. this morning. She was out in the rain all night on the riverbank. I think she fell in the river last night, then she fell in again this morning. She was shot twice. They had the first bullet out of her shoulder, looked like a cop shot her. They need a spinal surgeon for the other bullet that went into her pelvic area, it ricocheted and is next to her spine at the tail bone." Jordon was choking up as he was telling Steve.

"So, is she ok, have you seen her?" Steve was concerned.

"She was still in surgery waiting for the spinal surgeon at one p.m. I haven't seen her since the ambulance ride." Jordon was finding it hard to keep it together at that point.

"She will be ok, Jordon. I am sure of it. Just have faith; she is a strong stubborn little lady!" Steve was reassuring Jordon as well as himself.

Then in came a nurse to the room, and she said she was sent to give an update. "Cindy is in recovery. They got the bullet out. She will be an hour or two in recovery, depending on if they can get her temperature up. She will be fine, but they don't know about her baby. They don't think her pregnancy will last."

The guys looked stumped at each other; they were shocked. They asked the nurse, "How far along was she? We did not know she was pregnant." Steve was very concerned.

"Oh, she is only a week or two into the pregnancy, she likely didn't know either. She will be on the fourth floor when she leaves recovery. That's all I know at this time."

Jordon was in shock, and said, "When did she have time to get pregnant, and who would be the father? Why didn't she tell me she had a guy?" Jordon was getting worked up. He was hurt and felt betrayed.

"Jordon!" Steve shouted and winced from pain. "I doubt she has a guy! That nut Austin likely raped her the night of the attack. We just didn't think about it. Don't go getting upset. I see how she looks at you. I see how she looks at me as well, but Austin she can't stand looking at him. Relax buddy, she will be fine."

"I might just kill that SOB! D likely doesn't even know he violated her. He is a sick dude, that's all I can say about it." Jordon was pacing back and forth, he was upset.

"Jordon Smith?" A doctor walked in the room. "Hi, I am Dr. Stanly, I'm the Spinal Surgeon. I got the bullet from Cindy's tail bone. I just thought I would let you know she is in room four-twenty-six. She is asking for you. I have her heavily sedated. I want to keep her blood pressure low for now, as she may abort the fetus. She got extremely upset to find out you were told. We had no idea no one knew. I apologize. Ok, I am going, and I will check in tomorrow if all goes well."

Steve said, "What are you waiting for? Go see her, I'll be fine. Tell her I hope she feels better soon. Go, go see her."

Jordon was frozen in place and looked at Steve, "You'll be fine? Have the nurse call for me if you need me. I will just see how she's doing then be back up."

"I'm fine. Take your time. Don't rush your visit or she might think you are abandoning her. She needs one of us." Steve was serious about this. "With D she takes it to heart."

Jordon took off and went down the stairs, skipping the whole flight. With one jump and a second jump, he was on the fourth floor. D's room was right across from the stairway doors. Jordon knocked on the door and asked if he could come in.

"Of course, you can come in," D had a smile on her face, but there were tears there too. She had been crying. D used the blanket to wipe her face quickly. She did not know what to say to Jordon.

"Boy! I sure am glad to see you, and the case is done."

Jordon had a hard time looking into D's eyes. He did not know what to say either. "Ah, Steve says he hopes you feel better soon. He's upstairs in bed after his surgery. How are you feeling D?" Jordon was a bit shaky on asking that question.

"I am all right. I am in pain, but I will live. At least I'm not still in the cold river." D shivered just saying that. "Is Steve going to be ok? I don't know what happened to him, but I hope he is ok."

"He was shot in the shoulder; it just nicked his heart. He has a long rehab road to go through, but he will be ok." Jordon was holding D's hand finally, but it was ice cold. She was squeezing his hand and holding tight. "Are you ok? Warm enough? Any pain?" Jordon wondered.

"To tell you the truth, I am freezing inside. I don't think I will ever be warm enough. And I am in pain. The freezing they used is wearing off. The nurse should be coming soon. She was going to get a warm blanket for me." Then all of a sudden, D winced and squeezed Jordon's hand so tight his knuckles cracked.

"What's that for?" Jordon asked. "You're squeezing so tight, what's happening?"

D said, "Do me a favor and get a nurse. I am having pain, and it is every minute or so, please?"

D was on her side doubled over and crying in pain. She knew she was about ready to pass everything out. Then she was trying to breathe between the pain, but she was crying.

The nurse came in the room, "Ok Cindy, breathe through it nice and easy. I called the OBGYN to the unit, let's get you on your back!"

"My tailbone hurts when I am on my back." D was crying so quietly it was like little squeaks coming out of her. The nurse was coaching D and said to just go with it and the pain will not be so bad. The doctor came in the room and kicked everyone out including Jordon.

"How far along in this pregnancy are you?"

"I'm only a few weeks, why do I hurt so much? It's like giving birth!"

"Well, I am going to check and assess, just to be sure everything is normal."

"I don't understand. Oh My God, I feel like I have to push, why?"

"You had surgery for a bullet, right? Did they freeze you from the waist?"

"Yes, they did, and I had two bullets, one in the shoulder, one near the tail bone."

"Ok, you are dilated; you can start with a gentle push."

D just went with the flow. She let her body do what it needed to do. She was crying so silently the doctor hadn't noticed, and was encouraging Cindy.

"Ok, Cindy, you are doing good, that's really good, you are being brave!"

"I am not brave; I just don't understand." D had to push again and this time she felt a popping out of something.

The doctor said, "There we go, it came out all intact. Good job, Cindy!"

The doctor cleaned away the placenta sac and checked for any issues. "The fetus was just a peanut size. Everything came out, so no further surgery needed, monitor for infection. Cindy, I am sorry for your loss."

"Well, I'm not, it was a product of rage. I just didn't know I had been raped. I was out cold."

The doctor then said, "Well, I guess Mother Nature took care of this matter. Well, take care and goodbye."

The Nurse was trying to cover D, and she asked, "Are you ok, Cindy?"

"Just call me D. I'm freezing. Can I get a warm blanket? I guess Jordon left as well…That doctor has no compassion she's like a robot."

"I will see if he is waiting in the hallway anywhere, ok, and I will get you a blanket as well. You ring if you need anything D, ok?"

"Yeah sure, thank you for your help." D rolled over to her side and faced away from the door. She tried to be very quiet in her crying.

Jordon did not know what to do. He was in the stairwell. He was going to go see Steve, but thought no that would not be good. All he was thinking of was what Janet went through, but he never worked through his feelings. "Losing a baby is so personal," he thought. He walked back to Steve's room.

"Hey buddy, how you doing, how's D? Not good judging by the look on your face." Steve lost his smile on his face.

"I got kicked out. She was having pain; a doctor came in kicked everyone out and I think she lost the baby."

"Well, how is D after everything? Or is she still in labor?"

"Is that what they call it, she called it pain."

"What's wrong, buddy? Why are you not with D?"

"I don't know what to say to her or what to do."

"You abandoned her? You just need to be there for her, just hold her hand, keep her company, that's all. But don't leave her."

Jordon thanked Steve for his honesty and said, "I'll go see if she is allowed company then."

A nurse brought D a warm blanket, and she asked for a phone to call a friend. The nurse said she would see what she could do. D was feeling the warmth and started to fall asleep.

Jordon was walking the hall and a nurse saw him, "Are you here to see D?"

"Yes, I am. Can she have a visitor?"

"Why sure, she could use a good friend right now."

"I don't know what to do or say though."

"Just be there for her, hold her hand, let her cry. You don't have to say or do anything special, just be with her and support her."

Jordon entered the room. He took the chair and moved it to the side of the bed D was facing. He sat down, and then he felt for her hand under the covers. He held it gently. It still felt cold, so he covered it with his. He watched her sleep. She was quiet and just slept. The whole ordeal had taken all her energy.

A few hours went by, and the supper hour was on. The orderlies burst into the room, woke D, and placed a supper tray in front of her. She saw Jordon there and she sprung up, smiled, and said, "Hi, I thought you were with Steve?" D was trying to give Jordon an out for disappearing, with no judgement.

"I only went back to see him for a little bit to let him know how you were doing. I came back and sat quietly, watching you sleep."

"Aw, that was sweet of you. They gave me a warm blanket finally and it was so warm and cozy, I guess I fell asleep. How is Steve now?"

"He's good. He says he's sorry for what you went through."

"Oh, well I'm a tough bird, I can get through anything."

D had a tear rolling down her face and Jordon saw it. He reached his arm around her and said, "You don't have to be tough for me, you know. If you're hurting just admit it, I'm here for you. What are friends for? If you're scared, just tug on my arm, I am here for you."

"Aw, gee, thank you, Jordon," D said, "Well, I could use a really strong hug about now."

The nurse came in the room with a phone and plugged it in the wall. She told D: "You have to press nine to dial out."

"Thank you, nurse, you are great."

The nurse reminded her to eat supper before it got cold. D looked under the lid, and gagged once again, "I think I'm going to be sick."

She giggled, for a moment. It was some kind of mess under the lid. Just then, Zack came in with dinner for two -Poutine, burgers, salad, and two large real coffees.

D was delighted, and thanked Zack. She said, "You are a life saver, Zack."

Jordon agreed with D, as he did not want to watch her get sick. He'd seen it enough times to last a lifetime.

Zack visited for a few minutes and then said that he had to scoot he had other deliveries to make. Jordon thanked Zack and Zack left. He visited Steve for a few minutes, and then took off.

D ate, she was hungry, then she lay back in bed, and she said, "I have too much boredom time, my mind is going a mile a minute. I don't want sadness getting in." She was trying not to cry. She was fighting it.

Jordon said, "Why don't you want to be sad? It's ok to have sadness. It's not bad. Sometimes if you don't release it, it can build and then you can't control it."

"I don't want you to get the wrong idea about my sadness. It's not about losing a baby, it's about a violation. My trust was stolen. I feel sick that this happened to me, by a very sick and twisted individual." D began crying and she felt so sad.

Jordon held her in his arms, and said, "It's all right. You are allowed those feelings. It's your right."

"It's that I wish him dead, I wish him a tortured death. It's not good to wish bad things on another human being. It saddens me that I can have those hateful feelings."

"D, you are the most loving creature I've ever met. You sing to Mother Nature, and drum. You thank Mother Nature for all you receive. You let go of anger and forget about it, you hold on to positive thoughts and feelings. Let yourself have this indulgence for a short time, then you can pray and forgive if you want or just move on and forget." Jordon said all that with true heart, he didn't even know where it came from, but he knew his friend was hurting. He hugged D and kissed her forehead.

D cried for a while but, as she sounded tired to Jordon, he soon realized she had cried herself to sleep. He laid her down and tucked her in, he then sat there holding her hand and watched her sleep.

Jordon eventually fell asleep. He had not realized how tired he actually was, at one point he was semi awake, and he felt like someone was watching him. He lifted his head and saw D was watching. She had awakened.

"Hello sleepy head, did you get some rest? I hope your back and neck will not pay for how you slept. Thanks for staying with me."

"You are welcome." Jordon sat up and stretched himself, and then rubbed the sleep out of his eyes. "Did you have a good sleep; your hair says yes."

"Oh, don't look at my bed hair! It's a mop when I sleep." D blushed. "Maybe you should go home and get some real sleep."

"I think you look cute with bed hair." Jordon was grinning, and very happy to see D was happy.

D blushed and then let out a little giggle, "Oh I look like a drowned rat, especially after feeling like one falling in the river."

"How did that happen anyway? How did you not drown?"

"Mr. Nardelli took me into the tunnels, then he heard the police coming. He used me as a shield. He shot at the police, and kept me in front of him, that's how I got shot. He let go of me and took off. I reached under my gown, and pulled out my pistol. I shot one of Nardelli's men coming into the tunnels. I walked over to him and went up the steps to a house. Then I ran out of the house when the police ran in. I was so confused as to my direction, and from whom I was running. I jumped over the shrubs, and then stood up, I went to run, and I ran into the river. I was fighting the current, and got tired, then I let myself go with the current, I tried to move towards the shore. My gown got caught in a downed tree, I climbed up on the branches and then passed out. I woke up at dawn. I couldn't see, things were blurry, I got up and tried to walk towards the road. I don't remember anything else."

"Wow, you are lucky to be alive. You fell off a railway bridge when we found you, you weren't on the road. The Harbor Patrol fished you out of the river. Then we put you in the ambulance, and here you are. Very lucky little lady." Jordon was looking at D with admiration. "If your hairs a bit messy after that ordeal, I think it is very sexy." Jordon hugged D and gave her a long kiss.

"Wow, knock my socks off and rock my world." D grinned with a little giggle.

All of a sudden there was a knock on the door. It was Captain Shepherd and Steve in a wheelchair.

"Can we come in or is this private?"

"Come in, come in, Steve I'm glad to see you and you too, Captain Shepherd." D reached for Steve to hug him but carefully.

Steve hugged her back and said, "It's good to see you, kid." He had a tear and so did D.

She then hugged their captain. D welcomed them both to visit.

"How are you doing Detective Bishop," Capt. Shepherd asked.

"I'm doing fine, Captain Shepherd; I may be a while before I get a green light from the doctor," D answered. She did not catch what he had said.

Steve was staring at the captain and said, "Did I hear you correctly, Captain?"

Jordon also had a questioning look on his face, "Yeah, Captain, what did I just hear you say?"

D looked around and then said, "What did I miss? You all look gob smacked!"

"I asked you, Detective Bishop, how you were?" The captain reached into his jacket pocket and pulled out a badge wallet and chain.

D got excited and said, "You mean you're my boss now? I am official River City Police Department personnel?" She was reaching to see the badge and was excited. She squealed a high pitch giggle.

Both Steve and Jordon shouted, "Congratulations D!" and they high fived her.

"Thank you so much, Captain. I won't let you down." D was very excited.

The Captain said, "No, you won't as you will be working under these two detectives. I will be watching all of you." The Captain added, "I will see all of you in my office in a few weeks once the doctor has cleared you for duty. Jordon, you will be on desk duty next week. Don't come in till then."

The captain left, and everyone was happy.

"And the journey begins; case stories to follow."

www.ingramcontent.com/pod-product-compliance
Lightning Source LLC
Chambersburg PA
CBHW032101050726

47590CB00001B/373